# faded

Praise for FLICKER

## 1st Place Winner (MG/YA) 2015 — 3rd Annual Writer's Digest Self-Published eBook Awards

"In FLICKER . . . we are presented with a story that is heavy on the romance and teen drama while mixing in some supernatural thrills and interesting historical ideas as well. It mines this territory well — rather than seeming like one genre is mashed onto another, the blending works well here and it really feels like a cohesive and necessary story being told in the only way it possibly could have been."— *Judge, 3rd Annual Writer's Digest Self-Published eBook Awards*

"Biz is a likeable character with enough conflict about her powers to make her utterly believable. Most teens feel different ... she really is. Hooyenga does an admirable job with the wonder and horror that comes with a young woman both embracing and rejecting who she is. The secondary cast of characters is also really great and there's a twist at the end that will have readers breathless." — *Jesse Peterson, Explorer News (Tucson)*

"Hooyenga's FLICKER had me on the edge of my seat! A great who-done-it for YA fans, it had me guessing until the very end. Hooyenga had me (and my teenage daughter who loves this book) eyeing the shadows between trees a bit differently after reading FLICKER, it stays with you long after the last page." — *Stacey Graham, literary agent and author of The Girls' Ghost-Hunting Guide and The Zombie Tarot*

FLICKER by Melanie Hooyenga is a very gripping novel... With both contemporary and supernatural elements mixed in, FLICKER shows how anyone can have abilities beyond the grasp of the average individual... FLICKER comes highly recommended for those who love contemporary fiction, romance, time travel, and a fast, thrilling read. — *Staff Review, YA Books Central*

## Praise for FRACTURE

A gripping and relatable contemporary novel with an awesome time travel component mixed in, FRACTURE draws you in and refuses to let go. — *Staff Review, YA Books Central*

"The intensity increases as this unique storyline is carried forward by wonderfully imperfect multidimensional characters — no cookie-cutter stereotypes here. Fantastic all-around." — *Sher Bowie*

"More intrigue, more drama, more feels, and more jaw dropping page turns. I can't recommend this book or this series enough and I eagerly await the next book in the series." —*Amazon Customer "Lostgirl"*

"I read the last 180 pages in a day. I could not put it down, I had to see how it ended. FRACTURE ... leaves you open ended and waiting anxiously for the next book." — *Emily Klutts*

"Hooyenga keeps pushing the envelope and she delivers. FRACTURE is fast-paced, well-developed — and heartbreaking." — *Amazon Customer*

## Praise for FADED

"It is not always true that a series can get better with each new book, but it is certainly true of Hooyenga's writing. Anyone who loves contemporary young adult romance or the idea of time travel will want to go out and pick up this series right away."— *YA Book Central*

FADED is the perfect wrap up in this YA trilogy. Multiple story lines and problems involving new and past favorite characters are concluded beautifully leaving the reader with closure, unlike in some books! You'll find yourself unable to put this book down." — *M. Chittenden*

"Ms. Hooyenga hooks you from ... the first sentence. Her dialogue always rings true to the teen voice and her writing makes her books a quick and enjoyable read!" — *Montessori Mama*

Books by Melanie Hooyenga

*The Flicker Effect Trilogy*
FLICKER
FRACTURE
FADED

*The Rules Series*
THE SLOPE RULES
THE TRAIL RULES
THE EDGE RULES

*The Campfire Series*
CHASING THE SUN
CHASING THE STARS
CHASING THE MOON

*Anthologies*
LOVE ON MAIN
THE ART OF TAKING CHANCES

# faded

## Melanie Hooyenga

Left-Handed Mitten
Publications

FADED

Published by Left-Handed Mitten Publications

ISBN-13 978-0-692-72755-3


UPC

Book design, cover design, and formatting by Left-Handed Mitten Publications.

Author website: melaniehoo.com
Email: melaniehooyenga@gmail.com
Facebook: facebook.com/MelanieHooyenga
Twitter: @melaniehoo
Instagram: @melaniehoo
Newsletter: melaniehoo.com/hoos-letter/

*To my mom,*
*for everything*

# chapter 1

If your birthday has to land on a school day, having it on a Friday is far superior to the rest of the week. At least that's what I keep telling myself. Amelia, my best friend and biggest cheerleader, has planned a party to end all parties and she's convinced me to hang streamers from every permanent fixture in her house.

I grab a roll from the plastic bag. This one reads Happy Birthday. "Remind me why crinkled paper is essential at a party. Aren't we getting a little old for this?"

Amelia pouts, but it's quickly replaced with a huge smile that lights up her face. "That one goes over the kitchen table."

I tilt my head.

"For your cake!"

"Do we really need to announce that it's my birthday?"

"Biz, eighteen is a big deal. Huge. You should be excited!"

I sink into a chair. "I am excited. Sort of. I just wish..." I trail off.

She stops in front of me, clutching a roll of tape to her chest. "I can still invite him."

I shake my head. "No. I haven't spoken to Cameron since Katie's funeral. I don't think a party is the right time."

"When is? You can't go the rest of the year not talking to each other. You and Cam have been best friends since forever. Two months ago he told you he loves you. That doesn't just go away because his sister died."

My heart flinches. I thought I loved him, too, but too much has happened. "Sometimes it does. It's been two months since Katie killed herself. I have no idea if he still blames me for not trying hard enough to stop her, but I couldn't flicker three times." I shake my head.

We've had this conversation before and Amelia has yet to find a way to justify the fact that Cameron was willing to risk my life to save Katie. A double flicker—going back a second time before I've caught up to the time of the first flicker— already led to brain surgery once, and when I went back the second time to help Katie, we didn't know how close I'd cut the timing. Cameron knew the risks, and even though Martinez, my brain doctor, managed to fix me up without surgery, at the time Cameron didn't know if I'd need another operation. "I understand why he pressured me, but I'm still upset that he was okay with me getting hurt when I'd already failed to save her. Twice."

Amelia bites her lip. After a moment, she holds up the roll of tape. "I was hoping we wouldn't need it but—be right back." She sprints up the stairs to her room. Moments later, she's back at my side, hand behind her back.

"I told you not to get me a present."

"This isn't really a present. It's more of a celebration!" She pulls out her hand, revealing a flask of vodka.

"Seriously?"

"Seriously."

"Since when do you have alcohol?" Amelia drinks the occasional beer, but only when it happens to be at a party. She doesn't have her own stash.

"I know you're upset about Cam and I want to make sure you have fun tonight. If Mr..." she turns the bottle to read the brand. "...Stoli needs to help, so be it." She twists off the cap, sniffs the top, and wrinkles her nose. "I don't know who the crazies are who say vodka is odorless. It smells like paint thinner."

I laugh. "Don't offend Mr. Stoli. He's just trying to make us happy." I can't remember the last time I drank alcohol. My last brush with vodka was the first night Katie killed herself, when she was still alive, holed up in Maddy's room and refusing to let us help her. Before everything fell apart.

I grab the bottle from her hand and take a small sip, followed by another longer drink. The liquid sets my tongue on fire, burning my throat as it slides to my stomach, sending a warm glow through the rest of my body. I take another swig, then tilt my head back for one final swallow that's so big it almost makes me gag. I hand her the bottle. "Happy birthday to me."

The vodka pushes away the all-encompassing numbness that seems to follow me everywhere these days, replacing it with a different sensation that makes me more comfortable in my skin. I could get used to this, but I won't. I don't drink often, and when I do, I'm always responsible about it. Speaking of which.

"I should have my mom pick me up. I told her I'd meet them at the restaurant for dinner, but considering," I waggle the bottle in the air, "I probably shouldn't be driving."

Amelia leans forward, eyes wide. "You're still coming back, right? The epic party will lose its epicness if you're not here."

I pull the bottle toward me. "How much have you had?"

She giggles. "Just a couple sips."

I replace the cap on the bottle and tuck it inside a bag of party supplies. "Take it easy. You need to be fully alert to get me through tonight." I pull out my phone to text Mom.

> Me: Can you pick me up at Amelia's? I don't want to lose my parking spot.

"Will they know you've been drinking?"

"I don't think so. If they get suspicious I'll just say how super excited I am to finally be eighteen." I smile despite myself. The last few months have nearly sucked the life out of me—Katie's suicide, her funeral, then radio silence from Cameron ever since, plus the fact that Dad's health is getting worse every day—but maybe this birthday is the start of better things.

Or maybe it's just the vodka talking.

Amelia's face breaks into a smile that lights up her face. "That's the spirit!" Then she throws the streamers at me. "Now climb on the table and wrap this around the chandelier."

My phone dings as I'm taping the final piece to the light fixture. My heart jumps as a reflex, but I already know it's not him. I untangle myself from the long strands and pull my phone from my back pocket.

Mom: Sure. Be there in ten minutes.

I jump off the table, landing with a thud that shakes the dishes in the china cabinet. "Time to go. My mom's on her way."

"Is this..." she pauses, chewing her lip.

"What?" It's not like Amelia to not say what's on her mind.

"I was just thinking about your dad. Is he okay enough to go out to a restaurant? I mean, I know he has the wheelchair now so walking isn't an issue, but I wasn't sure if he has enough energy to go out."

Outside of my family, Amelia knows the most about my dad, including the fact that he's not actually dying from epilepsy: he's dying from years of flickering. Until he found out that I flicker, he'd never told anyone—including his doctor—the real reason for his seizures. He learned the hard way that there's a limitation to our ability. It's like we only get a certain number of flickers and once you pass it, your body starts to shut down.

"There's a Greek restaurant they've gone to for years so the staff is really helpful. Not like they'd kick him out or something because he has a wheelchair, but there's a whole new set of challenges to getting around when you can't walk." Dad's mortified to be seen in public in a wheelchair, but it's relieved a lot of Mom's stress since she no longer has to worry about him falling. He jokes that she just likes it because now she can push him around, literally. I like it because it keeps him contained if he has a seizure, so he's less likely to hurt himself.

"That's nice he can go out for your birthday, especially since..." she trails off again.

Since this is my last birthday he'll be alive for. A lump forms in my throat and tears spring to my eyes, the warm fuzzies from the vodka slipping away. "I know."

A car beeps in the driveway and I scan the mess on the table. "I'll help you finish up when I get back."

She wraps her arms around me and squeezes. "Are you kidding? I'll have this done in twenty minutes without you here to slow me down."

I laugh against her shoulder. "Thanks, Amelia." I sling my bag over my shoulder and head outside. The sunlight blinds me for a moment and I blink to clear my vision. Dad waves a thin arm out the window and I hurry to open the back door. "Thanks for picking me up. Amelia said half the school might show up and I didn't want to have to park a mile away."

Mom smiles at me in the rearview mirror. "It's no problem. We were already loaded and ready to go." Meaning she'd already helped Dad into the car and lugged his wheelchair into the trunk.

I lean forward to squeeze his shoulder. "How are you feeling?"

He presses his cheek to my hand. "I'm ready to celebrate." His voice, while sounding upbeat, comes out a whisper.

"You and me both, Dad." I lean against the seat and stare out the window, and my thoughts drift to Katie. I'm slowly learning to forgive myself, but I can't get past the fact that I brought this upon all of us. A photo I took for class led me to discovering that it was Mr. Turner, my teacher, who kidnapped Katie. Everyone was beyond thrilled that she was back home, but the damage was already done. After watching Katie die three times I didn't think I had tears left, but the sight of her small, white coffin surrounded by white lilies and roses, combined with the mournful music playing in the church and Cameron's parents sobbing in the front row, pulled on a reserve of tears I didn't think existed. After the service, I mumbled out an "I'm sorry" for the hundredth time, then left the church and haven't spoken to Cameron since.

I wipe my hand across the tears sliding down my face and study my fingertips in horror. They're tingling.

No.

I've been so wrapped up in the past that I'm not paying attention to where we are.

The sunlight filters through the trees and it's too late to stop the effects.

Please no.

Not when I've been drinking.

The tingling shoots down my legs to my toes, followed by the intense weight that nearly leaves me breathless.

What was I doing yesterday at this time? I think I was with Amelia and—oh crap!

Before I can grab Dad's shoulder to alert him, the crushing heaviness strikes. I have a fleeting thought that I should record this for Martinez, but there's no time. It's coming too fast. The weightlessness sweeps through me and I'm floating, floating and—

—the steering wheel jerks under my hands, sending the car straight toward a giant tree on the side of the road while Amelia's screams pierce through the fog in my head.

# chapter 2

"Biz!" Amelia grabs the wheel but it's too late.

It's like I flipped a switch to zoom my camera lens on the tree, but it's not slowing down. I slam both feet on the brake but in seconds the tree is looming over us, its branches pulling us closer into a deathly embrace. Metal screeches as the front of the car crunches into the massive trunk. I tuck my legs closer to my body as the passenger side buckles around Amelia and the airbags explode around us.

"Omigod! My leg!"

The car stops against the tree and the airbags slowly deflate. A hissing sound comes from the front of the car, but no smoke, so hopefully this is the end of it. I fumble with my seatbelt, my head still catching up with the fact that I'm no longer in the backseat of my parents' car, and reach for Amelia.

She's slumped over the deflating airbag. I gently move her hair off her face, not sure if she's conscious, and gasp. Tears stream down her face. She's clutching her legs, or at least I think that's what she's doing since her hands are out of sight beneath the mangled dashboard.

"Are you okay?" I know she's not. The acid in my stomach churns as she lifts her head to face me.

"M-my leg's stuck. I c-can't move it."

"Shit." I lean closer to try to see, but she pushes me away.

"Biz, what happened? We were just driving—" she takes a shuddering breath, "—then you jerked out of nowhere—" another breath, "—and drove us straight into the tree!" Fear and confusion battle on her tear-streaked face. Her lip quivers and her eyes seem to have trouble focusing as she reaches for her leg again and winces.

I rest my head on the steering wheel. "I flickered."

I hear a small intake of breath. "Just now?"

I meet her gaze. "Yes."

She exhales, and her shoulders slump. "I think I need an ambulance." Her eyes flutter closed, then open again. "I don't think I can walk." She pulls out her phone.

I touch her arm, stopping her. "There's more."

She pauses, waiting.

"We were at your house. Drinking."

Her mouth falls open. "Are you drunk?"

"Not drunk, but not not-drunk."

"Oh, shit."

"Yeah."

"Biz, I'm really sorry, but—" she takes a couple shallow breaths, "—we have to call for help. You know I'd keep quiet if I could, but..." she looks at her leg, her voice growing soft. Her jeans, which looked normal a minute ago, are now soaked in blood.

I close my eyes for a beat before pulling out my phone. "I did this. I'll call." I press 9-1-1, flashing back to the last time I had to call that number. Katie was unconscious on the bathroom floor, an empty bottle of pills by her side, Cameron cradling her head in his lap. That situation was totally different than this, but I can't stop the fear that crawls through me, wrapping around my throat and squeezing my lungs until I can't breathe.

"9-1-1. What's your emergency?"

I clear my throat. "I just had an accident. I hit a tree." I glance at Amelia, and gasp again. Her head rests against the window, eyes closed, her face ghostly pale. And her jeans are more red than blue. "My friend is hurt. She's bleeding and her leg might be broken." I reach for Amelia's hand, but she doesn't squeeze back.

A keyboard clacks over the phone. "I've got your location from your phone. Sit tight. An ambulance will be there soon."

"Please hurry." I end the call and press my hand to Amelia's face. Her eyelashes flutter, but there's no other reaction.

I reach for her leg, but stop, hand in midair. I'm not a medic. I've already done enough damage. I brush the back of my hand against the tears that burn my eyes. Amelia is my best friend and is always there for me. She has to be okay. I touch her face again and she moans softly.

"Amelia, I'm so sorry."

Her lips part, but no sound comes out. I lean my head against her arm and wait for the ambulance, anxious for them to hurry but dreading who will be shortly behind them:

The police.

They don't take long. One minute I'm telling Amelia silly stories in an attempt to keep her awake and distract her from her leg, and the next the red lights of an ambulance are filling the inside of the car, along with a steady stream of panicked thoughts: What if Martinez is in the ambulance? Will I be arrested? Will they take me to jail?

Amelia glances out her window and I rest my hand on her arm. "I don't think I'm gonna make it to the party tomorrow."

She faces me, fresh tears in her eyes. "Me either."

I cover my face with my other hand. "I'm so sorry. I'm always so careful about flickering."

Her gaze drifts to the window, eyelids half-closed. "W-what are you going to tell them? Won't it seem weird that y-you were drinking but I wasn't. That I let you drive?"

I push aside my fear of being arrested to come up with a story that will keep Amelia out of trouble. "We'll say that I picked you up and you didn't know I was drinking."

She leans forward, then winces at her leg and sits back. "But you're going to get in a shit-ton of trouble. Oh, wait." She grabs my arm, but her grip is shaky, her usual exuberance gone. She looks so weak I don't know how she's still talking. "Your birthday is tomorrow so you're still a minor. That will help, right?"

"Not with legal stuff. Seventeen is considered an adult."

"Maybe they won't realize—" she pauses to take a breath, "—alcohol...has anything...to do with this. It's still pretty early...for drunkies on the road. You big...lush." She pokes my side, a lazy smile on her lips, but it's wiped away by a sharp rap on my window.

I roll down the window and look into a pair of concerned, blue eyes. Not Martinez. Strong hands grip the door as the eyes peer further in and assess Amelia. He looks me in the eye again. "You hurt?"

I shake my head, hoping alcohol isn't oozing out of my pores. "My friend is." I am the stereotypical drunk driver: I don't have a scratch but I broke my best friend.

He moves around to the passenger side and tries to open the door. Metal creaks, causing us both to jump, but the door doesn't open. He taps the window and Amelia reaches to roll it down, but she doesn't have the strength. I unbuckle my seatbelt and lean over her, doing my best not to injure her more as I roll down the window. The EMT places both hands on the edge of the door and yanks with all his strength, shaking the entire car. I bounce against Amelia, who moans in pain. "Sorry," he mutters. "I've almost got it. Don't want to use the Jaws of Life if we don't have to."

Jaws of Life? How badly did I hurt her? Amelia's eyes widen and for the hundredth time in the past few minutes I wish I could undo this.

The car jerks again and the door opens with a screech of metal. The EMT crouches next to Amelia and slides a hand beneath the dashboard, examining her leg. I flinch at her sharp intake of breath, and another wave of guilt and nausea sweeps over me.

"Amelia, I'm so sorry."

She reaches for my hand, eyes closed. "I know."

"If I could—"

"Shh." Her jaw flexes as she presses her head against the back of the seat while the EMT pushes on the dashboard.

He pulls away from Amelia and she drags the back of her hand across her forehead, leaving a streak of blood on her pale skin. "We might have to wait for the fire department."

The color drains from Amelia's face as we stare at him. I lean closer and touch her face. Her skin is colder than it should be. "You can't leave her here!"

"They're already on their way. It should only be a few more minutes." He looks past us down the road, but the only other vehicles are bystanders who stopped to gawk. On any other day I might be one of those people, except I'd have my camera glued to my face, intruding on a situation I really shouldn't be a part of.

I turn my focus back to Amelia. Her eyes haven't opened. I squeeze her hand.

She doesn't respond.

Panic builds in my chest. Breaking a leg is bad enough, but what if it's something more serious? "Can't you do something for her?"

Before he can answer, a female EMT appears with a bundle of life-saving equipment. She swipes Amelia's arm with a piece of gauze, slides a needle into the crook of her elbow, and hangs a clear plastic bag from the open door.

I'm transfixed by her delicate fingers. They look like the same ones that slid a tube down Katie's throat as she laid unconscious on Sarah's bathroom floor. I start to ask her if she's the same person, but a small moan drifts from Amelia, pulling me back to the present.

"Is she going to be okay? Is it just her leg or is something else wrong?"

She tightens her lips. "We won't know until we get her into the ambulance. But don't worry, we'll take good care of her."

I feel like she's placating me, but I'm not in a position to argue. And once they find out I was drinking, any niceness they're showing now will be gone.

The color in Amelia's cheeks is a little better since they hooked up the IV, but she still hasn't opened her eyes. I lean forward until my forehead rests on her arm and whisper another apology. "I'm so, so sorry. If I could take this back, you know I would."

"But you can," she whispers.

I raise my head to peer at her half-opened eyes.

"You can," she mouths.

I shake my head. "I promised I wouldn't." And I can't risk another double flicker.

Her gaze drifts from her leg to the IV in her arm, before her eyes close again.

I can fix this. If I time it perfectly, I can flicker back to the moment before the crash and prevent Amelia from getting hurt and avoid all the trouble that's about to come down on me, but I promised my dad I wouldn't. He's dying because he flickered too many times, and while Martinez hasn't figured out why it happens, we all agreed that I need to learn to live with the consequences of my actions instead of always taking the easy way out.

A siren wails in the distance and the EMTs both stand.

I exhale in relief. Help is here for Amelia. They'll get her out of the car and to the hospital and she'll—

I freeze. The lights bouncing off the windshield aren't the red lights of the fire truck.

They're blue.

The police are here.

# chapter 3

The police car parks behind us and I close my eyes. This is the final moment before all the shit in my universe hits the fan. Gravel crunches outside the car and I open my eyes.

Two cops stands next to the EMTs, hands on hips, faces serious. I can only hear snatches of their conversation.

"Broken leg."

"Lost a lot of blood."

"Possible DUI."

My gut clenches. They know? How do they know? I put my hand in front of my face and exhale, then immediately cough at the smell. I may as well have a bottle of vodka taped to my forehead.

I am screwed.

The taller cop walks to my side of the car and bends forward so he's looking in the window, directly at me.

Sweat erupts from every pore in my body. I have never been in this much trouble.

"I'm gonna need you to step out of the vehicle."

Fuck. Fuck fuck fuck.

I unfasten my seatbelt and open the door. My legs tremble as I stand and I have to grab the door to keep from falling.

He catches my arm and holds me upright. "Have you been drinking?"

I glance at Amelia, unable to meet his eyes. "I'm freaked out from the accident."

"That's not what I asked." His deep voice forces me to look at him, but I focus on his name tag. BUSTER.

Seriously?

"Is this funny to you?"

I finally meet his eyes. There is no joking with him. "No! No. I'm really worried about my friend and sometimes when I'm panicked it comes out in really inappropriate ways." Shut. Up. Biz.

"I'll ask again. Have you been drinking?"

At this point I think it's pretty obvious, but he's not going to stop until I answer. I hang my head. "Only a little."

His grip on my arm tightens and I let out a yelp.

"Buster, take it easy," the other cop says from behind me.

His grip relaxes but he doesn't let go. "Come with me." He steps away from my car and heads toward the front of the cruiser, giving me no option but to follow. We stop so the headlights are shining on us—why are the headlights on since it's still light out?—and he releases my arm. He turns to face me, arms crossed. "How old are you?"

I swallow hard. This is really happening. "I'll be eighteen tomorrow."

The other cop steps closer to us, seeming ready to say something, but Officer Buster waves him off.

Buster points at Amelia, who's still trapped in my car. "Did you think about the fact that you could have killed your friend when you decided to drink and drive?"

"I didn't mean—"

"Stop," the other officer says, stepping between us. "She's a minor. You can't question her without her parents. You know this."

Buster clenches his jaw and exhales several times. I get that underage drinking and drunk driving are bad, but his reaction seems to have more to do with than just me and my arrest.

The other officer faces me and I finally see his name tag. Reece. "We need to bring you to the station."

My heartbeat kicks up a notch. "What about the hospital?" I peek at Amelia. Her head is drooped against her shoulder, the EMTs crouched next to her. I can't leave her here. I face Officer Reece. "Shouldn't I be checked out? You know, to make sure I don't have internal injuries or something?"

Buster scowls. "You don't look injured."

Reece holds up a hand, silencing him. "They can run a BAL at the hospital. But you'll ride with us since there's only one ambulance."

As if on cue, a siren pierces the air. The fire truck comes to a stop behind the cruiser—red lights flashing, horns blaring—and several yellow-clad firemen spill out of the middle. They carry a big hunk of metal that looks like it belongs in a Transformers movie—a large bitey claw on one end and an engine on the other—and introduce it to my car. And by introduce, I mean they shred the dashboard in a few quick movements. I expected there to be a loud grinding noise, but aside from a puff of air with each cut, the machine is eerily silent.

Which is probably a good thing because I can't tell if Amelia is conscious.

The fireman closest to the car tosses the mangled remains of the dashboard into the long grass, then steps aside to allow the EMTs to help Amelia. One crawls through the driver side door and together they lift her onto a stretcher resting alongside the car.

I watch, transfixed, as dread sinks further into my soul. I hadn't even noticed the stretcher—how drunk am I?

They secure her arms next her sides then lift the stretcher and gingerly move around the vehicle to the ambulance. Her eyes flutter open as she passes me and I reach for her hand.

"Amelia, I'm coming with you."

A small smile crosses her face, but it's gone as soon as they step past me.

My mouth goes dry. I face Reece. "Can I get some water?"

He twists to look into the cruiser, but Buster stops him. "No." He hitches up his pants and levels a glare at me. "Won't help your blood alcohol anyway."

"That's not what—" I stop. That is what I was thinking. The severity of this situation is freaking me out with each passing minute and I'm battling between my concern for Amelia and not knowing what this is going to do to my future. "Can I call my parents?"

Buster exhales. "Yes. Tell them to meet us at the station."

"Is the hospital okay? They might already be there." As far as I know Dad is at home, but he's been spending more and more time at the hospital so if I have to bend the truth to make this jerk feel an ounce of sympathy, I will.

Buster's glare softens for a moment, either out of curiosity or compassion, I'm not sure, but then he blinks and it's back to bad cop, hater of all things Biz. "Fine. But only them. No boyfriends or whoever else."

The comment stings, a fresh jab to my already bruised heart. The only consolation is he couldn't know that's what got me into this situation in the first place. "No boyfriends, got it."

The ambulance doors slam shut, spurring Buster and Reece into action. Buster reaches inside my car and retrieves my bag, while Reece opens the back door of the cruiser and grabs my arm, more gently than Buster did before. "We won't cuff you since we're going to the hospital, but they might later." He presses a hand to the top of my head and guides me into the backseat.

I tuck my feet behind the front seat and look out the window, sure that my heart is still out there, floundering near my car. My gaze drifts to where Amelia had been sitting. The overhead light is still on, reflecting in the pool of blood on the floor, and my photographer brain wonders how that would look in black and white. Most photos are taken in color, but black and white wipes away more than just the color, it wipes away the distraction, leaving more room for the layers of emotion hiding beneath the surface.

Like when you almost kill your best friend.

For the millionth time I wonder how badly she's hurt and wish I could take it all away.

Buster tosses my phone into my lap and juts his chin at me.

"Can't I call them while you drive?" I haven't begun to think about what I'll say to my mom.

"No. I need to take your phone away after you call."

Reece rests a hand on Buster's shoulder. "Let her keep it. I promise that if she makes a second call, you can stop the car and take it away from her."

Buster exhales before slamming my door. He climbs into the driver's side, Reece in the passenger. The ambulance siren wails, cueing Buster to make the cruiser wail in return. Another police car arrives as the ambulance pulls away, but no one gets out. Buster does a small salute at the other cruiser, then hits the gas and we lurch onto the road.

I feel numb, but I know this feeling won't last. On top of the migraine that's coming, I'm betting I'll have a wicked hangover in the morning. And from the way things look from the back of the cruiser, I couldn't flicker tomorrow even if I wanted to.

There's no sunlight in jail.

# chapter 4

My thumb hovers over Mom's name on my phone. I'd much rather call Dad—he knows that I flicker and could help me spin this so Mom doesn't freak out—but he's been so weak that even talking on the phone is sometimes too much for him. I take a deep breath.

Just get it over with.

I press the button and while it rings and I wonder what I'm interrupting. She's probably cleaning up after dinner, curious why I'm not there.

"Biz, you missed dinner."

"Hi, Mom. I know. Listen, I—"

"It's not like you not to call. I would have appreciated a little notice that you wouldn't be eating with us."

I close my eyes. She does so much for me and Dad, and I hate to think of her worrying about me. "I know, I'm sorry. Look, I'm in trouble."

She inhales quickly. She doesn't know about the truly dangerous situations that I've been in, but she's been more protective since Katie's death. "Are you hurt? What happened? Do you need me to come get you?"

Buster glances at me in the rearview mirror, brows furrowed.

I close my eyes and rest my head against the back of the vinyl seat. "I was in an accident. I'm okay but Amelia's hurt. They're bringing us both to the hospital."

"I'm on my way." Her keys jangle in the background and I picture her slinging her purse over her shoulder and heading for the door.

"What about Dad?"

"He'll be okay by himself for a little bit."

I get that he pretty much only leaves the house for doctor's appointments, but this would be a lot easier with him by my side. "Okay, I'll see you soon." I should tell her the rest of it, but I need a few more minutes of my mother not thinking I'm a delinquent. I end the call and open my eyes to find Buster glaring at me.

"Not telling her isn't going to change that you drove drunk."

"I know." I avoid his gaze the rest of the drive, preparing myself for the onslaught of lights in the ambulance bay. Sunlight is the only kind of light that makes me flicker, but artificial lights still do a number on my head. My eyes freak out and I get the lightness and heaviness, but instead of escaping the scene—like I'd really like to right now—I collapse in a heap on the ground. It's happened a couple times when we've brought Dad to the emergency room, and again when Katie killed herself, but this is the first time I'll have cops by my side. I just hope they don't think it's because of the alcohol.

The ambulance turns into the hospital entrance and we follow it up the long drive. The sirens cut off, but the lights continue to spin, bouncing off every surface of the bay.

I lift a hand to shield my eyes as the cruiser comes to a stop.

"No hiding now."

I don't bother correcting him. Better he thinks I'm only ashamed to be in the back of a police car.

My door opens and a strong arm jerks me onto the pavement. I keep my eyes focused on the ground and start to walk toward the doors, but Buster doesn't move.

"You just wait a minute. They need to get your friend inside first." He squeezes a little tighter. "You know, the one you could have killed."

I hear Reece sigh from the other side of the car, but he doesn't interject. We stand there, Buster's hand locked on my arm, as

Amelia is pulled out of the back of the ambulance, still strapped to the stretcher. The EMTs jerk their arms at the same time so the wheels hit the pavement. Once it's locked into place, they hurry her through the automatic doors. I glance at Buster, afraid to make eye contact and have him yell at me again.

He clenches his jaw. "Let's go."

Inside, I recognize the nurse behind the desk from the night Katie died, but she's too focused on the officers escorting me to pay much attention to my face.

"What have we got here?" Janie gives me a once over without truly looking at me, and I'm grateful for a few more moments of anonymity. I'm well known in the ER because of Dad and as far as I can tell, all the nurses like me. I couldn't bear for them to change their opinions.

"DUI. She was driving the girl who just came in."

"She injured?"

Buster shakes his head and slides a piece of paper with my information toward her. "No."

Okay, maybe complete invisibility is a bit much. Shouldn't she be asking me if I'm hurt, not him?

Janie types into the computer. "Curtain four has an open bed. A nurse will be in shortly."

Buster guides me past the desk to a row of beds divided by flimsy curtains. He steps into the first area with the curtain drawn back and nods at the bed. "Have a seat."

Reece joins us in the cramped space and gives me a curt nod.

It takes all my strength not to make small talk. I'm not typically much of a chatter, but throw me into an awkward situation and I'll tell you about my favorite green shirt if it means I don't have to sit in silence, wondering what the others are thinking. Especially now, since I know they're thinking about what a scumbag I am.

Instead I focus on the flurry of activity in the ER. Thursday evening doesn't seem like their busy night, but men and women in blue scrubs stride back and forth around the room, a chaotic dance choreographed to help people more urgent than me. One stops suddenly, her blond ponytail swinging. Her gaze bounces between the cops before landing on me.

I look away.

"Clement?"

I nod, staring at the floor.

She steps closer and yanks the curtain shut, enveloping us in a very cramped, very uncomfortable cocoon.

I don't think I'll be emerging as a beautiful butterfly.

Buster shuffles awkwardly out of her way as she moves to the head of the bed.

She pulls a sealed plastic bag from a drawer and reappears in front of me, tearing open the top and removing the instruments inside. "Sleeve up, please."

I push my sleeve over my elbow and inhale sharply at the cool swipe of alcohol on the inside of my elbow.

"Just a little poke."

Tears sting my eyes as the needle pierces my skin, and I close them so I don't have to see Buster or Reece. I wish I knew where they'd taken Amelia. I wish I'd paid more attention when mom picked me up from Amelia's house. I wish I hadn't had as many shots as I did.

"Biz, what's going on?" Mom's frantic voice interrupts my pity-party. I open my eyes and immediately wish I could close them again. Her wide eyes skate over Buster, then Reece. "You said there was an accident, so why are the police here?" It's like they're not real people, just fixtures in the ER and I happen to be in the room where they're stationed.

Buster clears his throat, but Reece speaks first. "Your daughter was in an accident, but she's not injured." He glances at the needle in my arm. "We suspect she'd been drinking so we're drawing her blood to check her blood-alcohol level."

If I thought her eyes were wide before, now they might actually bug out of her head. I expect her to yell, but her voice comes out so low it's almost a whisper. "You've been drinking?"

"Mom, can we do this later?"

The nurse deftly removes the needle then presses a cotton ball to the crook of my elbow. My blood looks almost black in the vial. She holds it up and faces Buster. "We'll have the results in a little bit." She looks at me, her lips firm, neither a smile nor a frown. "Sit tight."

Mom takes a step closer and crosses her arms. I've done some stupid things in my life—including getting caught cheating at school earlier this year—but I don't think I've ever seen this level of disapproval on her face. It's like I told her that I convinced the Easter Bunny to stab Santa Claus, then we went on a bender with the Tooth Fairy. "Biz, we've talked to you about drinking and driving. I can't—" she shakes her head, closing her eyes for a moment. "I can't believe you would do something so stupid."

The shame I've felt up to this point is no match for what I feel now. Heat flushes my cheeks and I long for my old hair to hide my face. On reflex, my fingers reach for a strand near my neck, but I come up empty-handed. My brain surgery was months ago but my hair is taking its sweet time growing back. I slide my hand over my face, covering my eyes. "I'm sorry."

I hear her exhale, but I can't bring myself to look at her.

The silence is excruciating. Buster doesn't move—arms locked over his chest, feet spread wide apart—he's in this for the long haul, but Reece fidgets, shifting his weight and shoving his hands in and out of his pants pockets. Mom just keeps staring at me.

When the nurse returns with a slip of paper, I'm so relieved for the break in the tension that I almost forget why she's here. My stomach plummets at her frown. "BAL is point oh-six-five."

Buster exhales slowly and Mom's head whips between him and the nurse. She hasn't figured out yet that he's determined to make this as awful as possible. "Is that good or bad?" She clutches her purse tightly, my fate resting in his answer.

I hold my breath.

"It's not above the legal limit, but since she's a minor, she's still in trouble."

The balloon of hope inside me pops.

"Is she being arrested?" Mom's voice comes out higher-pitched than normal and remorse washes over me for the millionth time. If I'd been more careful when she picked me up, none of this would have happened. A tiny voice reminds me that I also could have not drank when I knew I was going to dinner with my parents.

"Yes." Buster is either oblivious to my mother's panic or just doesn't care.

I start to stand but he freezes me with a hard glare. "Can I see Amelia before we go?"

Reece takes a tiny step closer and rests his hand on the edge of the bed. It's the closest to a comforting gesture I'm going to get, and I lock eyes with him, willing him to continue being the good cop to Buster's bad. "I'll find out where she is. Even if she's having surgery, I doubt they've started yet."

My mouth goes dry. "Surgery?" Mom and I say in unison as Reece moves the curtain aside and steps into the main room.

Buster doesn't blink. "That's what happens when you drive drunk. You hurt people."

That's it. I know I screwed up but I don't deserve this judgmental crap from a cop who—

"Who did you lose?" Mom asks, her voice barely above a whisper.

Buster's eyes widen and his lips part for a split second, then the stony mask falls back into place. He clears his throat. "My daughter."

My heart squeezes, but I don't have time to say anything because he grabs my elbow and steers me out of the room, his eyes locked on the exit. "What about Amelia?"

"I'm not doing you any favors."

I glance over my shoulder at Mom, who's trailing behind us.

She shakes her head and hold up her hands as if to say, "I don't know."

We're almost to the exit and still no sign of Reece. Worse than not seeing Amelia is the thought of riding to the police station alone with Buster. I try to slow down but Buster's grip doesn't loosen.

"Don't you need to wait for your partner?" Mom asks from behind me.

Buster doesn't turn his head. "He'll meet us in the car."

The automatic doors whoosh open and Martinez walks in, his white lab coat flapping against his thighs. He stops abruptly when he sees us. Or rather, when he sees Buster. "George," he says with a friendly nod.

Please don't let him see me.

He notices Mom first. "Mrs. Clement, what are you doing—" His mouth falls open when he finally sees me. "Biz?"

I hang my head. I can't look him in the eye.

Buster yanks me from behind him so we're standing hip to hip. "You know her?"

Martinez slides a hand over the stubble on his chin. "She's the project I told you about."

# chapter 5

"Your project?" My pulse races as I glare at Martinez, forgetting Buster, the accident, Amelia, my mom. He's told people about me? It's supposed to be a secret—or as secret as a research project about my whacked-out brain can be.

Martinez holds up a hand, a gesture I'm very familiar with. It's supposed to calm me down, but it rarely works. "Not the particulars. Just that we're working together." His dark eyes plead with me and I feel another familiar sensation: butterflies in my stomach.

Why the hell does he have to be so hot?

Buster loosens his death grip. "She's the case that's going to make you famous?"

Martinez's mouth drops. I can't remember the last time I've seen him at a loss for words.

Now it's Mom's turn to speak up. "Dr. Martinez, what exactly have you been telling people about my daughter, and how on earth is a study on migraines going to make you famous?"

Oh yeah, Mom doesn't know that I flicker.

Martinez looks back and forth between me and Mom. "I promise I haven't divulged anything pertaining to our research, I merely mentioned to my friend George here that I have a new project I'm working on." His gaze lands on me again, and he shrugs, a soft gesture that makes me think of our sessions in his office. Ever since Dad expressed his concern about how close I've become with Martinez, I've been aware of how he acts with me, and even though I know it's crazy because he's like ten years older than me, sometimes I swear he's flirting with me. "You know you can trust me."

Buster clears his throat. "I hate to break up this party, but Ms. Clement needs to come with me."

Martinez gives him a look that I don't understand—a small tilt of the head and a tightening of his lips—as Reece finally reappears.

"I found her." Reece touches my free arm. "You can see her for a minute."

Martinez lifts a hand like he wants to grab my arm, too, but I'm fresh out of arms. He settles for a hard glare instead. "What's going on?"

I can't look at him. "I hit a tree and Amelia is hurt." I raise my head to meet his stare, hoping he can read my mind and know I flickered, that I didn't do this on purpose. Tears spring to my eyes. "They're saying she might need surgery."

Reece nods.

Buster still hasn't let go of my arm. I try to pull it out of his grasp. "Can I please go see her? Just for a minute?" I expect him to scowl and yank me through the doors, but he closes his eyes, inhales slowly, and finally releases my arm.

Reece addresses Mom. "We'll just be a minute."

"I'm coming with you," Mom says.

We leave Martinez and Buster standing in front of the door. I follow Reece through a set of swinging doors and it's like someone hit the mute button. The brightness and activity are the same, but it's much, much quieter. More serious.

Reece stops in front of a closed door. "In here." He opens it and I hesitate. "Hurry up. Buster's gonna rip me a new one as it is."

Mom nudges me forward as she steps back into the hallway. Amelia lies motionless on a stark white bed, dwarfed by the machines that surround her. One tube runs from a clear bag suspended over her head into her arm, while another snakes from behind her pillow, feeding oxygen into her nose. A blanket is tucked tightly against her chest, making it impossible to see how badly she's hurt. Her hair is in the same ponytail from earlier, but chunks have come loose and hang limp against her face. I don't think I've ever seen her so still. Even when she's sleeping, she tosses and turns and talks so much that I can barely sleep during our sleepovers. A lump catches in my throat. I did this to her.

The door clicks shut behind us and her eyes open. A smile parts her lips. "Hey, what took you so long? Were you scoping for hot guys?" Her smile fades as her gaze shifts to Reece, who is leaning against the door.

His cheeks turn a shade of pink that looks almost salmon under the florescent lights. He clears his throat and nods in Amelia's direction.

"They're taking me to the police station but I wanted to see you." I move to the edge of the bed and carefully weave my fingers through hers. Her skin is cool and I'm reminded of holding my dad's hand in a hospital bed like this. But his sickness has nothing to do with me. Amelia wouldn't be here if I hadn't been so careless. "I'm so sorry."

"Stop it." She squeezes my fingers but there's no strength in the gesture. My heart aches at how weak she is. "It's not like you did this on purpose."

"If I could trade places with you, I would."

"You already had surgery this year."

I shake my head and smile despite myself.

"So you concede. Now run off with your handsome cop friend and we'll catch up tomorrow."

I start to pull away but she tugs me closer. I press my forehead against hers.

"I wish there was a way you could tell the truth," she whispers.

Tears sting my eyes. "Me too."

"Good luck."

I give her hand a final squeeze, then straighten and face Reece. He opens the door and I feel like he's walking me to a firing squad.

Mom's a flurry of questions as we retrace our steps to the ER entrance. "How is she? Are her parents here? Does she really need surgery?"

"Mom, I don't know. I barely had time to apologize." I'm shaken by Amelia's appearance and the uncertainty of what exactly she needs surgery on. I assumed it's her broken leg, but what if she has internal injuries or a severed liver or something? I stop in my tracks. What if she dies?

Reece slows his pace but doesn't stop. "Come on."

Buster stands at the entrance, his strong arms crossed over his chest.

Martinez is still there, but any concern he had for me earlier is gone. Now he just looks pissed. His scowl deepens as we get closer. "You left out a few details."

Anger burns through me at his accusation, but I swallow it. This is my fault. I can't get mad at Mom or Buster or anyone else for telling the truth. Even if I didn't mean to drive after drinking, those are the facts and by tomorrow everyone I know will have heard the news.

I throw back my shoulders, hoping the bravado masks the fear coursing through me. "You didn't give me a chance."

Buster nods at Martinez, then glares at me. "Time to go."

I fight an intense urge to run through the doors, past the cruiser, and into the night.

Buster must have noticed my hesitation because his hand finds its way back around my upper arm. No fleeing for me. "Ma'am, you can meet us at the station."

Mom nods like he told her she can rent a giraffe at the next corner. "O-okay."

I lock eyes with Martinez.

He blinks once, turns, and walks away as we step outside. If he's wondering if I flickered, he's not giving anything away.

Buster opens the back door of the cruiser. "Doesn't look like you're his pet project anymore."

I want to smack the smug look off his face, but I climb into the backseat without saying a word. Assaulting a police officer on the way to the station will not help this situation.

He slams his door harder than necessary. Once seated, he messes around on the dashboard and the blue strobe lights jump into action, bouncing off every concrete surface in the ambulance bay.

I sink lower into the seat in an effort to protect my eyes and whatever's left of my dignity.

Reece slides into the passenger seat and turns off the lights. They glare at each other for a moment, but whatever silent battle they're having ends in my favor: the lights stay off.

The ride is too short. Night has descended over the town, hiding everything in shadow so all I can see is the faint outline of trees before we pull into the police station. We repeat the scene at the hospital, except this time there are no concerned faces waiting inside. Buster nods at the man seated behind the counter as we push through a metal door that leads to a small room. It's empty except for a long table and a couple chairs. The lingering odor of stale coffee and something more pungent, more carnal, assaults my senses, making my stomach turn.

He points at one of the chairs. "Wait here." The door clicks behind him and I'm left alone for the first time.

This is real. I'm being arrested for drunk driving and who knows what other charges for hurting Amelia. I sink into the chair and rest my head on my folded arms. The promise I made Dad drifts through my head. No more flickering. We still don't know what makes us flicker—Martinez has made some progress but we still have a lot of research ahead of us—so I agreed not to flicker unless it's absolutely necessary. And since I'm in a flicker now, double flickering could kill me faster than whatever is happening with Dad.

I take a deep breath, trying to slow my heart rate. Amelia's face flashes through my mind. If there's ever a situation that's necessary, this is it, but if I've learned one thing over the past few months it's that just because I can change something, that doesn't mean I should. Sometimes it's better to accept what's happened and face the consequences.

I straighten my shoulders, readying myself for whatever comes next.

# chapter 6

The door opens after what feels like hours, but in reality is probably less than ten minutes. Buster and Reece enter. Buster takes the seat across from me while Reece stands in the corner. I really wish they'd switch places. I wouldn't go so far as to say Reece has been nice to me, but he hasn't been flat out hostile like Buster. Not that I can blame him. Just being in the same room as me is probably bringing back all kinds of memories of his daughter.

Buster pulls a notepad from his front pocket and glares at me. "Tell us what happened."

Just like that? I clear my throat. I've had plenty of time to come up with a story that doesn't include flickering, but it makes me sound like an irresponsible teenager. "I had a little vodka after school. It was stupid. I've had a really bad week and my birthday is tomorrow and I was feeling sorry for myself." That's all true, even if the timing isn't. They don't need to know that most of it happens tomorrow. Or did happen.

"Your friend didn't have any alcohol in her system. Why were you driving if she hadn't had anything to drink?"

Good question. "I don't know."

His brow furrows, making his eyes threatening, scary.

I want to scream, 'I would never drink and drive!' but I can't. Instead I go with irresponsible teenage logic, which is what he seems to expect. "I told you, it was stupid."

"Did Amelia know you'd been drinking?"

I shake my head, eyes down. My heart feels like it might burst with how badly I wish I could undo all of this.

"I need a verbal answer."

I raise my eyes and will myself not to cry. "No."

He sets down his pen and folds his hands on top of his notebook. His eyes narrow even more and I feel like his gaze could peel the skin off me.

I stiffen, not wanting to hear whatever he says next.

"Let me get this straight. You drank illegally because you were feeling sorry for yourself, then got into a vehicle without a care in the world about who you might hurt. Including your so-called best friend." He rubs a hand over his face, closing his eyes for a moment before resuming his attack. "Your blood alcohol isn't above the legal limit, and since your mother is here, you get to go home. But I want you to know that if it was up to me, you'd be spending the night in jail."

A shudder runs through me. Of all the possibilities of what might happen—being arrested, losing my license, Amelia needing surgery—going to jail never entered my head. Call it naiveté, but I've been more freaked out by what my parents will do to me. I risk making eye contact with him. "I'm sorry."

He stares at his notepad. "Tell that to the judge tomorrow."

"Tomorrow?"

"Yes. You have a hearing in the morning."

"Does that mean I can go now?"

"After we fingerprint you and get your glamour shot."

Reece opens the door and Buster stands. "Let's go."

The fingerprinting and picture were as humiliating as you'd expect. But they let me leave afterwards, my fingers stained and my ego bruised. Mom shoves the paperwork of my arrest and hearing tomorrow into her purse before getting into the car.

"Don't talk to me until we get home. I need a little more time to process this."

I get in the car and lean my head against the window, wishing for the millionth time that I could undo everything that's happened in the past few hours. I hate being judged for something that isn't true about me, and right now, everyone thinks I'm a stupid teenager who chose to drink and drive.

Mom exhales next to me. As mad as she is, Dad will be even more angry because I flickered—even though I didn't mean to.

A thought stirs, one that's occurred to me a lot lately: it's time to tell Mom the truth.

When we pull into the driveway, I grab my purse and follow Mom into the house. Dad's waiting at the kitchen island, his hands wrapped around a cup of coffee. He looks like he's settled in for a long night. Part of me wonders if he's already figured out that I flickered and didn't mean to drive, and is having the same thoughts as me about telling Mom.

I slide into the chair across from him and lower my eyes.

Mom busies herself behind me, putting dishes from the sink into the dishwasher before helping herself to a cup of coffee.

This is going to be a long night.

Dad takes a sip before speaking. "Do you want to tell me what happened?"

I meet his gaze, and to my surprise, there's no judgment there, only concern. My eyebrows raise and he gives a barely perceptible nod. He does know! "We need to tell her," I mouth.

He holds up a finger. "First tell me what happened."

I run through a shortened version of what I told the police. It's what's in the report, so I may as well get used to telling the same half-truth. "I was feeling sorry for myself about all the crap that's happened in the last few months and the fact that Cameron and I still aren't talking, so I had a little vodka."

"And then you decided to drive?" His voice comes out deeper, more gruff than I'm used to. Mom moves to his side and rests her free hand on his arm, a united front against me.

Why is he grilling me? Is this for Mom's benefit? Because if it is, we really need to just get the truth out right now. "It wasn't so much that I decided—I wasn't thinking."

"Clearly." Mom crosses her arms and I swear I can see steam coming out of her ears.

"Mom, there's more to it than that." I stare at Dad, but he closes his eyes. How do I ask Mom for a timeout to talk to Dad privately? He needs to be okay with this before—

"Well, let's hear it then." She puts her hands on her hips, then recrosses them, like anger is preventing her from standing still.

"I…" Dad, look at me! I'm screaming as loud as I can in my head, but he's still refusing to meet my gaze. I won't do this unless he agrees.

Mom looks so mad she could burst. "Biz, quit stalling. Say whatever it is you think will make this okay and make me not want to lock you in your room for the rest of the school year."

"Dad."

The desperation in my voice finally makes him look at me. He blinks once more, then whispers, "Okay."

Mom glances between us. "Okay, what?"

"Okay, she can tell you the truth."

She stills. "The truth? What are you two talking about? Why do I feel like I'm the only one who doesn't know what's going on here?"

I take a deep breath. So far I've told three people my secret—Cameron, Amelia, and Martinez—and instead of getting easier, each time has been more difficult. Maybe because the risk of that person not believing me has increased each time.

Mom leans her elbows on the counter, waiting.

Here goes nothing. "You know how the sunlight bothers me?" I look at Dad. "Bothers us?"

She nods.

"It does more than just give us migraines. It…" I close my eyes, fearing the betrayal my next words are sure to make her feel. We've kept this from her for so long—my entire life—and I would be devastated finding out after all this time. "It makes us travel back to yesterday."

Her head tilts to the side but she doesn't say anything.

I wait, but still nothing.

Dad moves his hand over hers and her eyes dart to him and back to me again.

"I don't understand."

I swallow hard. "The sunlight makes us travel back in time, to yesterday."

"That's impossible."

Dad shakes his head. "It's very possible."

She straightens. "Time travel isn't real."

His grip tightens on her hand. "It is for us."

"But I don't understand. How can you—" she focuses on me, "—you both...time travel," the words seem clumsy on her tongue, "without me knowing?"

A flash of disappointment crosses Dad's face. "You never suspected anything was off? A little different?"

I've always wondered if deep down Mom had an inkling that something was weird with us, but her utter confusion makes it clear that she didn't.

She slumps into the chair next to him. "I think you need to start from the beginning."

So he does. Starting with their first date, which he repeated to make it better, to when I was born, which was the first time he had a seizure. Then to when he first realized I was flickering—years before I ever told him—and how together we helped rescue Katie and the other kidnapped girls.

Mom's eyes widen. "You were involved with that?"

A lump catches in my throat. There are so many things I want to tell her, to fill in the gaps of what she thought she knew, but I don't know where to begin. "Yeah, I'm the big hero who stopped Turner, got kidnapped by him, and had brain surgery." Okay, so that may not have been the best way to explain it because her mouth has fallen open and her skin is decidedly paler than it was a few seconds ago. "Mom, are you okay? I'm sorry, I shouldn't have spit it all out like that."

She gives her head a little shake. "How does it—flickering—happen?"

Dad explains the strobing sunlight, the tingling fingers and toes, followed by the heaviness and the floating, and for a moment I have the sensation that I'm watching this happen to someone else. I've never heard another person describe flickering before. When he figured out that we both flicker we were too busy swapping stories than to talk about the mechanics involved.

Mom turns to me. "And it's the same for you?"

I nod.

She touches my hand. "Keep talking."

Now it's my turn to tell about all the little ways I've changed things over the years—reliving my first date with Cameron, unintentionally cheating on tests, and the big one: trying to stop Katie from killing herself. The overwhelming sense of grief that is never far from me surrounds my heart, making it too big for my chest.

Mom's eyes fill with tears. "I had no idea you were dealing with so much. I know it was hard when Katie killed herself, but I never imagined how involved you were."

Tears burn my eyes, and for once I don't try to stop them. "I feel like it's all my fault. I got her away from Turner, but I couldn't make her better." I shudder, remembering how angry and scared Katie was, especially in those last weeks before she died. "I tried three times to stop her, but her will to die was stronger than anything I could do or say to her."

Mom's face goes ashen. "Three times?"

Dad inhales, a wheezing gasp that snaps me back to the present. "That's when she ended up back in the hospital."

She's quiet for a moment, thinking. "So the last two times you've had to go to the hospital, it's been because you were trying to save Katie?"

I shrug. "Call it my personal mission. But I failed. She's gone, and now Cameron and I aren't even speaking. The only good thing is I didn't need surgery the second time." After unsuccessfully trying to stop Katie from killing herself, I thought for sure that Martinez would have to crack my skull open again, but he was able to stop my head from exploding with a heavy dose of steroids and a long list of other drugs I can't pronounce. So instead of getting my head shaved, I gained twenty pounds.

She moves around the island to wrap her arms around me. For a moment, I'm five years old again, safe in my mother's arms after a nightmare. "Why do you keep flickering if it hurts you?" She pulls back to look me in the eye.

Dad once called flickering an addiction, comparing it to drugs, and while I don't think I'm addicted, I've certainly done it for less than stellar reasons. "I'm trying to stop."

"Does Cameron know the truth?"

I nod.

She straightens. "Who else?"

My stomach sinks. "Amelia. And Martinez."

She releases me and whirls on Dad. "They know the truth, but me, your wife and mother, couldn't be trusted to know the biggest secret of your lives?" It's like we've pulled back a blanket by telling the truth and all her memories have shifted into something clouded by lies and deception.

Dad reaches for her hand but she pulls away.

Tears spill down her face. I've seen her cry plenty of times before, but it's always been out of concern for me or Dad, not anger or betrayal. Her head slowly shakes back and forth. "Our entire marriage, you've kept this from me. How can I..." she trails off, her voice low. "How can I ever know what you're saying is true?"

He rises from the chair and pulls her to his chest. "Nothing about my love for you has changed. Yes, there are some details that I've left out, but I'm still the same person you married, the same father to Biz, and I'll answer any questions you have for as long as I still have breath in my lungs." Despite his frail arms, he holds her as she struggles to move away, until she finally relaxes in his arms. Pressing a kiss to her temple, he strokes the back of her head, a gesture he's used to calm me down when I'm upset.

Suddenly I'm overcome with grief, a sweeping tidal wave that nearly knocks me out of my chair. What will become of our family when he's gone?

She wipes her eyes with her sleeve, kisses him lightly on the cheek, and turns to me. "I need some time to think about what you've told me. If this is true..." she shakes her head. "I don't know. I guess we have a lot more talking to do."

"I'm sorry to dump this on you, but I couldn't stand you thinking I would drink and drive."

The puzzled look on her face tells me that she hasn't made the connection between flickering and the accident tonight. "I guess I'm still not following."

I look to Dad for reassurance, but his eyes are glazed over, not focused on either of us. My heart quickens in fear that he's about to have a seizure, but after a moment his eyes clear and he's back with us. I run a hand over my face. There's no sense hiding the truth that I was drinking—the police have already outed me for that—but it's hard confessing that I was doing anything of which they'd disapprove.

"I was at Amelia's tomorrow—" I watch Mom to make sure she's getting it, "—and we had a couple shots of vodka. For my birthday." Tears blur my vision. That will be the only birthday celebration I get. "I was feeling sorry for myself because of Cameron and Katie and all the other crap going on in my life, so I might have had more than I should have."

Dad crosses his arms, his eyes dark. "Do you drink often?"

My heart clenches. It kills me to have him think badly of me, even if I earned it. "Not often, and not very much. Sometimes I have a beer at a party, but I'm not into acting like an idiot and I refuse to drive drunk. Ask anyone!" I realize too late that my argument is no longer valid.

"So how did you flicker?" Dad's working his jaw, clearly angry but not wanting to stop my story.

"I asked Mom to pick me up for dinner with the two of you so I wouldn't be driving and she drove through the Strand."

He closes his eyes.

"What's the Strand?" Mom asks.

"It's a stretch of tall trees where I can flicker pretty much any time of day. Assuming there's sunlight." I swallow, not wanting her to feel responsible for what happens next. "You drove through there and I wasn't paying attention. Before I could stop it, I was flickering and I ended up in my car, driving with Amelia. That's how I crashed." I hang my head. Even though I didn't mean to, I still wrecked the car and hurt my best friend.

Mom watches me but doesn't say anything. Neither does Dad.

The silence is unbearable.

I lift my head, tears sliding down my face. "You believe me, right? I would never do something so stupid, especially not with someone else in the car!" A sob breaks free from my chest and I put my head on my arms on the counter, unable to stop crying now that I've started.

I jump a little when her hand slides over my neck, gently kneading the muscles at the base of my skull.

"I want to."

That wasn't a yes, but it's the best we're going to get tonight. I lift my head as her hand drops away. "Can you do me a favor?"

She sighs. "What is it?"

"Would you mind calling the hospital and checking on Amelia? I don't think her parents will talk to me and I want to know how the surgery went."

"I'll call from upstairs." She brushes a kiss across Dad's cheek. "We can talk about this more tomorrow." She climbs the stairs, her hand tightly gripping the railing like it's the only thing keeping her grounded.

I face Dad, dragging a sleeve across my face to wipe the tears. "That went well."

The corners of his mouth turn down. "I've always imagined telling her the truth someday, but the thing that always stopped me was the fear that she would feel betrayed." Whatever strength has been holding him up since I got home evaporates—even his bones too tired to support his frame. His face seems thinner every week, but there's always been a glimmer of excitement in his eyes. Now that glimmer is gone.

"I'm sorry. She'll come around. We'll keep talking to her until she does." Dad doesn't have the luxury of time that I do. He needs Mom's forgiveness soon or the little time they have left together will be wasted.

He sighs, and I swear he deflates even more. "I know she will." His gaze meets mine. "I never wanted to lie to her, but it seemed too big, too farfetched, for her to believe me. For years, I didn't believe it myself, and even when I accepted flickering as part of who I was, I was afraid it would scare her away."

I certainly understand that. Before Cameron, I had a reputation for dropping guys when they got too close, but it was a survival method to keep my secret safe. Maybe the old way was better. Cameron was the first person I ever told, and we're no longer speaking.

"Biz, how often do you drink?"

The change in topic startles me. "Why?"

"You need to be extremely careful using any kind of substance that can alter your mind. As you learned today, even though you have a pretty good handle on flickering, there will always be times when you can't fully control it." His gaze drifts over my shoulder, staring into space, like he's having a hard time focusing.

"What happened to you?"

He shakes his head. "Another time. When I'm not so tired." He flattens his hands on the counter. "I may not be around to help if this happens again, so listen to me now. All the fun stuff that happens at college, like tailgating and pub crawls, can have horrible effects for you. And that's just alcohol—drugs bring on a whole new level of unpredictability."

"I don't do drugs." I feel a twinge of pride that I can say that much.

"But you do drink." It's a statement, not a question, and that momentary swell of pride bursts.

"Not often, and not a lot. Just a random beer at parties, like I said. It's not like I have a liquor cabinet in my room or anything." I don't mean to get defensive, but I hate the disappointed look on his face.

"Biz, this ability is a gift, but it's a gift that comes with sacrifice. You'll never be able to let loose like your friends without risking your safety and the safety of the people around you."

"I know." A small smile parts my lips. "Drunk flickering is bad."

He leans forward. "Biz, this isn't a joke."

"I'm sorry. That was stupid." I feel like I'm at the end of a bungee cord, being yanked from one emotion to the next, words blurting out of my mouth before I can stop them.

"I'm not saying this as some kind of punishment for tonight—you have enough trouble ahead of you without me adding to it—I'm talking about a change in how you live. The consequences if you don't..." He shakes his head, and once again I notice a sense of regret in his words.

"Did you hurt someone?" Part of me can't help but hope that he says yes so that I'll know I'm not the only one who's screwed everything up from flickering.

He closes his eyes. "Yes. But I wasn't as lucky as you. My friend didn't survive."

# chapter 7

My head hurts from last night, but I throw off the covers, determined to meet this day head-on.

I thought hearing that Dad had accidentally flickered after drinking would make me feel better, but it's further complicated how I feel about my ability. It's been almost five years since the orthodontist appointment that first made me flicker, and since then I thought I'd learned how to control it, or if not exactly control, to keep it in check. Dad's confession that he crashed a car and killed one of his best friends makes me realize what a fluke it was that Amelia didn't die.

The day of my hearing. My birthday.

I pull the covers back over my head. Maybe I'm not ready for this.

A knock on the door prompts me to pull off the covers again. "Yeah?"

The door opens and Mom peers inside. "Can I come in?"

I scoot closer to the wall to make room for her.

Instead of perching on the edge like I expect, she lies down next to me so her head is on the pillow next to mine. Her cool hand presses against my cheek. "I'm sorry that you've felt you had to keep this from me. I don't know if I fully understand everything, but I'm glad you told me."

The knot in my stomach relaxes ever so slightly. "Did you and Dad talk more last night?"

"A little. It's hard for him to stay awake once his body decides it's time to sleep, but he said enough to ease my anger." The corners of her mouth turn up, but it's a sad expression. Tears shine in her eyes. "He's always been able to charm me."

The sadness on her face makes me tear up, too. The swing of emotion dries my throat and I have to take a deep breath. "How much longer do you think he has?"

She closes her eyes, tears rolling onto the pillow.

I clasp her hand that's still on my cheek and nuzzle her palm. "I don't know how to go on without him."

Even while my heart is breaking, I can't help but feel a twinge of something—jealousy? regret?—that she didn't say how we will go on without him. Dad has always been her priority when he's had a seizure, and I understand that when he's in the hospital he should be her focus, but it hurts that I can be so easily overlooked by my mother. She squeezes my hand, but her presence is not as comforting as it could be, and I realize I feel the same way she does: Dad has always been my rock, and the person I'm left with will always be second-best.

I pull my hand back and wipe my eyes. "Do I have to go to school today?"

She smiles, but it's a wobbly effort, her lips trembling. "Consider it a birthday present." She props herself up on an elbow and presses a kiss to my forehead. "The hearing is at eleven, so be ready by then."

"Thanks, Mom."

The bed creaks as she gets up. At the door she turns to face me. "Happy birthday."

I lay in bed for another hour, but I can't sleep. The previous day keeps playing over and over in my head. The tree. Amelia screaming. And all the blood.

I reach for my phone, a little surprised my parents didn't take it away, and text Amelia for the hundredth time since last night.

Me: You okay? I'm sorry x 1000000.

Last night Mom couldn't find out any details since we aren't immediate family, and no one answered the phone in Amelia's room. I hope she hasn't answered because she doesn't have her phone, not because she's in a medically induced coma or something equally as scary. She could be in surgery or sedated or unable to write back for any number of reasons, so I may not hear from her—

    Amelia: Hey!

    Me: You're awake!

    Amelia: Surgery later this morning. Broken leg. :(

That can't be all. There was so much blood.

    Amelia: I guess I got a transfusion last night. The tree cut my artery or something.

    Me: Holy crap.

    Me: Can you have visitors?

    Amelia: You're not in school?

    Amelia: Oh! Happy birthday!

I smile. Leave it to Amelia to be thinking of others when she's laid up in a hospital bed.

    Me: Thx.

    Amelia: Parents are here. I don't think I can have visitors.

    Amelia: Plus you're grounded, right?

    Me: Not yet. We told Mom the truth.

    Me: And the hearing's this morning.

    Amelia: Big day.

    Me: Yeah.

    Amelia: Good luck. Tackle hug. xoxo.

    Me: xoxo

I rest the phone on my chest. Not many people would be as forgiving as Amelia, even knowing that the accident truly was an accident. I'm not sure what to expect from the hearing today. Some kids at school have lost their license and had to do community service, but the guy who caused an accident I once photographed had to spend a week in jail. I close my eyes, mentally steeling myself for whatever happens.

◆◆◆

Three hours later, a judge glares at me from atop a wooden desk on a wooden platform at the front of a wood-paneled courtroom. His gray curly hair seems ill-suited for a judge, but the black robe and scowl are plenty intimidating on their own.

"Your blood-alcohol limit was below the legal limit set by the law, but since you are only seventeen," the judge shuffles the papers in front of him and reads from the top of one. "Excuse me, eighteen, you are being charged with a Minor in Possession, in addition to causing an accident that resulted in serious bodily harm. Now," he looks up and steeples his hands beneath his chin. "I have the option of sentencing you to a jail time—"

Mom gasps next to me.

"—but as this is your first offense, I'm reducing your sentence to a one thousand-dollar fine, thirty hours of community service, a thirty-day suspension of your license, and one hundred-twenty days restricted license. That means you can only drive to school and work for another four months after the one-month suspension."

I let out a breath. No jail. The rest of what he says is a blur as relief courses through me. Losing my license sucks, but I can deal with it.

The gavel slams on the wooden desk and I jump. The judge is still staring at me. "Quite a way to spend your birthday, young lady."

"Yes, sir."

He points the gavel at me. "No more drinking until you're twenty-one. You hear me?"

"Yes, sir."

The public defender shakes my hand, and before I can get my bearings, we're outside on the sidewalk in front of the courthouse. The sun beats down on us from high in the sky, reflecting off a parked news van. It seems out of place on the deserted street.

"What do you think they're doing here?"

Mom studies the van. "I heard the pretrial hearing for Mr. Turner is soon. Maybe they're hoping to see him."

My already empty stomach feels hollow and my mouth waters like I might throw up. "Already? I thought it takes years for things to go to trial."

"Not always. It depends on the case. With him I suppose there's very little question that he's guilty so maybe it took less time."

"So his trial will be soon?"

"I heard April."

I shield my eyes with my hand, taking one last look at the van, then up the street. "Is there someplace nearby where we can eat?" Not that I'm hungry anymore, but I need to get away from here.

Mom slings her purse onto her shoulder. "There's a cute sandwich shop on the next street over. I think it's the same one where you photographed that accident last fall."

It's like I'm retracing every decision to flicker that led me to this point today.

◆◆◆

We go home after lunch and I spend the rest of the afternoon flipping through the paperwork from court, focusing on the sheet of options for community service. Picking up trash on the highway seems like the easiest, but I'm drawn to the ones that require interaction with other people: the food bank or helping at an office or library. As much as I'd like to hide from people until the accident is forgotten, I feel like I need to prove to everyone that I've learned from my mistake and that I can act like the adult I've officially become today and take responsibility for my actions.

I'm debating between sorting books at the library and distributing food to the needy when the migraine hits. For the first time in my life I'm grateful for the pain.

It's the only thing distracting me from the weight of everything in my head.

Hurting Amelia.

Disappointing Mom and Dad.

Letting down Cameron, even though deep down I know I couldn't have saved Katie.

I glance at my camera resting on the corner of my desk and a familiar pang stabs me in the chest. Since the first time I picked up a camera, photography has been my world, but it's like the connection was lost when Katie died. It doesn't help that every time I take a photo, Turner—the good Turner—whispers to me, instructing me on angles and shutter speeds and capturing the emotion of the scene, but then the bad Turner—the one whose evil I saw firsthand—crashes through my mind, threatening to pull me down into a spiral of depression that I don't know how to escape.

# chapter 8

By Monday morning my headache is gone, and I decide to push away the poor-me attitude and focus on Amelia. Mom finally talked to her mom, who reported that Amelia came out of surgery fine but not-so-gently suggested that I not visit her in the hospital. But I refuse to go another day without seeing her in person and making sure she really is okay. Since she's recovering and no longer in any real danger, her parents are probably going back to work today, which means no one will stop me from visiting her.

I take extra care getting ready for school—a touch of makeup and clothes that were actually in the dresser, not on the floor— even though deep down I know my efforts are useless: the kids at school will be brutal. The standard treatment for kids who get a DUI is beer cans taped to their locker, but hurting someone else is a whole other level. I don't even want to think about what they have in store for me.

"You look nice." Mom smiles as I come down the stairs.

I smooth nonexistent wrinkles out of my t-shirt.

"Nervous about today?"

I might be more nervous than I was the first day I went back after getting my head shaved last fall. At least that was a medical thing. "Yeah. High school really sucks sometimes."

She sighs, a soft sound that makes me look up. "I can't help but wonder how many times you've been punished for something that was caused by you flickering."

I try to smile, but it comes out lopsided. I join her at the kitchen island and take a sip of the coffee waiting for me. "Too many to count."

"I wish there were something I could do to make it easier."

"Well, there is one thing. Can we stop by the hospital on the way to school?"

She runs her finger around the rim of her coffee cup. "It's not exactly on the way."

"I know, but if we leave now we'd still have time. And I just need a few minutes so I can give her a squeeze and make sure she hasn't changed her mind about hating me."

"I thought you said she wasn't mad?"

"I'd like to see her face when she says it."

"How can I say no to that?"

We pull into the hospital parking lot fifteen minutes later. I climb out and look back in at Mom. "I'll just be a few minutes."

I hurry through the automatic door and find the elevator. I almost push the button for the second floor out of habit, but it's not Dad I'm coming to see. The doors slide open on the fourth floor and I glance at the nurses' station before beelining for Amelia's room. Her parents may not be here, but they could have told the hospital staff to tackle me on sight or something. But the coast is clear.

I knock lightly on the door before pushing it open.

Amelia is drinking orange juice from a straw. Her eyes light up when she sees me, but my heart nearly stops. Her leg is fully encased in a cast. She's paler than normal and the life seems to have been sucked out of her. "How'd you get past the Gestapo?"

"Super ninja moves I learned in the war." I pluck at the sheet that covers her uninjured leg. "You look good."

She snorts. "I look terrible."

The accident flashes through my mind and I fight back tears. "You look better than you did Thursday night. I was so scared you wouldn't...that you might not..." I can't say the words I almost killed you out loud.

"If it makes you feel better, I promise to never let you live this down."

The corner of my mouth turns up. "I missed you."

"I'm sorry my parents have been such jerks. I tried to tell them but—"

"I know. It's hard to explain without the truth."

She looks at her leg. "Yeah."

I move to the edge of the bed, unsure if I should sit. I rub the corner of the sheet through my fingers. "What can I do?"

"I fully expect you to get my lunch and carry my books for as long as I'm on crutches."

I straighten. "Done."

"And you shall drive me to and from school."

"No license. Or car."

She purses her lips. "Oh, right. Hmm...You will do my Trig homework."

I snort. "You really think that's a good idea?"

She smiles. "Can't be worse than what I'd do."

I laugh. I can't help it. Even lying here in a hospital bed, Amelia is the most amazing person I know. I lean forward to hug her and bury my face in her hair. "When are you busting out of here?"

"Later today." She smooths the blanket covering her legs. "They want me back at school tomorrow."

I hold out an imaginary skirt and curtsy. "Then I shall prepare for your arrival."

She smiles, but tears fill her eyes. "Thanks, Biz."

I touch her hand. "I'm sorry this happened. Look, I know I've said it already, but if I could take this back, you know I'd do it in a heartbeat."

◆◆◆

Mom and I arrive at school as the warning bell rings. A twinge of sadness stops me when I see my locker. Every birthday, Amelia has decorated my locker with streamers and balloons, but today it's covered with empty beer cans. Heat warms my cheeks as kids stare at me, waiting to see what I'll do.

Double J and a couple of the other guys who stopped talking to me when Cameron and I broke up stare at me as they walk by, but at least they don't say anything. The girls behind them aren't so kind. I catch the tail end of what sounds like "trailer trash" from Christina, the blond bimbo who tried to make my life hell last fall, as she accidentally on purpose bumps into me.

I turn away from them and face my locker. You'd think it'd be hard to get a roundish object to stick to metal, but duct tape holds everything. I yank off a couple near the combination and throw them on the ground. Once I get my locker open I pick up the cans and toss them into the bottom, but what if Stride Right thinks they're mine? I kick them back onto the ground. I'll find a garbage bag or something after my first class.

When I enter my first class, the conversation comes to a halt, but the whispers start back up when an aide from the office knocks on the door and I'm called to the front of the class. A chorus of "Oooohs" follow me into the hall.

"What's this about?"

"Mr. Walker wants to see you." The kid can't be more than a freshman. Why can't I ever get someone my own age to summon me to the principal's office?

By the time we arrive at Stride Right's office I'm sweating and struggling to breathe. Of course the school would know what happened, but I didn't think I could get in trouble here, too.

His secretary waves me through the open door, but I pause at the threshold. Wiping my palms on my jeans, I take a deep breath and step inside the wood-paneled room.

"Ms. Clement, have a seat." His large frame is concealed behind the desk, but that doesn't mean he's any less intimidating. He doesn't look up until he hears the crinkle of vinyl when I sit down. "I'll be brief." He sets down his pen and levels his gaze on me.

I try not to squirm.

"I take it personally when one of my students is arrested. I feel responsible for all of you and when you make poor choices, I feel like I've somehow made a mistake, too."

I nod, unsure what to say. This isn't the direction I was expecting him to take.

"This isn't the first time you've been in trouble—"

I was accused of—well, caught—cheating last fall and suspended for three days.

"—and I can't figure out where we've gone wrong."

I clear my throat. "We?"

"Clearly you have trouble following rules."

Sounds like most teenagers to me. "I didn't mean to drive." The excuse sounds worse every time I say it.

"But you did. And you nearly killed your friend."

"Killed? No!" Did I? "I saw her this morning. She's going to be okay."

"Regardless, your lack of respect for authority and the rules that exist to keep you safe are concerning. Now," he looks down at the paper in front of him. "Have you seen the judge yet?"

"Um, yeah..." Is he working with the legal system? Can they kick me out of school? I wrap my hands around the edge of the seat to keep myself from leaping out of the chair and bolting from the office.

"What was the determination?"

His formality scares me. "Uh, he suspended my license for a month, then I have restricted privileges for four months, and I have to do community service."

He doesn't flinch. "But no jail time?"

"No!" I flatten my hands on the desk, trying to steady my nerves. I can't get used to the idea that I could end up behind bars. "I was below the legal limit." Fear pulses through me and my voice comes out a whisper. "Did you really think I'd have to go to jail?" Most of the time I think of Stride Right as an out-of-touch principal who, despite his best efforts to get to know his students, doesn't really know much about our lives, but I suppose you see a lot dealing with teenagers every day for decades.

"With an accident like yours it could have gone either way."

My shoulders slump. I could be in jail right now. Some people—especially Amelia's parents—probably think I belong there. I should be relieved that the principal's office is the scariest thing I'm facing today, but a mountain of uncertainty lies before me. It will take a lot of work to convince everyone that I'm not oblivious to the consequences of my actions.

Stride Right interrupts my thoughts. "Do you have your community service schedule yet? It's best if you don't miss class, but if there are any conflicts, you'll need to bring a letter from the court."

I feel defeated. "I don't have it yet."

"Let me know if the harassment gets too bad."

My head snaps up. I'm not one to tattle on my classmates, no matter how douchey they are. Did he see the beer cans?

"I know kids can be rather...creative...when it comes to things like this."

"I could use a garbage bag."

"Check with Ms. Anderson on your way out."

And with that I'm dismissed, released back to the wild.

More beer cans await me after each class, and by lunchtime the garbage bag at the bottom of my locker is overflowing. Kids must have partied all weekend to empty that many cans. I eat my lunch in a back corner of the library, too chicken to face the student body en masse.

I get through my afternoon classes on autopilot, avoiding eye contact by staring either at the teacher or my desk. The only weird moment comes when I catch Cameron watching me in the hallway at the end of the day. He doesn't come near me, but his dark eyes stay on mine for longer than they have in months.

A small flutter moves in my belly, but I push it away. That's over.

I turn away before I can change my mind.

◆◆◆

On Tuesday, Amelia's allowed back to school so everyone's attention is on her. Trace, her soccer-star boyfriend, carries her books and makes sure no one bumps into her as she hobbles on crutches to her locker, where I'm waiting. Her face lights up when she sees me, but Trace is anything but happy.

I'm getting used to the dirty looks, but it hurts coming from someone I consider a friend. "Welcome back!" I force more enthusiasm into my voice than I've felt in days and wrap my arms lightly around her shoulders, careful not to knock her over.

"Thanks." She rests her head against mine for a second. "This is harder than I thought it'd be."

Her words punch me in the gut. I pull back. "Can I please help?" I nod at Trace and the gesture nearly bounces off the tension emanating off him. "You've already got a book carrier, so want to ride on my back?" I'd crawl on my hands and knees if it'd make this better.

She leans on one crutch and opens her locker with her free hand. "You can have lunch duty."

"Done."

The warning bell rings, sending kids scurrying around us. Someone elbows me and I whirl around, half expecting it to be Nate, the guy who used to torment me for my short hair, but it's a football player.

"Haven't you done enough to her?"

Before I can react, Amelia flips up her crutch and smacks him on the back of the leg. "This is none of your business. Leave her alone."

His eyes widen in surprise, and he continues down the hallway without another word.

Something tells me it's going to take more than Amelia's protection to get me through the day. "I'll see you at lunch. Text if you need anything."

The corner of her mouth turns up. "Maybe we can coordinate

bathroom breaks."

I snort. "Um, I might be busy then."

She points at me. "We do need to start planning for my birthday. Especially since we never had your party."

I dig deep for the enthusiasm she deserves. "Ten days!" I give her another squeeze and turn to leave, but Trace stops me with a hand on my arm.

"I don't get it, but I know she doesn't blame you, even though what you did was beyond stupid." He narrows his eyes and I take a half-step back. "At some point you need to start thinking about how your actions effect other people."

I want to scream 'That's why I had my parents pick me up for dinner!' but I just hang my head and mumble the hundredth apology since Thursday. I walk away, eyes to the ground, and run straight into a black t-shirt. "Sorry."

"Tough break." The voice is familiar and I look up in surprise. It's Nate.

I look over my shoulder at Amelia in case I need backup, but she and Trace are already hobbling the other way. I close my eyes and wish that Nate will be gone when I open them, but he's still standing there. "What do you want?"

He shrugs, but it doesn't have the same bravado that it had back when he and Katie were joined at the hip. I always assumed he was humoring her since she was younger than him, that he wasn't really that into her, but her death must have affected him more deeply than I realized. "Just saying it sucks is all." He nods at my locker where another beer can has already materialized.

"Oh." I'm not quite sure what to make of the Nate who isn't shoving me or calling me names, and I don't have the time or energy to worry about it right now. "Thanks, I guess."

He shrugs again and continues down the hall just as the final bell rings.

I hurry to class, shaking my head. Just when I thought my life couldn't get any weirder.

# chapter 9

Later that week, I'm standing in front of the school waiting for Mom to take me to my appointment with Martinez, and I'm reminded of the months after my surgery. Back then I wasn't allowed to drive for medical reasons, not my own stupidity. Cameron would wait with me, sneaking kisses before Mom arrived, and Amelia would tackle-hug me from behind when I least expected it. But now everything's changed and I'm all alone.

When Mom pulls up to the curb, I toss my bag in the back and sink into my seat with a heavy sigh.

"That bad?"

"It's not any worse than it was on Monday, I'm just getting tired of it." I could build a small plane with the amount of aluminum cans I've collected this week. At least Stride Right hasn't busted me for having empties. Even he knows there's no stopping the kids at school.

On top of feeling beat down from school, I'm nervous about my appointment with Martinez. I haven't talked to him since the hospital and I can't get the image of him staring at me as I got into the police car, disappointment clear on his face. Part of me is hurt that he judged me so quickly. I know he's a doctor and the only reason I see him every week is because he's studying my brain, but lately he's felt more like a friend, someone I can confide in. He's the one who pointed out that Cameron's actions when Katie died—

pressuring me to flicker even though he knew it could kill me—wasn't how someone who supposedly loved you should behave. The day she killed herself was the same day I decided to end things with Cameron, and I've barely spoken to him since.

"How do you know if you're going to flicker?" Mom's voice snaps me back to the present.

"What?"

She bites her lip, her eyes never leaving the road. "How do you know it's going to happen? Are there signs, or do you just suddenly flash back? Like poof?"

I smile. "Like poof?"

She swats at my arm. "Don't tease me. I'm trying to understand."

"There are signs." I close my eyes and imagine the sensations. "First the tips of my fingers and toes start to tingle—"

"Is that why you and your father are always flexing your fingers? I knew you got that from him but I figured it was a nervous habit."

"Yeah, I definitely got it from him. After the tingling, a heavy weight feels like it's pushing me through the seat. If I'm driving when it happens it's hard to even see over the steering wheel." I take a deep breath. It's weird, whenever I describe the feeling I have phantom reactions like I'm actually flickering. "Then the heaviness lifts and I feel like I'm floating. Then poof." I smile again.

"So there is a poof."

"More like a spastic reentry, but yeah, you could say that."

She tightens her grip on the steering wheel. "So will I know if you...if you're about to flicker?"

I reach across the space between us and rest my hand on her arm. "I'll tell you if it's happening."

"You promise?"

"Yes."

She exhales like she's been holding her breath, and I'm grateful that she wants to understand. I'll need her on my side after Dad—

I stop myself. I can't think like that. Not now. I've broken down too many times in front of Martinez as it is and if I keep thinking about Dad's impending death I'll be a blubbering mess before I'm on the examining table.

◆◆◆

I didn't need to worry about crying in his office. The anger rolling off him from the moment I step inside makes it clear we will not be having a heartfelt conversation today.

He gives me a curt nod as I climb onto the table.

The paper crinkles beneath me as I get comfortable, waiting for him to begin. Usually he starts by asking me if I've flickered since I last saw him or if I've had any other head-related problems, but today he won't even look at me.

After what feels like eons, he finally meets my gaze, but he just shakes his head and turns around to shuffle papers on the small counter that serves as his desk. His broad shoulders rise and fall as he inhales and exhales. When he flattens his hands on the desk but still refuses to say anything, I snap.

"What?" All the frustration that's been building the past week comes out in that one word, and he whirls on me.

"What do you mean, what?" His normally calm demeanor is gone, replaced with a red face, hooded eyes, and a pulsing vein in his temple. His disappointment is almost worse than standing before the judge. "How could you be so stupid?"

"Hey!" I hold up a hand. I may have to take this at school, but Martinez knows the truth about me. This is supposed to be my safe zone and he's looking at me like a child who made an impulsive decision—not the adult I feel like I am. "You do realize I flickered, right? I had a couple drinks with Amelia on my birthday. Remember, I'm eighteen now? And when my mom picked me up for dinner she drove through the Strand."

The tension in his face eases slightly, but his glare is still accusing. "Why were you drinking? You know the risks it could mean for your health."

I shrug. "I don't know. I'm a teenager."

"You're smarter than that."

I flop my hands on my thighs. "Can't I get a break from always doing the right thing? It gets exhausting. I thought I was being responsible by having Mom pick me up instead of driving myself and I still ended up driving."

He leans against the counter and crosses his arms. "Fair point. So when you flickered, you were driving with Amelia?"

I shudder at the memory of the tree. Amelia screaming. And all that blood. I drop my gaze. "Yeah. My body jerks when I jump back to yesterday and that was enough to make us hit a tree." I cover my face with my hands, fighting tears. I've never been much of a crier, but since the accident it seems like that's all I'm doing.

"Hey." Martinez touches my shoulder, and I jump a little. I hadn't heard him move. "I didn't mean to make you cry. Sometimes I forget you're still a teenager. That you're still figuring things out."

I pick at the seam of my jeans with my thumbnail, eyes still downcast. "What do you mean?"

He exhales a heavy sigh and his breath tickles my neck. "You act like you've got everything under control, even when you don't. Considering what you've been through this past year, I'd say you're entitled to a few moments of weakness."

"Gee, thanks."

He touches his thumb to my chin and gently lifts my head so I'm looking at him. "That was supposed to be a compliment."

Heat sears through my belly. Cameron used to do that when I wouldn't look at him. But this isn't Cameron. It's my doctor. He's only here because I'm his patient and my bizarre-o head is good for his career.

He's still holding my chin. Dad's voice suddenly warns me that this probably isn't appropriate. He'd been suspicious of

Martinez after coming to one of my appointments and made me promise that I would stay on my guard. I pull away and touch my hair. "I've never been good with compliments."

He presses his lips together before dropping his hand to his side. "How's Amelia?"

"She's on crutches and back at school. She knows the truth and doesn't blame me, but the kids at school are relentless so anyone who talks trash gets smacked with a crutch."

He laughs. He and Amelia have never met, but I've told him enough about her that he knows her personality. "And how are you?"

I shrug and give him the highlights: harassment at school, no license, almost killing my best friend.

"Do you know what you'll be doing for community service?"

"I hadn't decided."

"I can make a few calls if you want something at the hospital."

"Like a candy striper?" I've seen more than my share of perky teenagers when I've been at the hospital with Dad. Being pleasant to people who are miserable doesn't sound like something I'd be very good at.

He smiles. "Or maybe something less people focused?"

Now I feel like a brat. "I don't want to deal with bodily fluids or needles. What are the chances I can get credit for taking people's photographs?" An idea strikes me. "I've heard of people donating their time to photograph babies who are born really premature and have to stay at the hospital for months. Do you think I could do something like that?"

Martinez rubs his chin. I've learned this means he doesn't think I'm crazy and is considering what I've said. But if he runs his hand through his hair I'm toast. "I could talk to the hospital director, and she'd have to clear it with the judge."

I sit up straight. "Seriously? That would be amazing!" The first glimmer of hope I've felt since the accident expands inside me. Based on the list the court gave me I figured I'd be forced to pick up trash alongside the highway—I never thought I'd actually be able to do something useful.

"No promises."

"Yes, yes. Of course." I'm practically bouncing on the table.

He checks his watch, a flash of silver beneath his white lab coat. "We do have work to do today. I want to show you the video again. I've pinpointed where your pupil looks blown out, but since you weren't looking at the camera, it's hard to get an exact reading."

During the chaos of trying to stop Katie from killing herself, I managed to record myself flickering. It wasn't the most opportune time, but I did what I could in the name of science. "Can I see it again?"

You'd think I'd watch the video over and over again in an attempt to figure out this flickering thing myself, but I deleted it off my phone right after Martinez downloaded it. The last thing I need is for someone to grab my phone and find out about me. It's safe here with Martinez.

He opens a drawer and pulls out a tablet. With just a few swipes, my face fills the screen.

I slide off the table to peer over his shoulder. "Okay."

He taps the screen and the video plays. The sound is off so I feel detached from the me onscreen. It's different than watching myself in the mirror because it's a side view—right up until Amelia tosses the phone in my lap. The video stops after I've flickered to the day before.

Martinez swipes his finger again, rewinding to the moment where I'm crouched low in the seat, and zooms in on my face. My left eye is dilated so much that you can't even see the color, while the other eye looks normal. "That's what you looked like the night we met."

"I'm surprised you even talked to me." The words are out of my mouth before I can stop them, and a blush immediately warms my cheeks.

He quirks an eyebrow at me. "I am a doctor."

I nod at the screen. "So what have you determined from watching me go all cyclops?"

"It's clear there's a connection between whatever's happening in your brain and your optic nerve—"

"Obviously."

He shakes his head at me. "But what I haven't determined is why it affects your eye. And only the one." He rubs his hand over the stubble on his chin. This is his thinking mode and I sometimes wonder if he even realizes he's doing it. "In a perfect world I'd place sensors in your brain to record the activity when you flicker."

My mouth falls open and he holds up a hand to stop me from interrupting.

"I don't want to operate on you again unless it's absolutely necessary. This research is important but it's not a necessity."

I exhale, letting the memories of the tubes running out of my bandaged head slip back to the corner of my mind. I'd rather not repeat that. "So what are you saying?"

He crosses his arms and turns so he's looking directly at me. "I want more recordings of you flickering."

I have to give him credit for being direct. No beating around the bush here. "I thought we agreed I shouldn't flicker until we have a better idea of what's causing it?"

He does the chin-rub thing again and my eyes drift to his lips. "I said we should be cautious."

Cautious. Right. I blink, forcing myself to look away. The warning bells are clanging that I should run away—he's changing the rules to serve his own purposes—but he hasn't given me a reason not to trust him. And there's the fact that every time I'm in the room with him, it's like he's a beacon of light and I'm a helpless moth, wanting nothing more than to be closer to him.

Running away is not an option.

And if I can help Dad, all this will be worth it. Speaking of which. "I assume you've cleared this change of plans with my dad?"

He leans against the counter, arms still crossed. "I have not."

My brow furrows. "But don't you need permission..." the word dies on my lips.

"You're eighteen now," he says at the same moment I think it. His eyebrow quirks again. "I'm not suggesting that we leave your parents out of this, but legally you're an adult and anything we do from this point on is your decision."

The innuendo in that statement nearly knocks me over. I press my hands to my belly in an attempt to calm the butterflies, but it only draws attention to the heat that's spreading through my body. I touch my cheek, half expecting it to burst into flames right here in the middle of his office.

"Think about it." He reaches for my hand, but stops short of touching me.

Oh, I will. "Do you need it soon, or can I wait until the moment's right?" Oh my god, did I seriously just say that? "I mean, I don't want to flicker just to get a recording. I should probably wait until there's a good reason, right?"

A smile lifts the corners of his mouth, but he simply nods.

Am I imagining whatever is going on here? I've had boyfriends before but I am still in high school. Who knows what kind of experience Martinez has. He's probably smiling because I'm acting like such an idiot.

"Can I watch the video again?" I reach around him without waiting for an answer. He turns to grab the tablet and his elbow bumps his coffee cup. "Oh no!" I try to catch the cup but end up dislodging the lid, sending hot liquid all over the counter, the files, and finally, myself.

Martinez jumps back. A couple drops land on his white coat but otherwise he and the tablet escape unscathed.

I, on the other hand, am literally a hot mess.

He grabs the stack of papers and shakes them over the floor, sending rivulets of coffee streaming down the cabinets. A brochure with a city skyline slides across the floor. But he's not looking at the papers. He's watching me. "Are you okay?"

My jeans are soaked, but that's not a big deal. I hold up the hand that knocked over the cup. "This hurts a little."

He picks up the brochure and tosses it and the other papers

onto the examining table and grabs my hand. Before I can stop him he covers it with his sleeve.

"Stop, you'll ruin your fancy coat."

"I have a dozen of these at home."

And like that I'm imagining where he lives. Does he have a house, or maybe one of those fancy condos downtown that stand tall above the rest of our town? He always looks well put-together so it's probably decorated like something out of a magazine, all dark colors and sleek lines with metal accents on the furniture. I bet the condo has a doorman and you have to give your name when you—

"Biz?"

I snap back to attention. "Yeah?"

"I asked if you need ice for your hand."

Now that the excitement of spilling the coffee has passed, my hand really is starting to hurt. "Probably." I tug my hand away from his grasp. "While I appreciate the gesture, I don't think your coat is doing much to help."

"Wait here." He's out the door before I can say another word.

I have to give him credit—he doesn't hesitate when making a decision. Need ice? Boom, done. Want to record me even though it could put my life at risk? Well, of course, but only for the sake of science. A shudder passes through me. Is it really a good idea to put my trust in the hands of someone who's so focused on what he wants?

Martinez rushes into the room with a small plastic bag filled with ice and kicks the door shut behind him. EMT mode activated. He gently takes my hand and rests the bag on my knuckles.

While his attention is on my hand, I have one of those how-did-I-end-up-in-this-moment moments. His dark brows are furrowed in concentration, causing small lines to pinch above his nose. I feel detached, like I'm watching myself from the corner of the room.

"This should help."

"Thanks. I'm sorry I destroyed your office." I glance over his shoulder at the papers scattered on the counter and table. "I hope the files aren't ruined."

He adjusts his grip on my hand so we're palm to palm, and my heart stutters. "Everything's backed up on my computer but I prefer to take notes by hand." His fingers twitch beneath mine but this time I don't pull away. This is probably well over the line of appropriate doctor-patient behavior, but the ice is doing its thing by making the burn stop hurting, and frankly, it's been a long time since anyone has held my hand. Even if Martinez is just doing his job as my doctor slash guardian EMT.

After a moment of what can only be described as semi-awkward silence, Martinez shifts the bag and ever-so-softly runs the pad of his thumb along the side of my hand until it comes to a rest on my wrist. Electricity shoots up my arm and I quickly pull away, holding the ice with my free hand. This is definitely out of bounds. "Thanks. I think I can take it from here."

"Good, because I'm not helping you with your pants."

My mouth falls open. He did not.

He winks at me. "What, I can't tease you, too?"

"I...I guess." Words, Biz, use your words.

"I really just wanted to see you turn red again."

Kill me. Kill me now. I point at my cheeks, which I'm sure are the color of molten lava. "Mission accomplished."

"Speaking of missions." He clears his throat, professional doctor mode back on. "When do you think you'll be able to record yourself flickering?"

The uncertainty I felt earlier is back, now coupled with suspicion that his flirting is merely a way to get me to do what he wants, my health be damned. Martinez is the one who pointed out that Cameron was more concerned with his own motives than my safety, but now I feel like he's doing the same thing, except he's more skilled at manipulating people to get what he wants. It's not too late for me to back out of this, but the fear of ending up like my dad—combined with the hope that it might not be too late to help him—keeps me coming back.

I can only croak out a single word in response.

"Soon."

# chapter 10

Things at school calm down by the next week—I haven't seen a stray beer can since Friday and Amelia hasn't had to pummel anyone else with her crutch—but I'm still rattled by the conversation with Martinez and all these mixed-up feelings I seem to have for him.

I haven't said anything to Amelia about whatever craziness is going on between us. As far as she knows I'm still pining after Cameron, and I am a little, but there's something to be said about a grown man flirting with you, even if it is completely inappropriate.

I feel myself blush. I need to stop this.

At the moment I'm stuffed in the backseat of Trace's two-door car with Amelia's crutches, trying my best not to piss him off any further. The tension with us hasn't improved since the accident, and now Amelia's parents told her she can't have a party because they're worried about her health.

"That's two parties in two weeks that I have to cancel. People are gonna start hating me."

I poke my head between the front seats. "Everyone loves you. It's me they hate. Just tell them it's my fault."

Trace snorts. "It is."

I bite back a snotty comment and force a smile. "I really appreciate you driving me home."

He makes a noise in the back of his throat but otherwise doesn't acknowledge me.

Amelia gives me an 'I'm sorry' face and I shrug. I'll keep trying but without telling him the truth, I don't know what will convince him that I'm not a horrible friend.

I nudge his shoulder. "Soccer starts up again soon, right? That must be exciting."

"We've had practices all winter." His voice is flat.

"Oh." I flop back in my seat and get stabbed by a screw on the side of a crutch. That's what I get for trying to be nice. We ride the rest of the way in silence. When he finally pulls into my driveway, I brace myself for more attitude. Because Amelia can't move very well with her entire leg in a cast, Trace has to get out so I can escape the backseat.

I grab my bag and yank it through the small opening between the seat and the door. "Thanks."

He grunts again before getting back in the car and slams the door.

As I hurry to the front door, Amelia calls after me through the open window. "I'll call you later."

I turn to smile at her, but catch Trace's glare instead. "Bye." Part of me is glad she has someone who cares so much about her that he hates anyone who hurts her.

I pause before opening the front door. It's such a simple motion—put the key in the lock then turn the doorknob—but my entire life it's carried a hint of fear because I never know how I'll find Dad. Ninety-eight percent of the time he's either reading or napping, but that two percent...I take a deep breath. More and more these days I fear the two percent has come to dominate our lives.

A blast of warm air greets me, along with what should be a comforting silence, but instead it kicks my senses into high gear. I drop my backpack on the kitchen floor on my way to the living room. No Dad. I don't bother checking outside—the light bothers him the same way it does me, but it's gotten worse as his health has deteriorated. I resist the urge to climb the stairs two at a time, forcing myself to take slow breaths until I reach his bedroom door.

I knock lightly and press my ear to the door. The creak of the bedsprings tells me he's awake, so I open the door and tip-toe inside.

Dad rolls over to face me. "How was school?"

His voice, like the rest of him, is paper-thin. I see him every day so his appearance doesn't shock me, but he's so frail compared to the man I knew growing up. Aside from the weight loss, his movements have slowed, making him seem decades older than he really is. If anyone at school were to see us together they'd probably think he's my grandfather, not my dad.

I sink onto Mom's side of the bed and tuck a leg beneath me. "Better than last week. I've been replaced by the latest scandal so now the only person I need to worry about is Amelia's boyfriend."

"Still haven't won him over?" He shifts so he's leaning against the headboard.

I shake my head. I want to help him. He's so light it'd be easy to slip my hands beneath his armpits and pull him upright, but it'd be mortifying for him. So I watch him struggle.

"Give him time. There will always be people who are in your life but can't know the truth. The trick is learning to keep them close while also protecting yourself."

Like I did with Cameron and Amelia for so long. But that blew up in my face and I ended up confessing to Amelia to save our friendship. I would do it again in a heartbeat, but where do I draw the line? "I'm sure it's frustrating for Amelia, too, because Trace doesn't understand why she forgave me so quickly. I can't even imagine the conversations they have." I'll be sure to ask her when we talk later. "I hate that he thinks I'm evil."

Dad reaches across the bed to rest his hand on my knee. "Hang in there. I'd like to tell you that it gets easier, but this is your life."

I close my eyes, fighting the tears that come out of nowhere. "Sometimes I wish I could go someplace else and start all over.

I'd miss you and Mom and Amelia, but other than that..." I pluck at the bedspread. A couple months ago I couldn't imagine ever leaving home—but now running away to start over sounds more and more appealing.

"That reminds me." Dad points at a stack of magazines on the dresser. "Would you mind handing me those?" The cane he rarely uses is next to the bed but it's a lot faster for me to help him.

"Sure." I unfold myself and grab them, then set the pile next to him on the bed. "I'll leave you alone so you can read." It's not like him to dismiss me so abruptly, but he's on a lot of powerful drugs and maybe they're screwing with his head. I lean forward to kiss his forehead and he touches my arm.

"I'm not kicking you out. Sit down." He pats the space next to him and I obey. "I have something for you." He thumbs through the stack of magazines and pulls out a thick white envelope.

My heart speeds up. "Is that what I think it is?"

A smile creases his face. "Open it and find out."

I slip a finger beneath the flap on the back and tear open the envelope.

Dear Elizabeth Clement,
We're pleased to inform you that you have been accepted—

"I got in!" My whole body starts tingling, like I'm moving in slow motion. I can't believe this is really happening. Earlier this year I considered not even applying to college, or at the very least staying at home and going to community college, and now I've been accepted at the Rhode Island School of Design!

Dad taps the top of the letter. "Is that all it says?"

I scan the page. My mouth drops. "I'm getting a partial scholarship." A tiny piece of me is disappointed that it's not a full scholarship. I know my grades aren't good enough to qualify but I'd hoped maybe my photos were. I push away those thoughts because Dad's beaming at me. I can't remember the last time I've seen him so happy.

"Biz, I'm so proud of you. I know this hasn't been an easy decision, but your mother and I don't want you to forgo your dreams because you're worried about leaving us."

A lump catches in my throat. I'm happy, I really am. This is what I want, but all the reasons I don't want to leave home come crashing around me. Things are changing too fast. In the fall I'll go to the east coast, Amelia will be off at State, and Dad...I close my eyes. I can't even think about that.

"Hey." His thumb brushes my chin, then my cheek. "No tears. This is happy news."

I don't know when I became such a crybaby, but the mix of emotions bouncing through me sends tears running down my face. "I am happy."

He laughs, a soft exhalation that makes him cough several times. "I can tell."

I stretch out next to him and rest my head on the pillow so our heads touch. "I'm worried about you."

He shifts his arm so I can snuggle against his side. "Don't be. The doctors are doing everything they can to keep me comfortable." He kisses the top of my head. "Don't I look comfortable?"

I snort. "You are the picture of relaxation."

"Okay, so stop worrying." Another cough rattles his chest and I prop myself up on an elbow, not wanting the weight of my body to prevent him from breathing. He coughs several more times before closing his eyes.

"I should let you rest."

"That's all I do."

"Would you rather go downstairs?"

"No, then your mother will worry." He pauses to take a breath. "I'll stay here until she gets home."

"Okay." I set the magazines back on the dresser on my way to the door, where I pause to look at him. His breathing has steadied, the movement of his chest barely perceptible. He's already asleep. An ache grips my heart. I don't know how I'll go on without him. My entire life he's been my confidante, my cheerleader, my shoulder to cry on, and I wish there was something I could do.

I've suggested that maybe Martinez can help, but Dad thinks it's too late to make a difference. The idea of immersing Martinez even further into my life both frightens and excites me. Giving him a better understanding of flickering and its effects on the body could help me in the long run, but as I pull the bedroom door closed and head back downstairs, a tiny part of me still wonders if I made the right decision to trust my doctor.

# chapter 11

"Thanks again for letting me ride with you."

"Sure, no problem." Kaya, the brunette from my photography class smiles as she pulls into the parking lot of the *Chronicle*. She checks her reflection in the rearview mirror and adjusts her neon-green flowered headband before looking at me. "Sucks what happened."

I'm grateful that not everyone thinks I'm the antichrist. It's bad enough having to be driven to and from school, but my photography class is held at the local newspaper. Shelly Graham, a staff photographer, offered to pick up where Turner left off, so my last class of the day is held off-campus. It was great when Cameron and I were dating—sometimes we'd show up a little late after some quality time in his car—but it's a special kind of torture now that I'm single and not allowed to drive.

Speak of the devil. Old Berta, Cameron's hideous orange car, pulls in behind us. At least he has the courtesy to park at the opposite end of the lot.

Kaya nods in his direction. "That sucks, too."

"Tell me about it." We climb out of the car and follow Cameron inside. The cold weather means he's wearing a hoodie, but I can still imagine the muscles in his arms flexing as he pushes the door open. His back stays ramrod straight as he walks to the end of the room where our class is held, never turning to look at us. At me.

I slump into my chair and do my best not to look at him. I've had two months of practice, so you think it'd be easier by now, but part of me can't accept that not only are we not dating anymore, but we're not even friends. Yes, I'm the one who broke up with him, but that was because he wanted me to keep flickering to save Katie, not because I stopped loving him. I repeat the phrase I've been telling myself since that day in the hospital: He knew it could kill me but didn't care. I made the right decision.

And like clockwork, my eyes wander to his hands, which are resting casually on the table in front of him, and my body betrays me. My head understands that Cameron is now off-limits, but try telling that to the warm tingling sensation that spreads through me every time I see him.

I repeat my other mantra: Four more months.

Four more months until we graduate and another three months until I go to college and can put all of this behind me.

Shelly shows us the latest student photos that made the paper, and I smile and clap along with the rest of the class, but photography hasn't had the same pull since Katie's death. I've spent hours chasing down shadows, hoping something will be good enough to get the same attention as the one a few months ago that went viral, but like any good muse, the harder I try to capture it, the more elusive it becomes.

My lack of productivity hasn't gone unnoticed. Mom and Dad dutifully ask if another photo will be published, and I hate the disappointment on their faces when I tell them no. Shelly's kept me after class a handful of times in an attempt to snap me out of my funk, but so far it hasn't worked.

And it doesn't look like she's done trying.

As soon as Shelly dismisses class, she walks my way. "Biz, can you stay after class for a few minutes?"

Normally this wouldn't be a problem, but now that I'm relying on the mercy of others to get around, I don't want to end up stranded. "Umm..." I don't want to announce to the entire class that I can't drive, even though I'm sure they all know.

Kaya frowns and mouths, "I can't stay. Sorry."

Shelly checks her watch. "I can give you a ride home."

"But it's so far out of your way." In truth, I have no idea where Shelly lives. Her house could be around the corner from mine.

"I have plans in a couple hours. Nothing a quick drive around town will make me late for."

"Okay, sure." I give Kaya a half-hearted wave. "Same place tomorrow?"

"I'll bring the bells."

I open my mouth to reply, but she's already hustling for the exit. Kaya is the definition of quirky, but I like that she's not concerned with what other kids think. I face Shelly. "What's up?"

She sits in the chair across from me. "You know what's up. Isn't it about time you got back on the horse?"

"I've never been on a horse."

She rolls her eyes. Sometimes I forget that she's only a few years older than me. "The figurative horse, Biz. We all have crappy streaks now and then but—can I be blunt?" She rubs her hand over the back of her head, tousling her perfectly mussed pixie cut.

My stomach drops as I nod.

"It sucks that Cameron's sister died and then you two broke up, but life goes on. You can't wander around like a zombie forever."

She's said this before, but not—as she said—so bluntly. "Ouch."

"I say it out of love."

I smirk. "You love me?"

"I love your photos. I love your potential. I love that I get to help mold you before you run off to college, and hopefully off to a bigger town." She smiles and the sincerity I've come to respect is back. "What I don't love is you letting life get in the way of what you want. And I'm worried that this latest drama will push you even further from your dreams."

Her bluntness hits me in a way that Mom and Dad's hints haven't, shaking me awake. "Speaking of dreams, I got into RID."

"What!" She slaps the table with both hands and I laugh. "When did you find out? How did you not tell me the second you knew? Biz, this is fantastic!"

I wish I could bottle her enthusiasm and carry it with me when my confidence dips. Being around her makes me feel like I can handle anything. "A couple days ago, and I didn't think it was appropriate to text you after hours."

"For news like this I make exceptions."

Her smile is contagious, and I catch myself smiling harder than I have in weeks. Then she clears her throat. "But seriously, it's time for you to snap out of this slump. Even Cameron has had photos published, and it was his sister who killed herself. The pity party ends today."

She's right. Of course she's right. It's time for me to forget Cameron and stop dwelling on things I can't change. "It's not like I don't have things to distract me from him. The judge gave me thirty hours of community service, and Martinez, my doctor, suggested I might be able to incorporate photography into it. At the hospital."

Her face lights up. "Oh, like with babies?"

"You've heard of it?"

"A couple of my friends from college donate their time on the weekends. I could ask them how they set it up, then call your doctor to get it worked out."

Watching the excitement on her face, it's like I can see the thoughts as they come to her. "So you think it could work?"

"Definitely. And I think this will be a good project to push you out of your comfort zone."

"What do you mean?"

"No offense, but unless it's at the scene of an accident, people rarely make an appearance in your photos. You have a fabulous eye for capturing the emotion of a stressful moment, but I'd love to see what you can accomplish in a quieter, calmer setting."

I'd never thought of it that way.

"If you give me your doctor's number, I'll get the whole shebang set up for you."

I pull my phone from my bag, scroll past the new email notification to my contacts, and forward his info to Shelly. "Done."

She grabs my free hand and squeezes. "Biz, I'm really excited about this. No one can stay in a funk when you're surrounded by teensy tiny babies."

"Thank you for this. For not giving up on me. And for not making me feel worse about this whole drunk driving thing."

She shrugs and spins the bracelet on her wrist. "I did the same thing when I was your age and I turned out fine. True, I didn't send my BFF to the hospital, but I did a number on the neighbor's fence and mailbox."

"You?"

"You don't build character following the rules." She stands. "You ready to go?"

I grab my bag and follow her to the exit. We're halfway to my house when I remember the email. I don't recognize the email address, but most of my communication is by text, so it's not surprising that it's unfamiliar. I tap the screen, and everything inside me goes liquid.

No.

I wrap an arm around my stomach as everything around me goes fuzzy.

"Biz, you okay?"

"Yeah. It's just..." I blink several times and read the email again. *I know your secret, and it could kill you.*

# chapter 12

I mumble a thank you to Shelly and race inside the house. I'm sure I was a complete freak on the ride home, but after reading those words—I know your secret—small talk wasn't happening.

I burst through the front door and spot Dad on the couch.

He looks up at the sound of the door. His welcoming smile fades when he sees what I'm sure is pure terror on my face. He leans forward. "What's wrong?"

I drop my bag on the floor and sit next to him in a whoosh. "Look." I hold up my phone, showing him the email. I haven't closed the app since I was in Shelly's car.

What little color he has in his face evaporates. His eyes go wide. "Do you know who sent it?"

I shake my head. "It looks like it's from one of those anonymous email-address websites. I might be able to search the IP address to figure out where it originated, but—" I stop talking. Searching for mysterious email addresses is something Cameron is good at.

"You lost me."

"I don't know if I'll be able to figure out who sent it."

He takes a long, shuddering breath and covers his eyes with his hand. "What do you think they want?"

"I've been asking myself that same question since I opened it. The only people who know about me are Cameron, Amelia,

Martinez, and now Mom. I think it's safe to assume it's not Amelia or Mom. And even though Cameron and I aren't talking, he wouldn't betray my trust. Not after everything we've been through."

"Which leaves..."

"Martinez." My head spins and my mouth goes dry. My heart does that weird thing where it doesn't want to beat normally. "But why would he try to scare me like this?"

Dad drops his hand so it's resting on mine. "People do a lot of things for a lot of reasons. Money. Fame."

I can't wrap my head around this. Betrayal of this level is not something I've had much experience with and I keep falling back on childish protests. "But I trusted him."

"We don't know for sure that it's him."

An idea strikes me and while I know in my heart it's not possible, I say it out loud. "Amelia could have told Trace, but there are two problems with that theory. First, she would never betray me like that. And second, even though Trace hates me right now, I can't see him going through the trouble of sending an anonymous email. He'd just tell me to my face that I'm an ass." I sigh. "Martinez is the only one who makes sense."

"You can't accuse him without any proof."

I sit up straight. "Like hell I can't." I plan to rip him a new one and I will thoroughly enjoy it.

Dad smiles for the first time since I got home. "I almost feel bad for him."

"Don't. If he's behind this, he'll regret the day we ever met." I get off the couch. I can't sit still. Pacing the room, I try unsuccessfully to sort this out logically but I keep coming back to Martinez betraying me. It hurts more than I'd like to admit. Our relationship is supposed to be strictly professional, but over the past couple months—heck, even longer than that if I'm honest with myself—I keep wondering if there's something more there. Yes, he's ten years older and there's no reason he'd be attracted to me, but when we're alone in his office I can't deny the spark between us. What if he's been toying with me to get me to trust him, and this has been his plan all along?

My phone is still gripped in my hand. Before I can change my mind, I fire off a text to him.

> Me: We need to talk. Got a weird email that
> freaked me out.

I slide my phone into my back pocket and lock eyes with Dad. "I don't expect him to admit anything, but I have to at least ask."

Dad nods, his eyelids fluttering.

My heart lurches. "Dad, are you okay?" The anger lifts, replaced by concern. Once again I've been so wrapped up in my own drama that I didn't notice how weak he is. He can barely hold up his head. "Can I get you anything? Do you want to lie down?"

He cracks a smile, eyes still closed. "I liked it better when you didn't notice how badly I feel. Can we go back to figuring out how you'll confront Martinez?"

I kneel in front of him and gently lay my cheek on his knee. "I'm sorry I'm so oblivious."

"Never stop being you, Biz." His fingers run over my still-short curls, but they no longer feel like my dad's hands. It's like his heart and mind are still the same but his body's been replaced by an elderly man struggling in his final days.

Tears burn my eyes.

My phone dings against my butt and I straighten.

> Martinez: Busy now. Can it wait until our next
> appointment?
> Me: Fine.
> Martinez: You know you can trust me. But please
> don't plot my death in the meantime.

He knows me well.

> Me: No promises.

◆ ◆ ◆

Thursday can't come soon enough. I haven't told Mom about the threatening email so she's unaware of how tightly wound I am as we drive to Martinez's office.

"I was thinking the three of us could go to the lake this weekend. Get some fresh air."

"Do you think Dad's up for it?"

Her lips tighten, and it looks like she's trying not to cry. "He's been complaining about being trapped in the house. I know it's still a little cold to be picnicking, but it's what he wants."

I touch her arm. "Then of course we'll go." Her tears frighten me. We both know Dad doesn't have much time left, but it's like we're watching a clock without numbers and we have no idea when it's going to stop. If she's having a hard time keeping it together she must think we're near the end.

She takes one hand off the wheel to wipe beneath her eyes. "I don't mean to overreact."

"Mom, you're hardly overreacting. This whole thing sucks. I'd say you're entitled to cry."

She sniffles and forces a small smile. "I want to be strong for you."

I think back to all the times she's nearly forgotten me when Dad's been sick. Being strong for me is not something I would normally use to describe my mother, but if that's what she needs to think to get through this, who am I to stop her? Maybe I've been too hard on her and she's been doing the best she could.

We pull into the parking garage but she doesn't turn off the car. "Do you mind if I wait here? I'd rather people don't see me like this."

Plenty of people have seen her a lot worse, but I'm not going to argue. "You don't have to wait in the parking garage. Why don't you go get a coffee or something and meet me back here in an hour?"

She sniffs again, then presses her hands to her cheeks. "As long as you don't mind going up there alone."

A sarcastic comment dies on my lips as I realize she might be scared to go inside the hospital. "I don't mind." I lean over and kiss her cheek. "See you soon." I climb out of the car and throw back my shoulders, preparing myself to confront Martinez.

He's ready for me. Usually he's reading files or on his tablet when I arrive, but today he's sitting on his stool, facing the door, hands resting on his thighs. "Can you please sit down?"

His formality throws me off-guard. I sit, the paper on the table crinkling louder than normal.

"I don't know what's going on, but I need you to know that you can trust me. We can't do what we're doing here if you're not completely honest with me, and in return for that honesty, I give you my word that what we do here, stays here."

It's a little peculiar that he has a speech prepared when all I said in my text was that I got a weird email. "I haven't even told you what the email said."

"Biz, give me a little credit. We've spent a lot of time together. Do you think I haven't figured out that the idea of being exposed scares you more than anything?"

I still don't buy it. "So if what we're doing stays here, doesn't that make your research pointless? I mean, eventually you'll have to share what you find out, right?"

He steeples his hands, elbows still on his knees. "Yes, that's true, but I would never do anything without your approval. There will eventually be a report on my findings, but we're still a long way from that." He rests his chin on his hands. "Why would I betray your trust? I want to understand why you flicker almost as much as you do."

Considering he knows that my reaction to him betraying me would be to pull out of this whole thing, his argument makes sense.

He takes a deep breath and exhales slowly. "What did it say?"

"That they know my secret and it could kill me."

He shrugs, and I'm irritated that he doesn't seem more upset. "But you already know that."

"I guess, but that doesn't make it any less freaky." I bite my lip. I can't work up the nerve to ask him directly. "So who sent it?"

"Hard to say. How many people have you told?"

I sit back, stung by his accusation. "Three. Four counting you." Wait, we just told Mom. "Five."

He straightens, pulling his elbows back to stretch his chest before resting an arm on the counter next to him. His brows are furrowed in concern, but I can't shake the feeling that he rehearsed this. "The more people who know, the more likely it is that someone will tell. How long has it been since you've talked to Cameron?"

"It's not Cam."

"But you don't know for sure."

I shake my head, eyes on the floor.

The stool squeaks as he shifts and I jump when his hand grazes my knee.

My eyes meet his and my stomach does that stupid thing it does when a hot guy has crossed into my comfort zone.

"I'm not saying it's him, but you need to be careful who you trust. This is a big secret you're holding onto and while it seems like high school is a huge place, in a few months you'll graduate and realize how very small it actually is. What if he told someone, and now that person is trying to scare you?"

"But why would anyone want to scare me?"

"To feel powerful, like they have control over someone. I don't know." He shakes his head. "What about that kid who was bothering you last fall?"

I search my memory past the last few months. "You mean Nate?"

His jaw clenches. "Yeah. Maybe the punk is bored and needed entertainment." He straightens his shoulders and looks into my eyes. "Let me know if you need help getting him to leave you alone. I can be pretty persuasive when I want to be."

Tell me about it. "Thanks, but I don't think it's him. He's barely looked at me since Katie died. They were pretty close." Nate made my life hell after my surgery, but it's like Katie's death knocked the wind out of him and he still hasn't recovered. Siccing Martinez on him would just be mean.

"It could be anyone who knows you're still seeing me. You have drawn a lot of attention to yourself recently."

"You don't need to be an ass. I get it. I'm a stupid teenager who made a stupid decision. Again." I cross my arms, trying to hold back the tirade that's bubbling in my chest.

He expels a breath and shakes his head. "You're misunderstanding me. In the grand scheme of things, high school will be just a blip on the radar. Right now your friends—and enemies—are the most important people in the world, but you're going away to college. You'll meet new friends. So will they. Before long you only talk to them over email and see them every other Christmas."

For the first time it strikes me that when I go away and leave my friends behind, I'll also be leaving Martinez. I hadn't considered that there would be an end to our research. I know we can't do this forever, but I didn't think it'd be over in a few months.

He's focused on a spot over my shoulder and I wonder what he's thinking about, but with a quick shake of his head his eyes clear and he refocuses on me. "Not to change the subject, but I talked to your photography instructor. Shelly?"

Right, community service. "Do you think the hospital will let me do it?"

"I think so. There are privacy issues to deal with and you'll need consent forms signed by anyone you photograph, but once you submit a proposal to the hospital board I can push it through for you."

My head's spinning. "Board? Proposal?" I hate to rely on the old 'hey, I'm just a teenager,' but what the what? He chuckles and I reach over and smack his arm. "That's not funny! I've never done anything like this before. Doesn't the court have a form or something that I can fill out?" I realize as soon as I ask that he wouldn't know either.

He's still smiling. "I'm sure they do. But I've already talked to the board. They'll make a decision next week."

"Oh." My mouth hangs open a moment longer than necessary, and I snap it shut.

He drags a hand over his jaw, lingering on the stubble on

his chin. "I know I shouldn't tease you, but you're cute when you're flustered."

Heat races from my belly until I'm sure my face is the color of a tomato. This is not the first time I've heard this—Cameron used to say that, too—but it is the first time I've heard it from a grown man. "Shouldn't you be worried about how this is going to cut into our time, rather than making fun of me?"

He shrugs. "Our time is still a priority. Right?"

"About that." I take a breath. I'm sure he's thought of this, but I want to know what he's thinking. "What happens when I go away to school? Does your research just stop?" The corner of my mouth turns up. "Or do you become my long-distance doctor and we only see each other on vacations and holidays?"

"The grant expires at the end of the summer, right before you go to college. At the time I applied for it, you hadn't settled on a school or even decided if you were going, but I chose that date in case you came to your senses. And if you didn't, I planned to apply for an extension."

The heat from moments earlier becomes a rock in my gut. "So this ends when I go to college."

He slides closer on the stool so his knees are inches from my shins. "Don't focus on that. Focus on how much we can accomplish in the six months we have remaining."

"Five months."

He counts out the months on his fingers. "It's February. You leave in August."

I smirk. "You're crazy if you think I'm spending my last weeks here trapped in your office."

"Fine. Five and a half."

I hold out my hand. "Deal."

He grips my hand, and the warmth of his skin dissolves the rock until I'm a puddle on the table. Does he know he has this effect on me? I wish I could turn it off, but just when I think I've got the upper hand he does something ridiculous like take the hand I've offered and my will power bolts out the door.

Still holding my hand, he slides closer until his knees are touching my legs. "Since we're moving up the schedule, have you thought any more about what I asked you?"

At this point I'd give him whatever he wants. "What?"

"I'd still like to get another recording of you flickering."

I jerk back, taking my hand with me. "I thought we agreed I shouldn't flicker unless it's an emergency."

He glances at the floor, then looks back into my eyes. "We did, but knowing how much your Dad is deteriorating, don't you think it's worth the risk to help our research? I'd like another recording to compare against the first. One where you're holding the camera, not the driver."

Logically it makes sense, but the warning bells are clanging at full alert. "I should run it by my dad."

He straightens, moving slightly back so our legs are no longer touching. "What happened to Biz the adult? I thought you're the one who makes the decisions now?"

I cross my arms over my chest. I know he's manipulating me but my stubbornness won't back down. "Fine, I'll do it. But I can't drive and everyone who could drive me can't." Cameron, Amelia—and there's no way I'm asking Mom.

"What about right now?"

"Now?"

He checks his watch. "We still have fifteen minutes. And that won't matter once you flicker because you'll be in yesterday, right?"

"You and your logics."

"Is that a yes?"

# chapter 13

Five minutes later we're in the parking garage walking to Martinez's car. I can't say this is the smartest thing I've ever done, but considering I was able to escape a kidnapper's van while drugged and blindfolded, riding with my doctor should be relatively harmless. Martinez didn't say it, but maybe this could help Dad and somehow reverse what's happening to him.

Hopefully Mom's still at the coffee shop so we can leave without her seeing us.

Martinez opens the passenger door. "Oh, hold on." He reaches inside and grabs a silver bracelet from the seat and tosses it into the center console before opening the door wider for me to get in.

"Thanks." I've been in cars with boys before, and while this certainly isn't a date, the awkwardness is the same. My eyes settle on the bracelet he moved. It looks vaguely familiar.

He notices me looking and chucks it into the backseat. "It's my sister's."

You know how when you're a kid and you run into your teacher at the grocery store and suddenly your entire world flips upside down because you never imagined that Mrs. Greenbaum had a life outside her classroom? Every time Martinez makes an offhand comment about his private life, that happens to me. "It's pretty." I'm still looking at the console so I don't see him reaching for my hand until he's already holding it.

"Do you trust me?"

"Depends on the day."

His jaw twitches and he closes his eyes for a heartbeat, which gives me a split second to admire his long dark lashes. "Biz, I thought we covered this in my office."

"We talked about it, yeah, but five minutes of blabbering isn't enough to convince me." I must resist the pull of those lashes.

"Biz, I wouldn't do anything to hurt you." He lifts the armrest storage thing and pulls out a digital camera. He hands it to me. "Cue it up so it's ready to record. This may not work perfectly, but I think if you hold it instead of me, we'll be able to see your eyes better."

Like Little Red Riding Hood. "The better to see you with," I mumble.

"What's that?" With his dark hair and athletic build, he does resemble the Big Bad Wolf.

"Nothing. I'm super excited. No second thoughts at all."

He leans his head against the seat and stares at the ceiling. "What can I say to convince you?"

I stare at my lap. "That this will somehow help my dad."

"I can't promise that."

A lump catches in my throat.

"I can promise that I will use this to try to save you."

I look up. "Save me? You make it sound like I'm already doomed."

He doesn't answer right away. I soak in his profile as he considers his words. "Until we know why this happens, I have to work under the assumption that what's happening to your dad is the standard course of this...ability."

I smile that he used my word: ability.

"We can do tests every day for the next ten years, but without a control subject I can't say with certainty that anything we're doing will change your prognosis."

This is nothing new. I figured it out when Dad first told me that he used to flicker, but hearing it from a medical professional, my personal research guy, is a little scary. "So I'm doomed."

"You're not doomed."

"Okay, I'm semi-doomed."

He chuckles, but doesn't deny it. "That's why we're here."

"Very reassuring."

"The Strand is over by the river, right?"

I assumed he knew since he drives all over town in the ambulance. "Yeah, that stretch of tall trees just before—"

"Yeah, I know."

The camera is heavy in my lap. It's a third the size of mine, but knowing what I'm about to do and the fact that another video will soon exist of me flickering—more evidence to bite me in the ass if I'm not careful—makes me hesitant to pick it up.

"Put the strap over your wrist so it goes with you."

I do as he asks. The strap feels coarse against my skin. There's a little dial on top for the settings, and I spin it to the video icon. "Doom Master, I am ready."

He laughs softly beneath his breath. "Is there anything else you need to do to make sure you flicker?"

"Just keep my eyes open." We're nearing the final bend before the Strand. I press the power button and turn the camera so it's pointing at my face.

Martinez flexes his fingers against the steering wheel. "Do I need to do anything?"

"Don't go below fifty."

He quirks an eyebrow.

"You know? There's a bomb on the bus. Come on, it's a classic!"

"Yes, I know the movie. I wasn't expecting you to joke right now."

"I'm extremely anxious and uncomfortable. This is the perfect situation for joking. Oh shit, here it comes." Like he flipped a switch, my toes and fingers start tingling, the sensation crawling up my legs until I can barely hold the camera.

"Make sure it's pointing at your face." Martinez's voice is level and it calms the mild panic that often comes when I'm flickering.

I hold the camera close to my face. "Prepare for freakiness." I nearly drop the camera when the weight descends, but somehow manage to keep it up. I wedge my elbows against my side and force myself to stare at the camera. I have no idea what my eyes are doing right now but I hope I'm capturing it because now I'm floating and the camera angle bounces over my head. From the corner of my eye I see Martinez's hand reaching for me. "No. Don't." I never told Martinez that Cameron flickered with me when he touched me at just the right moment because he's so determined to figure this out he'd probably grab my arm and never let go.

"Are you okay?" There's a hitch in his voice that wasn't there before. Is he actually concerned about me?

No time to worry about that now.

"See you tomo—"

His hand wraps around my wrist just as I go back.

—I jerk upright on my bed, then flop back onto the pillow. "Thank god." The benefit of not being able to drive is that except for the days of my doctor's appointments, I'm home after school. And since I'm in my room, Dad won't know I flickered.

Or the reason why.

I touch my wrist. Did Martinez grab me in time? When Cameron flickered with me we both landed at my locker, but I was never sure if that's where we'd been at that exact moment the day before, or if it was because he traveled back with me. If Martinez did come back with me, his absence from my room proves that anyone who flickers goes back to their yesterday, not mine.

My butt rings. I twist to one side to pull my phone from my back pocket and read the display: Martinez.

I smile as I answer. "Pretty freaky, huh?"

He takes several breaths before speaking. "How is that—how did?" He clears his throat. "Did you know that was possible?"

There's no sense keeping the truth from him any longer. "It happened because you were touching me, and yes I knew it was possible." I imagine him running his hand over his face while he processes the fact that he just time traveled.

"How long have you known? Why didn't you tell me? I could have flickered with you months ago."

That's why I didn't tell you, I want to say. "Cameron flickered with me one of the times I went back to save Katie. There was so much going on at the time that I guess I didn't think to tell you."

"Biz, this is incredible."

I shrug even though he can't see me. The amazingness of my ability isn't as amazing as it used to be.

"Did the recording work?"

The camera's on the bed next to me, but I'm hesitant to pick it up. Part of me wants to smash it into a million pieces and put a stop to everything so I can go back to the way my life was before, back when no one knew my secret and no one was pressing me to divulge my every waking thought.

"Biz?"

"Let me check." I press the power button and switch to play mode. "Yep, there I am. Wonky eyeball and everything."

Martinez exhales. "Is there any chance we can meet tonight so I can see it?"

I smile again. "Nope. Part of flickering is the excruciating wait for tomorrow. Sleep tight." I end the call and press play again.

I knew that one of my pupils dilates really big, but seeing it close up, with the camera pointing directly at me, is totally different. It's like the color is completely gone from my eye. I lean closer and my chest tightens. I feel like I'm staring into my own soul. All the fear and uncertainty that I felt is clear on my face, but I never realized how transparent my emotions are. When the screen jumps to my bedroom, I hit play over and over until I can recall it with my eyes closed.

Then I download it to my computer. While I know deleting the first video from my phone was the smart thing—the safe thing—to do, I've regretted not studying it first. My computer never leaves my room so unless someone breaks in and hunts for a random video, it's not going anywhere.

Well, except for Martinez. The panic that I pushed down in his office claws its way back to the surface. I still don't feel right about agreeing to flicker. It's been a long time since I went back just for the sake of going back, without having something I'm trying to fix or relive—although technically I flickered so Martinez could get another video—and it's not sitting right with me. I know he said he needed the video since we don't have as much time—

Wait. Wait just a goddamn minute.

He said the grant for our research is only until the end of the summer. Which means he's known all along that we only have six—five and a half—months left together. So why did he act like we have to switch to an accelerated schedule? Even if he really was planning to apply for an extension, he should have said something about this timing when we started.

I look around the room, but everything is a blur. The walls are closing in on me. Did he flat out lie to get me to flicker? I'm probably not risking anything more than a migraine, but at least when Cameron pressured me he was trying to save his sister's life. Martinez had no reason other than to help his precious research. I press my hand to my chest, forcing the breath in and out. Did I seriously let my stupid crush blind me from his intentions?

And even worse, now I'm going to have a migraine on Amelia's birthday. I could fake my way through dinner but she'll see right through it and make me go home, so I may as well cancel.

I need to get out of here. I open the door to go downstairs, but the sounds of Mom making dinner stop me. I'm too pissed off to have a normal conversation, plus Dad's already suspicious of Martinez so telling him about this could push him past whatever small thread is holding him together. I shut the door and sink back onto the bed.

I made this mess, I need to deal with it.

◆◆◆

"I was thinking the three of us could go to the lake this weekend. Get some fresh air."

"Do you think Dad's up for it?"

Her lips tighten, and I know she's trying not to cry. "He's been complaining about being trapped in the house. I know it's still a little cold to be picnicking, but it's what he wants."

I touch her arm. "Then of course we'll go." I know she needs me to comfort her right now but I'm so pissed off at Martinez that I can barely concentrate on this conversation.

She takes one hand off the wheel to wipe beneath her eyes. "I don't mean to overreact."

"Mom, you're hardly overreacting. This whole thing sucks. I think you're entitled to cry."

She sniffles and forces a small smile. "I want to be strong for you."

We pull into the parking garage but she doesn't turn off the car. "Do you mind if I wait here? I'd rather people don't see me like this."

The words roll off my tongue and I wonder for the millionth time how my brain recalls the exact conversation from before. "You don't have to wait in the parking garage. Why don't you go get a coffee or something and meet me back here in an hour?"

She sniffs again, then presses her hands to her cheeks. "As long as you don't mind going up there alone."

I'm tempted to make her come inside since my migraine will hit while I'm in Martinez's office, but she looks so pitiful I can't bear to make it worse. "I don't mind." I lean over and kiss her cheek. "See you soon." I climb out of the car and throw back my shoulders, steeling myself for a different confrontation with Martinez.

He's pacing in the waiting room when I arrive. "Biz, hi!"

The stuck-up receptionist quirks an eyebrow but the scowl never leaves her face.

I look around self-consciously. Two other people are waiting, but they're focused on their phones and don't seem to realize that my doctor is acting completely unlike himself. "Hey?" It comes out a question, but what I really want to ask is 'why aren't you in your office like you normally are and should I be concerned about the smile that seems plastered to your face?'

He holds his arm out to me as he opens the door, gesturing for me to follow. "Come on, we have a lot to cover today."

Of course, the flickering. I've been so pissed off about being tricked into going back for no reason that I sort of forgot that he's probably OMG-freaking-out that he flickered, too.

He leads me into the office and shuts the door. I pace the small space, nearly bumping into him. "Sit down, sit down." He pats the table and I stop, arms crossed. I don't think I've ever seen him this excited, but it's not changing the fact that I'm royally pissed off. The smile fades a milliwatt. "What's wrong?"

"You lied to me."

His head tilts to the side and for a moment he seems genuinely confused. "When did I lie to you?"

"Yesterday. Well, today. When you convinced me to flicker for no reason."

"It was for a very good reason. Another recording of you flickering will help immensely with our research." He glances at my bag. "Did you bring the camera?"

"Yes, I brought the camera." I dig it out of my bag and set it on the counter, rather than throwing it at his head like I'd like to do. "So you admit you lied?"

"No. When did I lie to you?"

"You just said you lied for a good reason!" I throw my hands in the air and start pacing again. "Why do I feel like we're having two separate conversations?" Anger burns in my chest. I want to scream, lash out, but I can't say it's all Martinez's fault. I agreed to flicker and it's my own stupid fault for not thinking it through until afterward, but that doesn't change the fact that I'd like to throttle him.

He gestures to the table. "Will you please sit down?"

I lean against the table, arms still crossed.

"Biz, I'm sorry, but I don't know what you're talking about." He rubs his hands over his face, then back through his hair, making it stand on end.

"You asked me to flicker because we suddenly have an accelerated schedule since I'm going to college." I air quote 'accelerated', hoping the disgust on my face demonstrates how angry I am. "But you also said the grant ends when I go to school, which means you've known all along that we only have five months left."

"That's true."

I pause. I didn't expect him to admit it so quickly. "So you admit it."

He sighs. "I admit that I've known our research sessions might end in August, yes, but I wasn't trying to trick you. What purpose would pissing you off serve?"

"I don't know. Maybe you get your kicks off getting me all riled up."

He turns away, but not before I notice his cheeks coloring.

Do my eyes deceive me or is he actually blushing? "I feel completely used. It seems like you tell me whatever I want to hear just to get what you want. Sometimes I think you're worse than the boys at school."

He whirls on me, his face a mask of fury. Brows furrowed, eyes narrowed, and jaw clenched so tight I fear he'll pop a blood vessel.

I shrink away. I might have pushed him too far.

"Which ones? The ones who bully you or the one who said he loved you then pushed you to the point where you could have died? Or maybe the one who's sending you emails just to scare you? Because I've done none of those things." He picks up the camera and wraps his fingers around it, holding it in front of my face. "This will help us figure out why you flicker. It might even save your life. That's all I'm trying to do."

He sets the camera down and stands directly in front of me. "I'm not playing games. I'm not thinking up ways to trick you into doing something that you don't want to do. That's not who I am." He takes a tiny step closer. "I never said I'm perfect. I could probably say things nicer or gentler or whatever it is that wins physicians doctor-of-the-year awards, but I consider you an adult. I guess I figured you were mature enough to understand that." He lets out a breath and his shoulders slump ever-so-slightly.

"Oh."

He smirks. "Oh?"

"That's a lot to take in. Give me a minute." I knew pressing his buttons would get a reaction, but that was more than he's ever said to me all at once and the most he's revealed about what he thinks of me. I knew he didn't like Cameron, but I didn't know he gave two shits about the bullying, and I definitely didn't know he considered me an adult. I mean, he did say that when he was trying to convince me to flicker, but I figured he was taking advantage of me, not speaking honestly.

He's still standing in front of me, the same soft smile on his face. "Do you trust me?"

"Depends on the day."

He tilts his head again, as if recalling this conversation the first time around. "Does that always happen?"

"The repeating of conversations?"

"Yeah."

"Sometimes."

"It's strange how the exact same words come out of my mouth without me even thinking about it."

"Tell me about it."

"So are we good?"

I break his gaze to study the floor. I can't shake the feeling that once again, I'm giving in too easily, but what choice do I have? I want to solve this flickering thing and live a long, healthy life. Martinez is my best chance.

I look up and my pulse quickens. Why does he have to be so damn hot?

"Yeah, we're good."

# chapter 14

Knowing a little more about how Martinez thinks has changed my perspective on things. Yes, I'm his research project and he's using me to help his career, but I'm using him to save my life. I don't know if that makes us even, but it changes how I think about our relationship.

If that stupid email wasn't from him, then who sent it? I want to trust him that he only wants what's best for me, but sometimes it's hard to believe he doesn't have ulterior motives.

"Biz, you okay back there?" Mom catches my eye in the rearview mirror. We're on our way to the lake, Dad tucked securely in the front seat and me crammed in the back with my camera, the picnic basket, and enough blankets to keep a family of ten warm. "You can't be too sure," Mom had said when she ran back inside to get three more. It is barely spring, but I think we'll survive.

"Yeah, just thinking."

Dad looks over his shoulder at me. "Everything okay? You've been quiet since your last appointment with Dr. Martinez."

I choose to ignore the unasked question in his eyes. "It's not a big deal. I realized this week that our sessions will end when I go away to college."

"Are you making progress? It's been a while since you've shared anything new."

"Yes and no." I don't want to admit that I flickered. I managed to hide yesterday's migraine from them and considering how worked up Mom's been about this day trip, even though the doctors said it'd be okay, I'd like to keep them in the dark. "But let's not talk about me." I sit forward so my head is between their seats. "Mom, has Dad ever told you about your first date?"

Her head jerks as she looks at him. "Told me about it? I was there."

He smiles. "But you only remember the second one."

I settle against my seat, head resting on the window, as Dad launches into the tale of repeating the date to better impress her. Mom's giggles ease my tension, and soon they're both laughing, lightening what had started as a rather somber day. No one says it out loud, but we all know this could be one of Dad's last ventures beyond our town. His wheelchair, meds, and an emergency kit fill the trunk, which is why I have all the normal picnic supplies next to me.

"I always wondered how that conversation went so smoothly! You never missed a beat. And you brought my favorite flowers." Mom rests her hand on Dad's arm and he slides his fingers through hers.

"That part I got right on the first try. Not everything was changed." He smiles at her, eyes watery, and presses a kiss to the top of her hand. They fall into a comfortable silence, and we keep our thoughts to ourselves until we reach the turnoff for the lake.

Mom pulls into the handicapped spot closest to the path, and Dad sighs. "Really? It's only ten more feet to a normal spot."

"But the wheelchair."

"Humor me. Please."

She puts the car in reverse and moves us to a spot that's more than ten feet away but doesn't have other cars next to it.

"Thank you."

We do the wheelchair dance and she piles the basket and supplies into his lap. Mom pushes while I sling my camera around my neck and bear-hug the blankets. The camera digs into my chest, but I don't want to risk dropping it.

Dad points to a bench a good distance up the path. A pair of swans float near the edge, a dozen gray babies swimming circles around them. "What about there?"

Mom smiles. "Looks perfect."

"As long as there aren't any predators lurking in the bushes." I meant a fox, like in my picture that went viral last fall, but from the sharp look Dad gives me, I realize he's thinking about human predators. Like when I was kidnapped.

"I'm sorry we can't go farther away."

"Dad, that's not what I meant. Just ignore me."

Whenever we'd go on a picnic when I was little, Dad would pick a spot as far off the path as we'd tolerate, arguing that if he wanted to hang out with strangers, he'd take us to a restaurant. It pains me to see how much his body has changed and limited what he's able to do. I catch Mom's eye as she pushes the chair and I know she's thinking the same thing. But any picnic at the lake is better than being cooped up in the house.

I help Mom spread a blanket on the ground, then I choose the softest one and drape it around Dad's shoulders. She sits next to him on the bench, another blanket over her lap. I take a step back and laugh. "You two look like you're waiting for a blizzard."

Mom pulls the blanket tighter to her chest. "It's cozy."

Dad tilts his head toward hers and she mirrors the gesture, kissing him gently.

Without fully realizing what I'm doing, I unzip my camera bag, pop off the lens cover, and take their picture. *Click-click-click.* Dad's eyes slide toward me, but he doesn't turn his head. Mom's hand drifts to his cheek and I continue shooting until my heart can't bear it any longer. A sob builds in my chest, threatening to turn me into a blubbering mess right here in the park. How will she go on without him?

I push myself to my feet and swallow past the lump in my throat. "Okay, well, I'm going to walk around and take pictures."

I run my thumb over the stitching of the strap. I don't feel right leaving them. Dad looks like he can barely sit up on his own. What if he has a seizure? Will Mom be able to handle it?

And how am I supposed to go away to college when I can't even leave them at a park?

Dad lifts a hand to shield the sun from his eyes. "Biz, go. We'll be fine."

"Take your phone," Mom calls after me, the unspoken words ringing as loudly as the ones she said: Bring your phone in case something happens and we need to leave.

I walk away, one foot in front of the other, willing myself not to turn around. Mom hasn't said anything about the inevitable since the morning of my birthday, but we both know it's close, and as much as I want to soak up whatever time I have left with him, they need time alone, without me.

A broad willow tree drips over the path ahead, sheltering a flock of small birds picking at the ground. I lift my camera and ready the lens, but I'm not feeling it. I hit the shutter—*click, click, click*—and the birds startle, flying away in one smooth motion. The camera feels heavy in my hands. It's been months since it's felt like a part of me, like an extension of my body, and I don't know what I need to do to get that feeling back. I still love photography, especially the way light and shadows play together, but it's just not clicking.

I snort at my own joke. At least I can amuse myself.

Several families dot the grass farther up the path. I don't want to be a creeper and take their pictures, so I simply watch as a little boy runs in circles around his dad, arms spread out like an airplane, his lips flapping as he makes engine noises. The dad looks up and smiles at me. I smile back but hurry along the path.

I'm halfway around the lake in a more wooded area before I come across a potential subject. It's another father and son, but they're crouched at the shore, their backs to me as they concentrate on a toy sailboat the boy is readying to launch into the water. The trees behind us cast everything in shadow except the two of them and they sit in their personal bubble of sunshine, oblivious to anything except the boat. I lift my camera and start shooting, hoping the noise from the camera doesn't ruin the moment.

The dad turns his head and catches my eye.

I'm about to apologize, but he smiles and turns his attention back to his son. Longing punches me in the gut. I'll never have a moment like this with my dad. Everything we've done together is all we'll ever do. There won't be any new moments, no new memories to store away to think of later.

Tears burn my eyes but I brush them away. I crouch lower to the ground so I'm shooting at the same level as them. The boy pushes the boat into the water and I capture the boat as it moves beyond his shoulder, framing it between them. *Click-click-click.* The knot in my stomach loosens, but I can't stop the tears from running down my face.

My knees pop when I stand. "Thank you," I say under my breath. The wannabe professional in me wonders if I'm supposed to get permission to take their picture, but he would have stopped me if he wasn't okay with it, right?

I continue around the lake, but the glimmer of inspiration I felt with the sailboat boy is gone. I'm aware of the trees around me and how pretty it is here, even though things are barely starting to bloom, but I feel numb inside. I can't stop thinking about Dad. I know he's going to die, and I know it'll be soon. What I don't know is how I'll go on without him.

As if on cue, my phone vibrates in my back pocket.

Mom: Hurry back.

That's all I need to know. I tighten my grip on my camera strap and run the rest of the way to where they are. They're both on the ground, Dad's head cradled in Mom's lap. A familiar scene, but this looks more desperate.

"Biz! Go get the car."

My stomach drops. "Did you call an ambulance?"

"They'll take too long."

"I'm not supposed to drive."

Her normally calm voice is nearly a shout. "I don't care. Right now your Dad's health trumps whatever the judge said."

That's all I need to hear. I grab the keys from her purse. The parking lot is at least two hundred yards away so I start running. My thoughts fall in sync with the pounding of my feet.

Don't let him die. Don't let him die. Don't let him die.

I hit the button to unlock the car as I get closer and glance over my shoulder. Mom is still cradling Dad's head in her lap. Dad's not seizing, but his stillness is even more terrifying.

I stop in front of the car, breathing hard. Backing the car out of the spot, I look around to make sure no one's watching, then press the gas and drive over the curb and onto the grass to get around the metal barrier that's supposed to keep cars off the path that runs next to the lake. The bottom of the car scrapes against concrete, but it doesn't sound like anything important fell off so I keep driving.

Mom's watching me, her face frozen in a mix of fear and panic. I hope she's able to help me get Dad in the car.

I bump over terrain not intended for vehicles, the car creaking and groaning its protests for not being on a smooth road, and come to a shuddering stop a few feet from the blanket. I'm out of the car and at Dad's side in seconds. "Can you walk?"

He moves his head from side to side, his eyes locked on mine. He's not having a seizure, but he doesn't seem to have control over his body. I look around to see if there's anyone to help us but the people who were walking nearby when we arrived have either moved to the opposite side of the lake or are too far away to see what's going on. "Do you want to be in the front seat or back?"

His eyes widen and he glances in the direction of the car, and although he opens his mouth, nothing comes out.

"You can't talk?"

"He hasn't said a word in ten minutes."

"What the hell, Dad?"

His eyes close briefly, and when he opens them, a tear leaks from the corner.

Mom rests her hand on the side of his face, her tears mirroring his.

I freeze for a moment, but we don't have any time to waste. I need to get us out of here. I open the front passenger side door and lay it back as far as it will go, then return to Dad's side. "I'll get one side, you get the other. We'll put him in the front seat so the seatbelt can keep him in place. Have you called the hospital yet?"

She shakes her head, eyes still focused on Dad.

"Mom!"

She looks up, eerily calm for how panicked I'm feeling. I've never seen Dad so bad. Seizures are scary as hell, but I've seen them my entire life so I know how to handle them. This...this stillness...I don't know what to make of it.

"Dad, are you in pain?"

A slow nod.

I crouch on the ground so I can slide my shoulder beneath his. "Mom, get his other side."

She finally moves, copying my position.

"Count of three. One. Two. Three!" I use one hand to push off the ground, shifting to my knees until Mom is off the ground. Dad moans. I touch his chest, tears burning my eyes. "I'm sorry."

We get to our feet at the same time but turn different directions and I stumble back to the ground. My shoulder jabs into Dad's ribs, and a whoosh of air escapes him. "Crap, I'm sorry. I'm terrible at this."

"Biz, we can do it." I don't know how Mom managed to stay on her feet, but if she can do this, so can I.

I stand again, keeping an arm wrapped around Dad's back. Mom's hand is pressed against mine, and the pressure is reassuring. I'm not in this alone. We shuffle toward the car, straining under Dad's weight. He's so frail that I expected him to be much lighter, but he's completely limp. We get to the open door and I falter. I've helped him into the car a million times, but he's always been able to help with his legs. I try not to think about what this means. We've known the end is coming, but here? Now?

Another reality sets in: we're hours from home. We may not get him to the hospital in time. "I think we should call an ambulance."

"But his doctors aren't here."

A surge of anger sparks inside me. "I'm calling 9-1-1." I sink to my knees, tightening my grip on Dad so he lowers with me. Mom has no choice but to follow—she can't support him on her own. I press the all-too-familiar buttons and am connected with an eager young man.

"9-1-1. What's your emergency?"

"My dad, he's—" I press my fingers to the hair brushing his forehead. How do I explain in two seconds what's going on? "He needs to get to the hospital."

"What's wrong with him?"

A lump forms in my throat, making it hard to talk. "I'm not sure. He has seizures, but he's not having one now. He can't talk or move."

"Is he conscious?"

"Yes. Barely."

"Okay, ma'am. What's your location?"

I tell him where we're at and he instructs me to stay on the line while he contacts the ambulance. "Please hurry," I whisper.

To say the wait for the ambulance is agonizing would be an understatement. With Katie we were fighting to save her life, but with Dad, there's nothing we can do except try to keep him comfortable. Mom's repositioned herself so Dad's head is back in her lap, so I busy myself putting everything into the car. A few people have walked by, casting concerned looks our way, but no one has stopped or offered to help.

I close the back door and sit on the other side of Dad. "Do you—" I stop, tears filling my eyes. Dad's eyes are closed. It looks like he's sleeping but I don't know if he can hear us.

Mom looks up, waiting for me to continue.

"Do you think this is it?"

Her lower lip trembles. She nods. "I don't know."

I reach for her hand. She slides her fingers through mine and we rest our hands on Dad's chest. His faint heartbeat thrums against my wrist. Or is that my pulse? He's so weak I don't know if his pulse is even strong enough for me to feel.

When sirens sound in the distance, I swear we've been sitting here for hours, but the sun has barely shifted from its perch directly above us. I stand, my knees stiff, and jog to the parking lot, waving my hands above my head when the ambulance appears.

It turns toward me, lights flashing but the sirens mercifully silenced, following the same path over the curb that I took and coming to a stop behind our car. Two blond, broad-shouldered men burst from the cab and rush to Dad's side. Mom moves backward so they can go to work, and in moments they have him on a board with a neck brace stabilizing his head.

The blonder EMT faces Mom. "You said he had a seizure?"

"I don't think so. There wasn't anything. He just stopped moving."

"We'll take good care of him. One of you can ride in the bus."

Mom gives me an expectant look that crushes my heart.

"I'm not supposed to drive."

"Biz, please."

I glance at the sky. The sun is still pretty high, but I don't know where the hospital is or what kind of trees we'll pass on the way.

I don't have long to worry because they've already got Dad in the back and the less-blond EMT is helping mom over the tailgate. I follow them over the grass and past the small crowd of people who've gathered in the parking lot. A few people have their phones up, documenting the spectacle, and I feel that familiar mix of anger and doubt. That will be me someday. That has been me, photographing horrific events for posterity.

I push those thoughts away and focus on the spiraling red lights in front of me. I cannot get into an accident or do anything else stupid to get pulled over. And—I take a deep breath—I cannot flicker.

# chapter 15

Amelia: How's he doing?
Me: It doesn't look good.
Amelia: Want me to come to the hospital? I can
have Trace bring me.

I look around the deserted waiting room. Mom hasn't left Dad's side. Not at the hospital in the town near the lake, not in the second ambulance as we came home, and not since he's been admitted and his regular doctors have checked him out. The nurses have been their usual helpful selves, but it'd be nice to have my best friend here.

Me: I am hungry.
Amelia: I see. I'm only good for food delivery?
Me: There's a good tip in it for you if you hurry.
Amelia: lol. See you soon.

I settle back into the padded chair, resting my head against the wall. The doctors at the first hospital weren't sure why Dad couldn't talk, but decided he was stable enough to make the two-hour trip home. Since getting here they've run so many tests I'm surprised he's got any blood left.

I run my thumb over my phone. I wish I could talk to Dad. Mom said she'd let me know if he's able to speak, but it's not just that. If this is really it, there are things I want to say to him, things I want him to know before he dies.

Me: Any change?

Fresh tears slide down my face and I wipe them away with my sleeve. Maybe I should just go in there. I'll never forgive myself if I wait too long and miss the chance to see him. I push out of the chair and walk past the nurse's station. My legs feel like lead. The man behind the counter glances up as I pass and gives me a weak smile. This isn't the floor for optimism and happy chitchat.

I pause in front of the door to Dad's room and take a deep breath. I knock lightly, then push the door open and step inside. A light burns dimly over his bed, casting eerie shadows across the room. Dad's lying beneath a thin blanket, tubes running into his arms, beneath his hospital gown, and up his nose. Mom's sitting next to the bed, her head resting next to his arm, eyes closed. Her cell phone is on the small nightstand.

"Got room for one more?" I drag the other chair to the opposite side of the bed.

Mom lifts her head. Her bleary eyes seem unfocused and it's like she's forgotten where she is. "What time is it?"

I check my phone. "A little after seven."

"Have you eaten?"

"Amelia's bringing food. Want me to have her grab something for you?"

She shakes her head. "I'm not hungry."

"Mom, you have to eat."

"I'll eat later."

Me: Can you grab something for my mom too?

I rest the phone on my leg and reach for Dad's hand. His skin is warmer than I expected, but he doesn't react to my touch. "Has there been any change?"

She shakes her head again. "His eyes have opened a few times but he doesn't seem to be aware of where he is or what's going on."

My heart sinks. I knew this was coming but no matter how much I tried to prepare myself, watching your father in his final days—hours?—is completely surreal. I'd like some time alone with him but A, I don't know how to get Mom to leave, and B, I don't know if he'll even hear me.

    Amelia: On it.

"Did they...do they think we'll know when it's time?"

Mom runs a hand over Dad's chest. "They won't say exactly. But I've read that there's often a period of lucidity shortly before—" she presses her hand to her mouth as she starts to cry. "I just hope we can say goodbye."

We sit in silence until Amelia texts that she's here. "Be back in a minute." I wind my way through the corridor to the elevator, my mind in a fog. I feel helpless. I'm used to doing things for Dad but now all I can do is sit by and watch as he fades away.

Amelia's waiting by the elevator on the main floor, leaning on one crutch, a white paper bag of food in her hand.

"I'm so sorry I missed your birthday."

She smiles, but it doesn't reach her eyes. "You get a pass. This time."

I can't believe I let her down again.

"Am I allowed up there?"

I shrug. "No one's paying much attention to us, so sure." I take the bag so she can maneuver with her crutches and she follows me into the elevator. "Did Trace leave?"

"He's waiting in the car. But he's got his phone so I can stay as long as you want." She frowns. "Is there any change with your dad?"

"He still hasn't woken up."

She rests her hand on my back. "I'm so sorry."

I force a smile. "It's not time for that yet."

"Okay." She drops her hand and I peer inside the bag. "There's cheeseburgers, chicken nuggets, and ten pounds of fries."

My stomach grumbles as the aroma of fried potatoes hits my nose. "Ketchup?"

"Obvi."

"My stomach thanks you."

The elevator opens and I lead Amelia down the hall to Dad's room, but stop outside the door. Aside from the occasional nurse, the hallway is deserted. I tilt my head toward her and lower my voice. "There's something else I need to tell you."

She mimics my posture. "This sounds serious."

"It is." I glance behind me to make sure no one is coming and she stops smiling. "I got an email a couple days ago that said 'I know your secret, and it could kill you.'"

"What?!"

"Shh!"

"What?" she whispers.

"I don't know. That's all it said."

"I assume you don't know who sent it?"

I shake my head. "Only five people know the truth, and that includes my parents and you. That leaves the boys."

"You think Cam would sell you out?"

"No, not really." Part of me wants it to be him because even though it would hurt worse than when we broke up, I could continue being mad at him. But most of all, if Cameron is the one trying to blackmail me or whatever is going on, that means it's not Martinez.

"So that leaves...the doctor?"

I appreciate her not saying his name out loud, especially in the hospital. "He denies it, of course, but who else could it be?"

She adjusts her grip on the crutch. "I don't get why he'd do that."

"Me neither. I've wracked my brain trying to come up with a reason, but nothing makes sense. I see him every week. What could he want to know that I haven't already told him?"

Amelia glances at the closed door. "What about your dad?"

"He has no idea who it could be."

She shakes her head. "No, I mean, does the doctor want to know about him?"

I hadn't considered that. Martinez knows that Dad used to flicker—knowing what it's done to his body is what keeps us motivated to find answers—but Dad has never talked to him about it. "He knows a little. Maybe he thinks that by pressuring me, I'll talk to Dad, who will...what? Confess his life's secrets? It still doesn't make sense."

"It's gotta be something big if he's resorting to cryptic emails." She bats her eyes. "Maybe you could use your feminine wiles to get it out of him."

"What?! Amelia!" I smack her arm.

A passing nurse gives us a stern look.

Amelia lowers her voice. "Oh, like you haven't thought about it."

"That's beside the point."

"So you have thought about it? I was just giving you shit, but this could get interesting."

I rub my hand over my face. "I need to learn to keep my mouth shut."

"No, just the opposite. Open it up and see what happens."

"Ohmigod, you are disgusting."

She waggles her brows. "I'm just saying. If he doesn't suspect that you're on to him, you could trick him into divulging his deepest, darkest secrets. Or at least admit what he's up to."

"I'll think about it." I grab the doorknob. "Ready?" She nods, and I push into the room. Nothing has changed since I left.

Mom lifts her head from the bed. "Amelia, hi sweetie."

"I brought food."

"Oh, you girls go ahead and eat. I'm not hungry."

I set the bag on the small table on the opposite side of the room. "Mom, you need to eat. There's enough food here to feed the entire floor."

"Maybe in a little while."

I move closer to her. "He still hasn't woken up?"

She shakes her head.

"He will." I join Amelia at the table and grab a burger from the bag. I peel back the paper and the greasy scent of grilled meat makes my stomach grumble louder than before. I take a huge bite and groan. "Mom, I take it back. There might not be enough for you."

"Don't talk with your mouth full."

"I hope you saved some for me."

We all whirl around at Dad's voice. His eyes are open and he's staring at the bag of food.

Mom presses her hand to the side of Dad's face, fresh tears in her eyes.

I swallow my bite, but the lump remains in my throat. "You might have to wrestle me for it." I'm probably supposed to rush to his side and coddle him, but we've been doing that for years and it always drives him crazy. Based on the way his eyes light up, I'm guessing teasing was the better choice.

"Biz."

Mom's voice holds a warning, but Dad smiles. "Can you put one arm behind your back?"

"For you, yes." I pull out another burger and the container of chicken nuggets and move to Dad's side. I reach over him to set the chicken on the bed in front of Mom while he untangles himself from the blankets that are tucked tightly under the mattress. I hand him the burger and he has the paper off and is taking a bite in a matter of seconds.

Mom still hasn't touched her food. "Are you sure you should be eating that?"

He takes another bite. "Absolutely," he says with his mouth full.

I smile and for a moment, we eat in silence.

Dad smiles at Amelia, who's doing her best to be invisible. "I assume you brought this?"

She nods and gestures toward the door. "I can go. Let you guys be alone."

"Nonsense. I spend my days hiding inside alone. It's not like when you kids were younger, running all over the house from morning 'til night. I miss the activity. The noise." He gets a faraway look in his eyes and I notice Mom chewing on her lower lip.

Is this the lucidity they told us about? That would mean we're at the end. I fall into the chair near the bed and clasp Dad's hand in mine.

"I'm gonna go." Amelia hobbles to my side and gives me a weird backwards hug. I move so she can lean over Dad. "It was good to see you, Mr. Biz. I hope you liked the burger." A tear slides down her cheek and she wipes it with the back of her hand.

"Hey, none of that."

She wraps an arm around his neck and gives him a hug, then hops backward until she's steady on her crutches. "Biz, call if you need anything."

I jump up to help with the door. "I will." I give her a real hug, both arms wrapped around her middle, and squeeze. "Thank you for coming."

"Keep me posted."

The door whooshes closed behind her and I return to the chair next to Dad.

"Mom, do you mind if I—"

"Sure, honey. I'll be here." She's nibbling on the end of a nugget, but her other hand is still resting firmly on Dad's leg.

"No, I was hoping I could have a few minutes with Dad." I pause. "Alone."

She straightens. "Oh."

"Just for a couple minutes."

Dad pats her hand and gives her a soft smile. "I'll still be here when you get back."

Her lower lip trembles like she's not so sure, but she pushes back the chair and stands. "I should probably check with the nurses about your medication anyway." She presses her hand against her mouth as she moves quietly into the hallway.

"I didn't mean to kick her out, but I want to talk to you privately."

"She'll be fine." This time Dad pats my hand. "Are you going to get mushy on me?"

"Maybe." I sniff.

Tears spring to my eyes. "I'm not so sure."

Now his eyes are watering. I half expect him to ask what I

want to talk about, but he simply watches me, waiting for me to find my words.

I'm not one hundred percent sure what I want to say, but I'm not sure talking about the email is a good idea. If he only has a little time left, I don't want him to spend it worrying about me.

"What's on your mind?" His voice is gentle, softer than normal. Is it because of the illness or his concern for me?

"Everything."

"Biz, you'll get past this."

"How do you know?"

"Because I've had the honor of watching you grow into an intelligent, determined, beautiful young woman. You have so much to live for." He pauses to take a breath and my heartbeat accelerates, thinking this is it, but he continues. "I'm just sad that I won't be here to see it."

I'm overwhelmed with all the things he won't be here for: graduation, college, walking me down the aisle when I get married, holding his first grandchild if I ever have kids. A sob breaks in my throat and I rest my forehead on the bed next to his side, my shoulders shaking with everything I can't say.

His hand grazes the back of my neck, his touch so light I almost don't feel it.

I lift my head to look at him. My entire head feels clogged and I can barely breathe, but I need to tell him how I feel. "Dad—" my voice breaks and I close my eyes for a moment. "You've been the best father I could ever ask for. I promise I'll make you proud." And I mean it. I may lack motivation on my own, but knowing what Dad wants for me, envisioning this future that he sees, gives me the boost of courage I need to stay focused on my goals.

"I know you will. I wouldn't expect anything less."

"And I'll do my best to take care of Mom."

His lips tighten into a firm line. She's spent her entire adult life taking care of him. What will become of her when he's gone?

I lean forward and press a kiss to his knuckles, then rest the side of my head on his arm.

We're still sitting like that when the door opens. I don't lift my head, but when several moments pass and Mom doesn't appear on the other side of the bed, I look up. Martinez is standing in the open doorway, wearing his EMT clothes.

"Mind if I come in?"

A thousand emotions swirl through me—anger, suspicion, and curiosity among the strongest—but a tiny part of me is grateful he came. I turn to Dad, who nods.

"Where's my mom?"

"She's still talking to the nurses." He crosses the room in several long strides and sits in Mom's chair. He lifts his hand like he's going to touch Dad, but changes his mind and rests it on his knee. "I'm not good at this but—"

"You have bad bedside manner? I feel shocked." Okay, that was probably snottier than necessary, but I don't trust his intentions.

Dad squeezes my hand. "Biz, why don't you give us a minute."

My mouth falls open, but I'm not going to argue with Dad, not now. I stand and look between them for another moment before turning on my heel and opening the door. I glance back once more, unable to shake the feeling that we're playing right into Martinez's plan.

# chapter 16

I'm pacing in front of the door to Dad's room when Mom returns.

"Why are you out here?"

"Martinez wanted to talk to Dad."

She looks at the door as if she can see through it, a frown creasing her forehead. "And he couldn't do that with you in the room?"

I shrug. I suspect Martinez is trying to get whatever information he can from Dad while he still has the chance, and I'm torn on whether or not that's a good thing. Yes, I want to prevent myself from ending up in the same situation, but not if it means exploiting Dad in his final days.

"Well, I'm not standing here in the hallway. Whatever they're talking about can be said in front of me." She pushes the door open without knocking and steps inside. Martinez is huddled in the chair, his back to us so we can't see his face. Dad's lips are moving but his voice doesn't reach us.

Then the door closes, leaving me alone in the hallway.

I wait, arms crossed, not sure who the first person will be to leave. I can't imagine Martinez asking Mom to give them more time alone, but I don't think he'd be comfortable grilling Dad in front of her.

Minutes pass, and I'm still alone. "This is stupid." I knock once on the door before pushing my way inside. Martinez hasn't moved. Mom is back in her chair, leaning forward, holding Dad's hand, but his focus is still on Martinez. No one looks at me as I enter.

There are only two chairs in the room so I resume my position from the hallway at the foot of the bed. The sense of panic that Dad might die while I was in the hallway lifts, but only enough to allow me a deep breath.

Martinez's clasped hands rest on the edge of the bed. "Did the severity of the headaches get worse? Or was there some other indication that your health was failing?"

Dad grimaces. "Other than the seizures? No."

"So you had no way of knowing that a change was coming."

Dad shakes his head.

Which means I won't know that I've passed the point of no return until it's too late. My knees buckle and I grab the railing at the foot of the bed to stop myself from falling.

Martinez half-stands. "Are you all right? Do you need to sit down?"

I'm tempted to say yes to get him out of here so Mom and I can be alone with Dad, but something deep inside niggles me to stay standing. This might be my last chance to get answers about flickering. I rest a hip against the end of the bed. "I'm okay."

My earlier conversation with Amelia flashes through my mind. It's a stupid idea. If Martinez is planning something other than helping me, why would he tell me? I don't have that much confidence in my womanly wiles.

The door opens, interrupting my thoughts. Dad's doctor breezes in, stopping short when she sees Martinez. "Rick, I didn't realize you're close with the Clements."

Martinez stands and nods at Dr. Matuszak before touching Dad's hand. It's the first physical affection I've seen and the seed of suspicion grows stronger. He turns to Mom. "Please let me know if there's anything else I can do." A look of disappointment crosses his face when he looks at me. He must not have gotten what he wanted. "Biz, same for you. I'll be on call all night."

The room feels colder once he's gone. But maybe that's just my dread at what's to come.

Dr. Matuszak checks the monitors near the bed before touching Dad's chest. "How are you feeling?"

Dad shrugs, closing his eyes for a moment. When he opens them, the sparkle that normally lights them is gone. "I'm tired."

Dr. Matuszak presses her lips together. "I know."

"Isn't there anything else you can do?" Mom asks, her voice strained. Now that she knows the truth about Dad, she finally understands our frustration that the doctors don't actually know anything about what's wrong with him, and that the efforts they're making to save him are probably wrong.

Dr. Matuszak sinks into the chair Martinez had been sitting in. Her jaw clenches. "I wish there were."

For the first time I see her as a person, not just a misinformed white coat blindly fighting something she can't possibly understand.

"Hey, no talking about me like I'm not here." Dad tries to lift his hand, but it barely makes it a few inches off the bed before he gives up. He looks from Mom to Dr. Matuszak to me. "No tears."

Mom sniffs. "No promises."

They sit quietly for several minutes, long enough that I start to feel self-conscious. "Dad, can I get you anything? I hear they have kick-ass Jell-O in the cafeteria."

I'm rewarded with a smile. "Red or green?"

"Red, duh."

"I'd love some."

I don't know if he's even allowed to have Jell-O, but as much as I don't want to leave his side, I need to get out of this room. "Be back in a minute." I push out of the room and head for the stairs. I need to stretch my legs. But once I'm in the stairwell, all the energy drains from me and I collapse against the concrete wall, sobs wracking my body.

He can't die.

Not yet.

I don't care that we've known this was coming. And if I let myself be honest—be truly selfish—I don't care that he's miserable and ready to let go. I'm not ready to say goodbye.

I bury my head in my arms, allowing the weight of my grief to swallow me. For a moment I forget where I am—all that exists is the uncontrollable sadness that I have to go on without him. I struggle to catch my breath, but the tears are coming too fast, too hard. I've gone full-on ugly-cry mode and for once I don't care. I need to get this out now because once Dad is gone, I'll need to be there for Mom, to help her go on.

A door to the stairwell opens above me and I press my head against the cool concrete. I drag an arm across my face, tears and snot darkening my sleeve.

A man and woman in scrubs appear on the landing. They pause when they see me, and for a moment I'm self-conscious, but I brush it off. This can't be the first time someone's been caught crying in a hospital.

The guy leans forward, the smile dropping from his face. "Sweetie, are you okay?"

"Yeah," I say, shaking my head. They seem nice enough, concern clear on their faces, but I don't need to drag strangers into my drama.

"You sure?"

I drag my hand under my eyes and wipe it on my jeans. "No, but I will be." I don't know if I believe it, but right now I cling to those words.

"Okay, but we're here to help, so if you need to talk to someone, you just let us know."

My heart clenches at his kindness. It's not the first time someone at the hospital has taken pity on me, but it always catches me by surprise. If this happened at school I'd be ridiculed.

They continue down the stairwell. I don't move until I hear the door close below me, then I slowly rise and make my way to the cafeteria.

◆ ◆ ◆

I'm waiting for the elevator, three cups of red Jell-O tucked into one of the compostable containers that are supposed to help cut down on waste. The woman behind the register scowled at me when she realized I was using it to transport more potential garbage, but I don't have time to worry about her.

The light for the elevator dings just as a low voice startles me. "Sugar fix?"

I whirl around to find Martinez, arms crossed. The serious expression on his face contradicts the playful tone he used to scare the bejeezus out of me.

He nods at the box. "Jell-O?"

I push my shoulders back. "You have a problem with Jell-O?" I don't know why I'm so defensive with him.

The corner of his mouth quirks. He peers inside the box. "Is one of those for me?"

I pull the box closer to my chest as the elevator door closes. "No." I don't think he's actually making fun of me. We've joked like this a million times—he's probably just trying to take my mind off the serious shit going on upstairs—but my nerves are so frayed that I'm ready to argue with anyone who looks at me the wrong way.

He takes a tiny step back, giving me space. "Biz, I'm just teasing."

I drop my gaze to the floor. His boots are scuffed and I instantly imagine the different scenarios that could have caused the marks: lifting a stretcher into the ambulance, kicking in a door to rescue whoever's inside, ripping the door off a mangled car.

"Biz?"

I meet his eyes, my breath hitching at the intensity in his gaze. "Sorry, I guess I've got a lot on my mind."

He touches my arm, the heat from his fingers sending a jolt from my elbow to my shoulder. "I can be done for the night if you need to talk."

The impulsive side of me wants to say yes, but this isn't the time to indulge in my whacked-out fantasies—regardless of what Amelia might say. "I should be with my dad."

"Text if you change your mind." His hand is still on my arm. I glance at it and he drops it to his side, but he raises it again, waving in the space between us. "I almost forgot. You're approved to take photos here."

"Really? Just like that?"

He smiles. "Just like that. There's some paperwork you need to sign with the administrator, but you can do that after—" He stops.

"Yeah. After." After Dad dies. When I'm supposed to go on with my life. The lump that retreated after the scene in the stairwell crawls back into my throat. If I'm not careful, I might start crying in front of Martinez, which might make him hug me and then I'll be dealing with inappropriate hot flashes on top of crying for my dad. No, it's better if I flee now.

"I'm sorry."

"I know." I press the button for the elevator. "I'll text when I'm ready to talk."

# chapter 17

At some point during the night, I make the decision to flicker in the morning. Logic argues that I should wait until Dad dies so I can go back to see him, but I've decided against that for several reasons. First, after watching Katie die three times, I don't know if I have it in me to go through that again with Dad. Second, and more importantly, I need to warn him about the conversation with Martinez. I don't know what they talked about, but I'm growing more and more suspicious about Martinez's intentions and even though it could help me in the long run, I don't want Dad spilling his guts on his deathbed. Third, maybe I can stop our trip to the lake. Dad will end up in the hospital regardless of what I do, but at least if he's at home it will be less stressful for Mom.

But there's one thing I need to do before I flicker. Something I can erase once I go back.

I text Martinez.

Me: Are you still here?

It's 3 a.m. Odds are he's at home in his luxe bachelor pad, sleeping or watching TV or whatever he does to unwind after EMTing all night. I rest my phone in my lap. It'll be hours before I hear back from him. It's a stupid idea anyway.

Martinez: Yes.

My stomach drops into my lap. It's now or never.

Me: Can we talk?

Martinez: Meet in my office in ten minutes.

I press my hand to my belly, willing the butterflies to settle the eff down.

Me: ok

I unfold myself from the chair next to Dad's bed. He fell asleep shortly after we ate the Jell-O and hasn't woken since. Mom's passed out in her chair, her head in its permanent spot next to Dad's unmoving arm. I don't bother leaving a note. If Mom wakes up she'll assume I left in search of a couch to stretch out on and won't look for me.

Plus I should be back before she wakes up.

I will be back before she wakes up.

The door clicks as I open it, but neither of them stir. The hallway lights are muted in an effort to lull the terminally ill patients to sleep, but the nurse behind the desk is wide awake. She smiles as I walk by.

I take the stairs in an effort to burn off the surge of energy racing through me, but my heart is still doing a weird dance with my stomach when I reach the door to his office. For a moment, the lack of sleep catches up with me and I rest my forehead against the door, but that jittery feeling you get from too much caffeine or too little sleep, or, I don't know, plotting something you know you shouldn't even be considering, jolts through me. I pace in a small circle in front of his office until I hear the elevator ding.

Martinez appears at the end of the hall, a cup of coffee in each hand. But that's not what makes my breath catch. He's changed into street clothes—jeans and a dark t-shirt—and his hair looks different. As he gets closer I realize it's still wet from what I can only imagine was a very hot shower. He holds out a hand and I take the cup, averting my gaze while he unlocks his office.

Maybe this wasn't the smartest idea.

He steps into the office, but instead of hitting the switch for the overhead light, he turns on a small task light on the counter. I follow him inside, but pause. Normally I'd climb onto the examining table, but between his different clothes and the fact that it's the middle of the night, that seems too intimate. He turns to face me, back to the counter, his hands resting on either side so his biceps are flexed.

Is he doing this on purpose?

"How's your Dad?" His voice is raspier than normal.

Suddenly I feel selfish for keeping him at work. "He hasn't woken up since his Jell-O."

"I'm sorry."

"I shouldn't have bothered you. You look exhausted."

He lifts one shoulder in a half-shrug, reminding me of the guys from school. "Ain't no thang."

I snort, nearly spilling my coffee. "Did you just use improper English?"

He smiles. "The rules go out the window this late at night."

He's totally doing this on purpose.

I'm also still standing in the middle of the tiny room. I mimic his stance and lean against the examining table, but realize I'm pushing my boobs out and quickly fold my arms over my chest. Well, one arm since I've got a cup of coffee in the other.

He quirks an eyebrow. "You okay?"

I take a sip of coffee and the warm liquid slides down my throat, building my courage. "I guess I'm out of sorts. I've known this day was coming for a long time, but now that it's here I don't know what to do." As soon as the words leave my mouth I realize that could be totally misinterpreted, so I quickly add, "with my Dad." How is he standing there so calmly when I feel like I'm about to burst out of my skin?

He looks down. "Losing a parent is never easy."

"Did you—" From the solemn look on his face, I don't need to finish the question. "I'm sorry, I didn't know."

He lifts his gaze. "It's not something I talk about."

Am I supposed to ask more? We're venturing into uncharted territory, even without my scandalous intentions, and I'm realizing how little I actually know about Martinez. "How old were you?"

"Twenty-two. I'd just started med school when my mom died of a brain aneurism."

"Oh, wow. That sucks."

The corner of his mouth lifts in a small smile. "Yeah, you could say that."

"Is that why you went into neurology?" I've never thought about why he specializes in brains. I just figured that at some point in med school you have to choose a specialty and since he thinks he's such a smarty-pants, he'd concentrate—hah!—on brains.

"Now you're analyzing me?"

For a second, I think he's pissed, but then the smile broadens and I realize he's just giving me shit. I lean forward and smack his shoulder. "What goes around, comes around, right?"

"Not usually. Not for me." My heart sinks as he clears his throat. "At least not here in the hospital." And my heart bounces back up where it belongs. I knew he was cocky, but the level of narcissism I thought I just saw had me about to run for the door. "Most of my patients don't fight me the way you do."

If I'm going to confront him, now's my chance. "What were you and my dad talking about earlier?"

He takes a sip of coffee, then lets the cup linger near his mouth.

If I didn't know better I'd think he's stalling.

He sets down the cup. "Mostly clinical things. How long he flickered without serious side effects. When things started changing. If anything ever happened to change his flickering."

"Like my surgery."

"Right. He was describing being diagnosed with epilepsy when Dr. Matuszak kicked me out." There's a tension in his shoulders that wasn't there before.

"You don't like her?"

"We've had our differences. She's in the explore-every-option-before-surgery camp, while I'm a firm believer in going in and fixing things."

I smile. "I can see that about you."

He tilts his head. "How so?"

"Isn't it obvious? EMTs rush into crazy, unpredictable situations and restore calm. The first time we met, your immediate reaction was to find the problem and stop it."

He rests his head against the cabinet above the counter, appraising me. "You sure you're only eighteen?"

"Last time I checked."

"Noted."

"So that's all you talked about?" I trust that Dad has told me everything I need to know about flickering, but part of me is scared that maybe there was one small detail he's left out and for whatever reason, he decided to trust Martinez with it.

And what if, the tiny voice in my head wonders, what if Martinez really was behind the threatening email?

"Biz, what's this about?"

I turn my back to him and rest my coffee on the table. When I'm looking at him, my resolve fades and I need to be absolutely certain he's telling the truth. "Like I said, I'm feeling out of sorts. With more than just my dad."

"With me?"

"Yeah."

"You know you can trust me."

"How can I be sure?" I turn back around and my breath catches. He's moved closer so less than a foot of space separates us.

"Have I done anything to hurt you?"

I shake my head. I'm sure he's made comments that have pissed me off or made me storm out of his office, but all I can think of is how close he's standing. Amelia's words run through my mind.

"You're dealing with a lot right now. It's understandable that you're feeling uncertain about other relationships in your life when—"

Whatever brainiac analysis he was about to make is cut short when I close the gap between us. My pulse races in my throat as I breathe in the scent of his body wash. I lick my lips, still not sure this is the smartest thing I've ever done.

His pupils widen, making his already dark eyes almost black. "Biz."

My stomach drops to my knees and heat flares through me. This is supposed to be calculated, manipulative, but right now I want this more than I ever imagined. Before I can think about it any longer, I rise on my toes and brush my lips over his.

He sucks in a breath and pulls his head back ever-so-slightly. I stare at his lips, unable to breathe. He mutters something in Spanish, then dips his head and presses his lips firmly to mine.

Kissing Martinez is nothing like kissing any of the high school boys I've dated.

Not even Cameron.

His lips are firm, confident, and they move over mine like we have all the time in the world. My hands, which have been hanging at my sides, move on their own to rest on his hips. My touch must encourage him because his hands glide up my neck, pulling me closer. His fingers trace through my hair until he finds the scar, the one he made, and I stiffen. But before I can pull away, his lips part and his tongue finds mine.

This might be the best bad idea Amelia has ever had.

I trace the contours of his spine until I reach the back of his neck, and the kiss grows deeper until we are full on making out.

Holy shit, we are making out.

And I don't want it to stop. My fingers find their way beneath his shirt and I revel in the smoothness of his skin. I want to feel more. I want to rip off our clothes and feel him against me. All of him.

He breaks away and exhales softly before pressing a kiss next to my mouth. "We shouldn't be doing this."

He's right. We shouldn't.

And by tomorrow, this won't have happened.

# chapter 18

"I should get back to my parents."

"Of course."

I'm still pressed against him, our chests rising and falling together as I wrap my mind around what just happened.

He pulls away first, stepping back until he bumps into the counter. His eyes haven't left mine. "I'm sorry."

I shake my head. "I'm pretty sure I'm the one who kissed you."

"But I know better. I shouldn't have kissed you back."

Heat flushes my cheeks. When I imagined this situation I knew it would end awkwardly, but knowing it—expecting it even—and experiencing it are two entirely different things. I move toward the door. "I guess I'll see you later."

Part of me hopes he'll stop me, but I make it out the door and into the hallway without another word. I look over my shoulder at the closed door, but it remains shut. I pull out my phone and fire off a text to Amelia.

Me: Mission accomplished.

I press the button for the elevator, telling myself that I'm skipping the stairs because I'm tired, not because I want to give Martinez another chance to stop me. The doors slide open and I step inside as my phone buzzes.

Amelia: What? For serious?

A half laugh, half sob bursts out of me. The plan was that kissing him would make him, I don't know, confide in me or something, but all I managed to do is further confuse myself. He kissed me back, which means he wasn't just teasing all those times in his office, but what now? I don't know any more about what he and Dad talked about, and I'm still not convinced he's telling the truth about the email. Being an amazing kisser does not mean you're trustworthy.

I stumble out of the elevator, grateful for the dark hallway. I peek inside Dad's room to make sure nothing has changed, then curl up on a couch in the waiting room.

Me: I'll tell you about it tomorrow.
Amelia: Tease.
Me: It was hot.
Amelia: Well duh. Have you seen him?

Yes, yes I have. But nothing can ever come from it, and after tomorrow, he'll never know it happened.

Amelia: Did you find out about the email?
Me: No. Too busy making out.
Amelia: You would make a terrible spy.

I smile. When you look at it that way—that I'm undercover trying to protect my dad—it doesn't feel so calculated.

Me: Maybe I should go back in.
Amelia: As long as I get the blow by blow.
Me: Shut it.
Amelia: Only until tomorrow.
Me: Good night.

I rest my phone next to my head and close my eyes, but all I see is Martinez. My lips are still tingling, not to mention other parts of my body that weren't even part of the action. I flop onto my back and throw an arm over my eyes in an attempt to block out the memories.

I must have fallen asleep because the next thing I know, the lights are brighter and a fresh shift of nurses is bustling in and out of rooms. I get up from the couch and stretch my arms over my head. With all the activity around me, it almost feels like last night didn't happen. I touch my fingers to my lips, remembering the feel of Martinez's stubble, and freeze. What if my face is red? I can't explain road rash to my parents!

There's a bathroom in Dad's room, but I need to see what I look like before facing my parents, so I duck into the restroom closest to the nurses' station. I rush to the mirror, preparing for the worst, but I look exactly like I do every day. My eyes are a little red from lack of sleep, but the one benefit to super short curly hair is I don't get bedhead. Or, hey-I-was-making-out-with-my-doctor head. And there's no evidence on my face. It's like it never happened.

I arrive at Dad's room at the same time as Dr. Matuszak. She nods as she pushes her way into the room ahead of me, and I can't help but wonder what she would think if she knew what I did. I doubt it would make her like Martinez any more. Part of me is tempted to bring him up to see how she reacts, but she's all business.

By the time I reach Dad's bedside, she's already flipping through his chart.

I touch his arm but he doesn't stir. I catch Mom's eye. She's still clutching Dad's hand. I doubt she's let go all night.

"He hasn't woken up since you left."

And I know she won't leave in case he does. "Do you need anything? Coffee? Breakfast?"

Mom shakes her head and looks at Dr. Matuszak, silently pleading for good news.

Dr. Matuszak tucks his chart against her chest. "His counts have continued to drop overnight. I wish I could give you better news, but I think you both need to prepare yourselves for the end. I can't predict an exact time, or even day, but he's simply not bouncing back the way he has in the past. I'm sorry." She gives Mom a curt nod, then turns on her heel and leaves.

She shakes her head, a slow back and forth motion that seems to take all her energy. It won't be long before the tears start. I know I need to be here for her, to sit by her side and hold her hand and assure her that she won't be alone, but I'm losing Dad, too. And I don't deal with grief the same way she does. She folds into herself and lets it overwhelm her.

I run.

"I'm gonna go get some fresh air." If I leave now, I can flicker in time to stop us from going to the lake. I'm on my feet and at the door when her voice stops me.

"Can you sit with me? I know I'll need to get used to this, but right now I can't bear to be alone."

"Of course." I drag my chair to sit next to her and the metal squeals on the worn linoleum. "Sorry!" I say to Dad, expecting the noise to wake him, but he doesn't even flinch. I settle in next to Mom and rest my head on her shoulder.

Time seems to stand still. Several nurses come and go, checking the machines that beep steadily. I know the beeps will eventually stop, but will it be sudden, or will he slowly wind down, leaving us waiting for one more breath?

I squeeze Mom's hand. "I'm going outside for a bit."

This time she doesn't stop me.

I find the car in the parking lot and head straight for the Strand. The drive to the lake took a couple hours, so if I'm calculating correctly—I don't remember what time we left home—I'll land in the backseat of this same car. Clouds mar the sky, challenging the sun for dominance. If the sun doesn't win, I'll drive back and forth until there's a break in the clouds. There's no way the weather is stopping me today.

As luck would have it, the clouds lessen closer to the Strand and I only have to double back once. The tingling comes quickly, then the heaviness, the floating, then—

—my foot slams into the back of Dad's seat. "Sorry!"

Mom glances at me in the rearview mirror.

"I fell asleep and had one of those dreams that I was falling." When we told Mom about flickering, we didn't get into all the particulars, like the whole uncontrollable jerking when I land in yesterday.

But Dad knows.

I lean forward in my seat so my head is between them. "We need to go home."

Mom sighs. "Don't be silly. We're almost there."

Dad looks at me, brows furrowed.

I nod, even though he can't know what bad thing I'm trying to prevent.

Mom doesn't turn the car around so I'm unable to change how Dad will end up in the hospital, but this time I don't wander as far away on my walk, and I'm right there when Dad collapses.

And this time Dad and I still talk about his hopes for me and our worries about Mom, but instead of resting my head on his arm and sitting there quietly, I push on.

"There's something else."

He tilts his head.

"In about ten minutes, Martinez is going to come in here and kick me out so he can talk to you. I tried to find out what you told him, but I don't think he told me the truth." Heat burns my cheeks but if Dad notices, he doesn't comment.

He's quiet for a moment, thinking. "Do you think he's behind the email?"

I press a hand to my forehead. Too much has happened in the past twenty-four hours. "I don't know. I want to believe that I can trust him, but I trust the other people who know...well, I trust them more."

"And you don't think I should confess to him on my deathbed."

"Dad!" I smack his arm, then immediately jump up and pet him like a wounded bird. "Oh shit, Dad, sorry! But quit saying things like that."

He fights a smile, his eyes twinkling. "I'll rephrase. You don't want me spilling my secrets to Martinez because you're afraid I'll tell him something I've never told you."

I pick at the blanket. How does he do that? "That might be part of it."

He rests his hand on mine, stilling me. "I promise I've told you everything important. I've left out a few things from when I was younger, but no parent wants their child knowing the details of their sordid past."

I raise an eyebrow. "Sordid?"

"Well, maybe not sordid. More like mildly debaucherous."

"This I want to hear!"

"I don't think so." He glances at the door and I remember how little time we have.

"I'm beginning to worry—well, I've been thinking..." I need to just spit the words out. "I'm not sure if I want to continue my research. I know it could help me blah blah, but I'll be going away to school in six months so it will have to end anyway, and I'm worried that you might inadvertently tell him something that would somehow take the choice away from me." I hadn't formed that specific thought until this moment, but now that I've said it, it makes sense.

"If you're worried, I won't say a word. I promise."

"Thank you, Dad."

"I do have one question."

"What's that?"

"Why didn't you just ask me what we talked about after he left?"

My mouth drops and the heat that flushed my face earlier vanishes.

His gaze drops to his lap. "Oh."

I stop breathing as the weight of what I've told him settles over me. "Y-you haven't died yet. But when I left you'd been unconscious for almost half a day."

He looks up. "You didn't wait to flicker until..."

"No. I've repeated enough deaths. I chose to spend more time with you while you're still here." I clasp his hand in mine and rest my head against his arm. Moments later, the door opens.

"Mind if I come in?" Martinez asks.

I turn to Dad, who nods.

Memories of last night pulse through me. I can still feel his hands on me. "Where's my mom?"

"She's still talking to the nurses." He crosses the room in several long strides and sits in Mom's chair. He lifts his hand like he's going to touch Dad, but changes his mind and rests it on his knee. "I'm not good at this but—"

"You have bad bedside manner? I feel shocked." I'm not passing up a chance to say that a second time.

Dad squeezes my hand. "Biz, why don't you give us a minute."

My mouth falls open, but I'm not going to argue with Dad. I trust that he won't tell Martinez anything valuable.

◆ ◆ ◆

When 3 a.m. hits, I have to fight the urge to text Martinez. As mind-blowing as our kiss was, nothing good can come from it. Worse case, it somehow screws up his job. Best case, things get super awkward between us and my appointments become worse torture than they already are. No, it's best that I don't relive that.

But I do need a migraine pill. I usually carry some with me, but I ran out of the stash in my backpack and I haven't been home in what feels like forever. Martinez isn't a pharmacist, but I know his office gets samples from those reps that drag around the rolling suitcases full of drugs.

Me: Are you still here?

Even though I know he is, I still imagine him in his luxe bachelor pad. A girl can still fantasize, right?

Martinez: Yes.

My stomach drops into my lap. Nothing will happen. Nothing will happen. Nothing will happen.

Me: Do you have drugs in your office?

Martinez: Excuse me?

Me: Migraine drugs.

Martinez: Meet in my office in ten minutes.

I press my hand to my belly, willing the butterflies to settle the eff down. We are NOT kissing.

Me: ok

The entire way to his office I repeat the same mantra over and over: Do not kiss him. Do not kiss him. Do not kiss him. When he appears in the hallway with two cups of coffee, I almost lose my resolve. No one should be allowed to look that hot, especially in the middle of the night.

"How's your Dad?" His voice is still raspy, but now I'm imagining him whispering in my ear.

"He hasn't woken up since the Jell-O."

"I'm sorry."

"I shouldn't have bothered you. You look exhausted."

He shrugs. "Ain't no thang."

Even though I know it's coming, I snort. "Did you just use improper English?"

He smiles. "The rules go out the window this late at night."

I need to keep this conversation on track. I lean against the table.

He quirks an eyebrow. "You okay?"

I take a sip of coffee. I should ask for the meds but I want him to tell me about his mom. A few more minutes in here won't hurt. "I guess I'm out of sorts. I've known this day was coming for a long time, but now that it's here I don't know what to do." I pause. "With my Dad."

He looks down. "Losing a parent is never easy."

"Did you—" This is where I always feel uncomfortable. I know what he's going to say, but if I change the conversation it might not play out the same way. "I'm sorry, I didn't know."

He lifts his gaze. "It's not something I talk about."

"How old were you?"

"Twenty-two. I'd just started med school when my mom died of a brain aneurism."

"Oh, wow. That sucks."

The corner of his mouth lifts in a small smile. "Yeah, you could say that."

"Is that why you went into neurology?"

"Now you're analyzing me?"

I shrug. "It makes sense. So, speaking of brains, do you have any samples of my meds here? I thought I had some in my bag but I don't."

He tilts his head, studying me. "Are you getting a migraine?"

Oh shit. I was so focused on not kissing him that I didn't think of an explanation for why I'm getting a migraine when I've been in the hospital all night. "I think so."

He closes his eyes and exhales slowly. "Did you flicker?"

I pick at the edge of the paper cup. Telling the truth about flickering doesn't mean I have to tell the whole truth. But what if he uses some voodoo brain doctor magic to get me to confess?

"Biz, this isn't a trick question."

"I wanted to spend more time with my dad." It may not be the whole truth, but it's true.

"Is there something else going on?"

I throw his words back at him, hoping to get him off topic. "Now you're analyzing me?"

He shrugs. "It's my job."

Right, his job. What's not his job is making out with me in a dark office in the middle of the night. "I'm fine. I'm still freaked out about that email, but it's nothing I can't handle." I don't expect him to admit to being involved, but I can't leave without asking again.

"I'm sure it's nothing."

"You actually believe that?"

He glances over my shoulder. "Why would someone want to threaten you?"

My stomach shifts. "I don't know."

"If you figure that out, you might be able to figure out who it is."

If it is him, he sure is confident I won't figure it out. Right now, the past two days are catching up with me and I'm too tired to think about this any longer. "So do you have my meds?"

He sets his coffee on the counter and opens one of the overhead cabinets filled with drug samples. He finds mine and grabs several packs. "Try to get some rest. The next couple days could be rough."

I palm the pills, suddenly overwhelmed with everything that's happening. Dad and Martinez and worrying about Mom, the uncertainty over the future, and the idea that my secret might be exposed. Before I can stop them, tears slip down my face.

Martinez moves closer, pulling me against his chest. Heat stirs in my belly, but it's nothing more than a hug. I allow myself to breathe in his body wash and a flood of memories from the first tonight nearly sweep me off my feet. He pulls back. "You okay?"

I glance at his lips before meeting his gaze. "I better go." I hold up the pills. "Thanks for these."

"Text if you need anything."

This time I don't look back.

# chapter 19

I've faked my way through headaches since I first started flickering, but today will have to be the mother of all performances. Dad's the only one who knows I flickered, and since he hasn't woken up since last night, I need to act like I'm my same old happy-go-lucky self.

Okay, that might be pushing it a bit, but I don't want anyone to know I'm suffering. The pill Martinez gave me helped a little, but the harsh lights the hospital insists on using have not been friendly to my head.

Mom and I haven't left Dad's side since this morning. Dr. Matuszak gave the same prognosis as last time, so now we're left here waiting for him to die and trying to imagine our lives without him.

Well, I assume that's what Mom's thinking about. I can't stop remembering the kiss with Martinez. Technically it never happened, but try explaining that to my body. The feel of his mouth on mine and his hands on my face are permanently burned on my skin and no matter how many times I tell myself it didn't happen, I know it did. This feels worse than cheating on a silly test. Which brings me down another rabbit hole: what if we'd done more? I've stopped or changed plenty of things in the past, but I never thought about something like sex. What if we'd had sex and I ended up pregnant but didn't find out until after I undid the deed? They'd start calling me the twenty-first century Virgin Mary. Well, aside from the virgin part. But conception without sex would be hard for a lot of people to swallow, especially the man who has no idea he slept with you.

This is not helping my headache.

We didn't have sex. I can forget a kiss. Right now I need to concentrate on Dad and do whatever I can to keep Mom from losing herself inside her grief.

I track the hours by the pattern of nurses who check on Dad. When the night shift comes in, Mom stands, stretching her arms over her head, making her joints pop. "I'm going to get some dinner from the cafeteria. Do you have any requests?"

I'm surprised she's leaving his bedside, but I guess you can only sit in a chair for so long. "Whatever you're having is fine. Are you sure you don't want me to go?"

She smiles down at Dad and smoothes his hair off his forehead. "No, I'll just be a few minutes."

The door clicks behind her and I shit you not, Dad opens his eyes. I start to go after Mom, but Dad's voice stops me.

"Where're you going?"

"What? Nowhere." I return to my chair. I should press the call button so the nurses can check on him, or text Mom to come right back, but I'm hit with a surge of selfishness. I want him to myself, even if it's just for a few minutes. "Mom went to get dinner."

"How long have I been out?"

"About a day."

He studies my face. I don't know if he realizes that I'm wearing the same clothes from yesterday, but his mouth presses into a firm line. "Is this it?"

Tears burn my eyes. I press my hand to my lips, which start to tremble.

He lifts his hand to touch my cheek and I lean into his touch.

"I don't want you to die."

"I don't think we have a say in this."

"But who am I—" I sniffle, and flinch at the pressure in my brain. "Who's going to talk sense into me when I want to do something stupid?"

He smiles. "I'm trusting that I've taught you well enough over the years that you'll know the right thing to do."

Right. Like last night.

"Otherwise I'll come back and haunt you."

I smile through my tears. There's so much love for him inside me and I don't understand where it will go when he's gone.

"I'm so proud of you, Biz, and I'm pissed off I won't be around to see everything you'll become. I'd wish you luck with photography but you don't need luck. Your talent will take you far. It's your Mom I'm worried about."

My tongue feels so thick I can barely speak. "I'm not ready to say goodbye."

His mouth pulls into a wobbly frown. "I'm not either, but—" He takes a slow, shaky breath. "—I don't think I get—" Another breath. "—a choice." He glances at the Styrofoam cup of water on the nightstand and I hold it so he can sip from the straw. "Thanks. There's one other thing I want you to do."

"Anything."

"Patch things up with Cam."

That's not what I was expecting.

"I'm serious. You've been a part of each other's lives for too long and you've been through too much to throw it away."

"But, Dad. He was willing to risk my life—"

"To save his sister. I know it's awful, but I can understand it."

I sometimes forget Dad had a sister. She died years ago—I only met her a handful of times—and we don't really talk about her or the husband and son she left behind.

He squeezes my hand. The pressure is so light I can barely tell he moved and my heart clenches. "Just give him a chance. If you decide he's a douchebag, at least you tried."

I snort. Leave it to Dad to make me laugh on his deathbed. "Your dying wish is for me to make up with Cam?"

"Who'd have guessed?"

The door opens behind us and Mom steps into the room, a tray of food in her hands. Her mouth drops opens when she realizes Dad is awake and I jump up to grab the tray. She rushes to his side but doesn't sit in her chair. Instead she kind of hovers over the bed, her face close to his, whispering while pressing kisses to his face. I feel like I should leave them alone, but I want to be here when it happens. I set the tray on the table across the room and poke at a sandwich, my back to them. This is the most privacy I can give them right now.

After a few minutes, Mom calls me over to the bed. I bring the food and we eat quietly. I can't even taste what I'm shoving in my mouth, but the pounding in my head lessens, so I keep chewing.

"Dad, do you want anything? There's some applesauce."

He shakes his head from side to side before his eyes drift closed. I set my food in my lap, my appetite gone. I lock eyes with Mom, who looks terrified. For as long as we've known this is coming, we haven't talked about the specifics, about what we'll actually do when he dies. I know there will be a funeral—I've heard them talk about that—but then what? Are we supposed to just go back to work and school and act like nothing happened?

He takes a shallow, raspy breath and we both exhale.

"What's on your mind?" Mom's voice is hoarse, like she's already spoken all the words she can.

I sigh. "I don't know what to do."

"We're not supposed to know what to do. Just follow your heart. If you want to hold his hand, hold his hand. If you'd rather not be here, that's okay, too."

"I want to be here."

"Then that's what you should do."

I continue to track the time by the patterns of nurses who check his machines. At some point during the night their frequency increases, but on the outside nothing changes. Every so often he takes a deep, shuddering breath that rattles his chest, and his eyes flutter open a few times, but he hasn't woken up again.

Mom is in a weird place between sleep and zombie. She hasn't closed her eyes since she returned from the cafeteria, and I don't think she's even gone to the bathroom.

"Mom, if you want to sleep for a little bit, I can keep watch and wake you up if anything changes."

She doesn't react, her gaze locked on Dad's face.

"Mom?"

She blinks rapidly before focusing on me. "No, I'm fine."

"You're not fine."

"Okay, I'm not fine. But I don't want to sleep."

"Okay."

We fall back into a hypnotic silence, interrupted by the quiet beep of the machines monitoring how much life is left in Dad. When the next nurse comes in, she lingers by his bedside. "I don't think he has much longer."

Mom and I sit upright in our chairs.

"I'm not supposed to say that, but his BP has dropped significantly and his breathing is very shallow."

Mom touches his chest, which to my eyes hasn't moved in minutes. "Is he in pain?"

"Not that I can tell. We can increase his pain meds if you're concerned, but he doesn't appear to be suffering."

Mom sucks her lower lip into her mouth in an attempt to not cry. "Thank you for telling us."

The nurse nods, then rests her hand on my shoulder before backing out of the room.

"I've always said Dad is a master at drawing out the silences."

"Biz!" Mom's tone is scolding, but one corner of her mouth turns up in a smile.

I smile, too, the heaviness in my chest lessening ever so much. "He is! I swear he took a class on how to keep quiet in an argument until the other person spills their guts. He's probably lying here listening to everything we say, just waiting for the right moment to jump in."

She looks at his face, the tension fading from around her

eyes. "I can see him doing that."

But he doesn't open his eyes. He doesn't sit up and join the conversation. He simply lies between us, his breaths growing weaker with every passing minute until that awful moment when they stop.

Forever.

# chapter 20

After Dad passed—this is apparently the word we're supposed to use; saying he died is "too blunt"—Mom and I finally went home to shower and sleep. Mom and Dad made all the arrangements months ago so all we had to do was call people. Which, by the way, sucks. I offered to call the family since I'd never met a lot of his friends and I thought it'd be weird giving sad news to strangers. Mom slept in my bed with me, either because she didn't want to be alone or couldn't bear to sleep in their bed, I don't know, and Amelia brought my assignments from school so I don't fall so far behind during the week of "bereavement time" that I risk not graduating. When friends and family started arriving, we slapped on our game faces like we were going into battle.

The funeral was a funeral. Let's just say there were lots of tears (by Mom—I'm trying to be the strong one), lots of sympathetic hugs from friends of Dad who, until today, I'd only seen in pictures, and altogether too many sad faces watching my every move. Amelia sat next to me, her arm linked through mine. The sun did not cooperate by making it a gloomy, overcast day. Oh no, it was out with bells on, shining off every glass and metal surface and shimmering off the small pond at the edge of the cemetery. But the service was nice. Not over-the-top, not overly religious, just a few pretty songs and a brief message from the minister-guy about making the most of every day. I know Dad died with regrets over things he didn't get to do, especially in the last year, but I hope he felt like he lived a full life. Flickering gives you a unique appreciation for which events are worth reliving, so I would think a lifetime of repeating things makes you realize how lucky you are.

Two details from the funeral stand out. Or more specifically, two people. The first is yet another person who I haven't seen since I was a kid: my cousin Quinn. At first I didn't recognize the tall, lanky boy with a dusting of dark curls. He looked vaguely familiar, but I assumed he was the son of one of Dad's many college friends. When he smiled and said hello, I returned the smile and waited for the standard outpouring of sympathy.

"You don't remember me?"

"Should I?"

He presses his hand to his chest. "I'm hurt."

I look closer. His eyes crinkle in the corner the same way Dad's does—did—when he was recounting a story from when he was younger. "Quinn?"

He smiles.

I step closer, resting my hand on his forearm. "We haven't seen you since—"

Since I was eight years old and he was ten, before his mom—Dad's older sister—died of an illness I never understood and his dad remarried and moved them to the other side of the country. Portland, if I remember correctly. By then, Dad's condition was getting bad enough that he didn't want to travel (side note: I've still never been on a plane) so my and Quinn's relationship was reduced to letters and Christmas cards. The last time I saw him he was a scrawny kid with braces, glasses, and a mess of wild hair. The braces and glasses are gone, but he is still skinny and a closer cut keeps his hair under control.

I look around. "Is your dad here?"

His smile fades and he clenches his jaw. "No, just me."

"But how did you—" I shake my head. "That's not important. I'm so glad you're here." I remember my manners minutes too late and step closer to give him a hug. He isn't awkward like some tall guys I know. He leans gracefully into my arms, bending low enough so I can hug him without getting a face-full of shoulder.

I step back, happier than I've been in a long time. "You're like bonus family."

He smiles, revealing gleaming teeth and a dimple in his cheek, then his eyes shift to something over my shoulder.

I turn around and encounter detail two: Cameron.

He's wearing the same dark gray suit and somber expression from Katie's funeral, but there's a hint of curiosity in his expression as he watches me and Quinn.

My throat goes dry. I admit I've been secretly hoping he'd come, but now that he's standing in front of me with his hair falling perfectly in his eyes and his shoulders filling out his suit jacket way better than any teenage boy's should, I don't know what to say. Or more accurately, I'm unable to say anything. My tongue is a useless blob in my mouth.

Cameron seems to be suffering from the same problem. He runs a hand through his hair, which only makes it look better. He starts to reach for my arm but lets his hand fall to his side.

Quinn wraps an arm around my shoulder and gives me a quick squeeze. "We can catch up later. It, uh, looks like you two need to talk." He walks away, his long legs carrying him gracefully to where Mom's standing with a group of Dad's friends.

I face Cameron, willing my throat to open long enough to say something, anything. "Thanks for coming."

"Yeah. Sure."

"There's gonna be food later at our house. You can come if you want. Or whatever." Good lord, this is brutal. Can't he just say whatever he wants to say then go back to where the group of kids from school are huddled?

Tears well up in his eyes. "Is this really what we've become?"

I bite my lip.

"After everything we've been through." He shakes his head, looking at the ground for a moment. He toes a clump of grass between us. "I miss you."

He says it to his feet, but my heart flip-flops anyway. When he raises his head it's like nothing has changed between us and I'm thrown back to when we first started dating: all nerves and butterflies and the inability to look him in the eye. The vulnerability on his face nearly breaks my heart. But things have changed. I can't forget how he was willing to risk my life for Katie's. "I miss you, too. But it's not that simple."

"You never gave me a chance to explain."

Dad's final wish comes back to me. I may not be able to forget, but I might be able to forgive. "Maybe we can talk?"

No one is standing close enough to hear us, but Cameron looks around like he's realizing this probably isn't the place for the conversation we need to have. "Just tell me when. Are you grounded or anything from the—uh—thing with Amelia?"

I smile, but it's a smile of sadness. I can't believe he hasn't figured out the truth about the accident. "No, I got grounded for like two seconds, but I didn't mean to drive so Mom and Dad weren't too mad at me."

"Didn't mean to—" he lowers his voice. "You flickered when you were drinking?"

My shoulders tense at the memory of landing in the car after doing shots. "Yeah."

He runs a hand through his hair again. "So what'd you tell the cops?"

I sigh. "That I was a stupid teenager and did a stupid thing."

"I didn't hear but—" he pauses, "—did you go to jail?"

I break out into a sweat at the memory of being in the police station, unsure of what would happen. "No, thank god. Unfortunately I couldn't use flickering as a defense with the judge either. I lost my license for a month and have to do community service, but Martinez figured something out at the hospital to let me serve my hours taking pictures of newborn babies." My stomach twists when I say Martinez's name. Looking into Cameron's eyes while remembering the erased kiss makes me realize just how dangerous it is playing with Martinez. I'm still in high school. What was I hoping to accomplish?

Cameron shifts his weight between his feet and jams his hands in his pants pockets.

I'm not used to seeing him nervous. Has he been wanting to talk to me for a while or would our silence have gone on forever if Dad hadn't died?

"So you're allowed to go out after school and stuff?"

"Yeah, but I think we should start on the phone." I'm not giving in that easily. He frowns, and the disappointment on his face almost makes me take it back.

"Okay then, I guess I'll call you later." He glances over at Quinn, who's entertaining a group of Dad's friends, hands waving in the air while he talks. Cameron's face grows dark, just for a second, and I decide to let him wonder who Quinn is.

"Thanks for coming. I really appreciate it."

Before I can mentally prepare for it, he steps closer and pulls me into his arms. He smells safe, familiar, and my traitorous body relaxes against him. I rest my head in the spot beneath his shoulder, and for a moment it's like the last three months never happened. His hand moves from my waist to the back of my neck, running his thumb over the exposed skin, before he presses a kiss to the top of my head. Then he lowers his head and whispers in my ear.

"I never stopped loving you."

# chapter 21

"He said WHAT?" Amelia smacks my arm. It's the day after the funeral and we're sitting on my bed, surrounded by textbooks that we're completely ignoring. Everyone else has returned to their lives and I'm doing my best to follow their lead.

"He said he still loves me. Well, technically, he said he never stopped loving me, but that implies he still loves me, so same difference." Saying it out loud doesn't make it any less surreal. After not talking to Cameron for so long, it never occurred to me that he still had feelings for me. I figured he pushed me out of his mind and that was the end of the Biz and Cam show.

Amelia sticks her pen in her mouth and chews on the cap. "What about you?"

"I love myself more than ever."

She smacks me again, then pokes me with the pen. "Do you still have feelings for him? You've had a lot going on and the Biz confessionals haven't happened as often as I'd like, so I feel like I'm in the dark here."

I mentally slap myself. I'm a sucky friend. "When he hugged me goodbye, it was like nothing had changed. I've missed him a lot and it's been awful not being able to talk to him. He didn't even know the truth about our accident until yesterday."

She pokes me again, a soft smile lighting her face. "So that's a yes?"

"That's an I-think-so-but-things-are-complicated."

"Because of Martinez?"

"Yes and no. I've decided there's no way that can happen again. I stopped him from stealing Dad's secrets, which was my goal. The kiss was just the cherry on top."

She snorts, and this time I smack her.

"There was no cherry exchanging."

This makes her laugh harder, and she falls over on the pile of books.

"Speaking of cherries, how are things with Trace?"

A dreamy look sweeps over her face and she clasps her hands against her chest. "Absolutely perfect." She pushes herself back into a sitting position. "Seriously, who knew guys could be so sweet and charming and awesome?"

I did with Cameron, but I don't say that. "I'm really happy for you. You're sweet and charming and awesome so I don't want anything less for you. I just wish..." I pick at the seam of my jeans.

"What?"

"I wish there was a way he could know the truth about the accident without me having to tell him about flickering. That stupid email has me terrified to tell anyone else, but I hate that he thinks I'm nothing more than a stupid drunk driver."

"He doesn't think that. I won't let him. I know I can't tell him about flickering, but I have other ways of making him see things my way."

"I suppose if anyone can convince him, you can. I guess I'm just feeling sorry for myself. Seeing Cam has me all topsy-turvy and now I'm wishing things were back the way they were and we could double date and just be normal teenagers."

Amelia lifts her arm and smacks a book on the bed between us. "It has been decreed!"

"What?"

"If that's what you want, we'll make it happen."

"I don't know if that's what I want. I was just rambling. You know I say things without thinking about whether or not I should really say them."

"You? Noooo."

I laugh. "Okay, maybe I want that a little bit."

"I'm not saying it'll happen next week. But give it time. Talk to Cam and I'll work on Trace."

"Oh, I'm sure you will." I barely have the words out before she whacks me in the head with a pillow.

◆ ◆ ◆

When I said everyone else returned to their lives, I left out one person. Quinn has slipped into our world like he's always belonged here. When Amelia leaves, he's in the kitchen stirring a pot on the stove.

"Don't you have someplace to be?"

He thumps his fist to his chest and throws his head back. "I'm hurt. Here for two days and you're already sick of me."

Laughter bubbles out of me. Between Amelia and Quinn, I almost feel like my normal self. "That's not what I meant. Don't you have school or a job or, I don't know, your dad, wondering where you are?"

He touches the side of his head with his forefinger. "Yes, no, and no. School can wait and Dad knows where I am."

"So you're skipping class to make us dinner?"

"Biz, Biz, my sweet, younger cousin. I came to the funeral to pay my respects, not intending to stay more than a day, but one look at you and I knew you needed my help."

I grab a towel off the counter and throw it at his head, but he catches it before it hits him.

"I'm teasing. It's been forever since we've seen each other and when your mom told me you have a week off school, I figured I'd stick around so we can hang out." He holds up his hands. "No agenda, I swear."

I shake my head, but I'm smiling.

"What? I can't stay?"

"No. I'm wondering how I've gotten along without you in my life."

He points the spoon at me. "That's what I like to hear! Let me tell you, when you taste this sauce you're gonna beg me to never leave."

I lean against the counter, thinking. "There is one thing I could use your help with."

"Name it."

"I have to go to the hospital and take pictures of newborns with their parents."

His brows furrow. "And you need me to hold the babies?"

"Ha, no. I'm—how do I say this?" I take a quick breath. "I'm a little freaked out about going back to the hospital so soon after Dad passed." I roll my eyes at the word.

"I hate that word. You can say he died."

"Thank god. Anyway, I know I won't be anywhere near where he died, but I could use some moral support going in there."

He leans against the counter and looks me straight in the eye. "Just tell me when and I'm there."

'When' turns out to be the next morning. Quinn's driving Dad's car—I swore I'd tell him the story of why I can't drive after we're finished at the hospital—and I'm navigating, doing my best to keep us away from the Strand. At one point he shields his eyes with his left hand, a gesture so familiar that I almost don't notice it. Almost.

But I don't have time to dwell on it because the hospital is up ahead and I suddenly can't breathe. I don't think I'm ready for this.

Quinn looks at me out of the corner of his eye. "You okay?"

"No."

"Want me to go back?"

"No."

He drives past the emergency entrance and I force myself to stare straight ahead. It's a weekday. Martinez won't be there.

We park in front of the main entrance—the non-scary front with revolving doors meant for people who are walking on their own, not being rushed in on a gurney.

I sling my camera over my shoulder. "This entrance is always so much calmer."

Quinn squeezes my shoulder and we stop at the front desk. A young woman with bright red hair smiles at us from behind the counter.

"I'm here to see—" I read the slip of paper in my hand. "Dr. Ward."

She types into the computer and smiles again. "Seventh floor. Suite 702. Take the elevators around the corner." She points away from the main entrance, but I already know where they are. I may not come in this way, but I've explored every inch of this hospital over the years.

"Thanks." I lead Quinn around a corner and press the button for the elevator.

"How're you doing?"

"Aside from the brief moment in the car when I couldn't breathe, great."

The doors slide open and we move aside to let an elderly couple pass, then step inside. He leans against the wall. "So why are you taking pictures of newborns?"

"Community service."

"Lost your license. Community service." He ticks my transgressions off on his fingers. "Something tells me you've been a bad girl."

The elevator dings when we reach the seventh floor. I step into the hallway and face Quinn. He's family but I still barely know him. I'm not sure if I'm ready for another person to know my secret. "Not as bad as they think."

He touches a finger to his lips. "I'm intrigued."

But that has to wait. We find Suite 702 and a less-friendly receptionist asks us to wait while she calls him. A few minutes later, a middle-aged man with a round belly, bald head, and graying goatee steps into the room and looks around. His face lights up when his gaze lands on us. "Either you're the youngest parents here or you're Biz Clement."

I stand. "That's me." I hold out my hand and he wraps both his around it.

"I'm so excited to have you here. We've talked about how nice it'd be for the families to have memories of the early weeks, so when Rick told me about your situation, I said it was like an angel answering our prayers." He's putting off an overly-religious vibe that normally makes me uncomfortable, but there's no feeling uncomfortable around him. Dr. Ward oozes love.

"Weeks? I thought I was taking pictures of newborns."

"Yes! In the neo-natal ward."

"Neo—like preemies?"

"Exactly like preemies."

I take a step back, nervousness tensing my shoulders. "I don't know if I should be around preemies. What if I, I don't know, break one or something?"

He smiles, a broad grin that nearly splits his face in two. "I can assure you that you will not break any of our babies. Next question."

I scramble for another protest, but can think of nothing. I straighten my shoulders. "Where do I start?"

Dr. Ward claps his hands together and his smile gets even bigger. "Right this way." He leads us down the hallway toward a set of swinging doors.

Quinn nudges my side as we walk. "You got this."

I didn't know what to expect when I thought I was photographing regular newborns, so I couldn't have prepared myself for the neo-natal ward. The beeps and whirring machines remind me of Dad's last stay here, but there's a quiet activity that makes it clear this room is about life, not death. A team of purple-scrubbed nurses glide between the half-dozen incubators spaced throughout the room, each holding a baby too small to be real. Two babies have parents huddled near them, but the rest are alone.

A man from the purple crew stops when we enter. Dr. Ward nods at him and he approaches. His light brown hair flutters when he walks, and recognition strikes me: he's the nurse from the stairwell. The one who caught me crying.

Dr. Ward gestures to the nurse. "This is Jonathan. He runs the show here. Jonathan, this is Biz. She's the photographer I told you about."

We shake hands, and I have to fight off tears. I was doing really well not thinking about Dad, but now I'll have to work with the one person who saw me at my weakest.

Make that two. The female nurse who'd been with him that day strides by, pausing long enough to give us a curious smile.

Jonathan dips his head to look in my eyes. "Nice to officially meet you, Biz. I hope you're doing better than the last time we saw each other."

I bite my lip. I can't cry on my first day. "I'm—it's nice to meet you, too."

Dr. Ward claps his hands together. I'm beginning to think that's how he ends all his conversations. "Okay, now that that's settled, I'll leave you to it." He walks away, leaving me in a silence so uncomfortable I'd rather run into Martinez than have to dig my way out of this.

"I didn't mean to upset you."

I shake my head. "It's okay."

Quinn steps forward, hand thrust out. "I'm Quinn, Biz's assistant." They grasp hands and it's like someone threw a firecracker at us. Quinn launches into a ridiculous story about an aunt who delivered a baby in a snowstorm and before I can figure out if the story's even real, I'm laughing as hard as Jonathan. Except Jonathan has an expression on his face much different than mine. His head's tilted to the side, and his eyes never leave Quinn's face.

Quinn's hands never stop moving while he talks, and he alternates between touching my arm and Jonathan's. By the time he finishes the story, he and Jonathan are just standing there smiling at each other. I tilt my head as if seeing Quinn for the first time. How did I miss that he's gay?

Jonathan touches my arm, pulling me from my thoughts. "The McCombs family has agreed to be your first subject." He nods towards one of the couples sitting near their child, and for the first time I realize the mother is wearing a dress.

My palms start to sweat, but I push away the nerves. No matter what's going on in my life, my camera has always been there for me and it's never let me down. As Quinn said, I got this.

# chapter 22

"So you got to take pictures of tiny babies?"

Cameron and I are having what can only be described as a phone date—he texted to ask if he could call, then asked what time, then I got all nervous and even put on a clean shirt, so yeah, a date. "Yeah, it was pretty cool. Scary, but cool."

After Jonathan introduced me to Mr. and Mrs. McCombs, he released their tiny baby, Lucas, from his incubator, put him in his mother's arms and without another word, left me alone to do my thing. I stood frozen for a moment, but when the couple looked at me expectantly, their son dwarfed in his blanket, my instincts kicked in. I may not have known what I was doing, but they didn't know that. To them I was a photographer, nothing more, nothing less.

I've never shot people before, not in a portrait-type setting, but I know light and shadows so I had Quinn drag their chairs next to one of the windows. There was no hiding the fact that they're in a hospital, so I tightened the focus on their faces, letting the background blur.

The first few shots, let's just say they weren't my greatest, but Quinn suggested I squat so I was at Lucas's level and the entire perspective changed. Suddenly Lucas became the star, not his mom or dad, and certainly not the machine hovering behind them, attached by a bunch of tubes and wires tucked out of sight beneath his blanket.

I researched traditional baby pictures online to get an idea of what to do, but a lot of the most popular photos would be impossible given the situation—no naked baby on a blanket, or balanced on his daddy's hand, or sleeping atop his mommy's now-flat belly—so I stuck with group shots and close-ups of Lucas: his itty bitty nose peeking out from the blanket, his translucent fingers gripping his dad's pinky, and finally, mom pressing a kiss to his fuzzy head.

Before I left, I scribbled my email onto a piece of paper and told the family I'd get the proofs to them the following week. I still needed to talk to Shelly about the best way to do this, but at least they didn't know that I'm figuring this out as I go along.

"So Quinn went with you?" Cameron remained quiet while I described the session, and I'm surprised this was his first question.

"He doesn't have anything else to do right now so I let him tag along. I'm glad I did, too, because his suggestion for the different angle totally made all the difference." It's not lost on me that there was a time when Cameron helped me that way. When we'd go out together to shoot assignments for Turner's class, we would look at each other's work and suggest things that the other wasn't able to see. But it's been ages since we've done that.

"He doesn't have, like, school or something?" His voice sounds strained.

"He took the week off to hang out with me and Mom. It's actually been nice because he's doing all the cooking."

His pauses, and the silence is excruciating. After several moments, he finally speaks. "So how did you two meet? He's not from our school, right?"

Realization smacks me upside the head. I never told Cameron who Quinn really is. "Oh shit. Cam, Quinn is my cousin."

He exhales loudly. "Oh."

"And," I laugh. "I think he's gay. Not that it makes a difference. Because he's my cousin." My heart quickens. Cameron was jealous! I feel a tiny prick of regret for letting him think the wrong thing at the funeral, but it didn't hurt anyone. "His mom died when he was a kid so it's been good to have someone to talk to. Plus, it's worked out really well having him here this week because I still can't drive, although it sucks having to tell another person why I can't drive without giving them the full story."

"You don't trust him enough to tell the truth? Even though he's family?"

I chew my lower lip. "I do trust him, but I got an email a couple weeks ago that totally freaked me out and now I don't want anyone else to know."

"What email? What happened?" Protective Cameron is back. I can almost picture him straightening his shoulders to scare off whoever's done me wrong.

"It came from one of those untraceable email sites and said 'I know your secret, and it could kill you.'" A shudder passes through me at the thought of this unknown jerkface sitting in a dark room, plotting my demise, or whatever it is they're hoping to gain from all this. "Only a handful of people know the truth so—"

"Well, it's not me."

"I didn't think it was."

"I would never betray you like that."

Dad's advice to give Cameron a chance rings in my ears and I bite back a snarky reply. But my silence speaks for me.

"Okay, I guess I did betray you, but I swear I've never told anyone your secret."

I wish he was sitting next to me so I could see his face. I'm ninety-nine point nine percent certain he's telling the truth, but it's easier to lie on the phone. I'd be able to read that point one percent if I was focused on more than just his voice.

"You believe me, right?"

"I do."

"I know it's been rough for us since Katie…but just because we stopped talking doesn't mean I stopped caring about you."

I close my eyes, relishing the words I've been aching to hear for months. I should probably tell him how I feel considering this is now the second time he's professed his undying like for me, but something holds me back. "Cam, I trust that you're telling the truth, but I need more time to fully trust you again."

The phone is silent.

"You can understand that, right?"

He sighs, and I imagine he's holding me against his chest, his breath tickling the back of my neck. "Yeah."

"I just need time."

"Can I call you tomorrow?"

A second date! I try to suppress a smile but there's no use. Cameron still makes me googly-eyed. "Yes."

"Then goodbye until tomorrow. I—" he pauses and my heart nearly leaps out of my chest. "I'm really glad we talked."

Okay, not what I thought he was going to say but I did just tell him I need time. "Me too." I hang up and fling myself backward onto my bed. Give this time, I remind myself. But part of me—the part that knows how amazing it feels to have Cameron pressed up against me, his lips on mine, arms holding me close—wants to throw my rules out the window and beg him to come over. Thinking about him means there's no room in my head to think about Dad, and I'm afraid if I let myself stop moving the tsunami of despair that's been nipping at my ankles since Dad died will finally catch me and pull me completely under.

So I keep moving.

I check the time on my phone and text Amelia.

Me: Phone date complete.
Amelia: Did you sleep with him?
Me: Almost.
Amelia: We'll be there in twenty. Is Quinn coming?
Me: Yes. See you soon.

I head downstairs to find Mom in the kitchen and Quinn sitting on the couch, flipping through a magazine. "You still want to go to the movie?"

He looks up and smiles, and I stumble. He's in Dad's spot, with Dad's magazine, avoiding the TV like Dad. Add in his strong resemblance and it's like he's still here, just in a younger, healthier body.

My eyes blur.

"You okay?"

"You remind me of my dad."

"Is that a good thing?"

I move around the coffee table to sit next to him, and the eerie similarities continue. How many times did I plop onto the couch next to Dad to talk about my problems? "Yes, definitely a good thing. It's so weird that he's gone. I keep expecting to come downstairs and find him here on the couch, reading a magazine."

Quinn studies the magazine in his hands. "That explains why you looked like you saw a ghost."

"How long did it take for you? After your mom died?"

"To stop expecting to see her everywhere I went?"

I nod.

"I haven't stopped. It's not as bad as it was right after she died, but every now and then I'll see someone from behind who looks so much like her that I'm sure she's found a way to come back to see me."

"That sounds awful." I couldn't imagine being a kid when Dad died. It's bad enough being eighteen.

"It's actually the opposite. For a second, before the stranger turns around, I remember what it was like to have my mom with me and I'm filled with the briefest moment of relief."

"So it gets easier?"

"It does."

I lean so my arm presses against his. "I didn't mean to bring us down. You ready to go?"

"Lead the way."

We head outside and wait on the porch until Trace pulls into the driveway. Trace gets out so we can climb into the backseat, then once we're situated, backs onto the street.

Amelia twists around to look at me. "Food first?"

Quinn pokes me. "What is this, a date?"

"Nah, she already had one of those today."

I roll my eyes, but Quinn pokes me again. "The hottie from the funeral? Please tell me you told him who I am because the way he was staring at me, I thought I'd have to watch over my shoulder the rest of the time I'm here."

I can't stop the blush that colors my cheeks. "Yes, I told him. But not right away."

"You're evil."

Amelia laughs. "Biz, I like him. Can he stay?"

Trace's head jerks toward her and she rests a reassuring hand on his arm. "Don't worry, baby. You're the only one for me."

Quinn cocks his head at Trace and mouths, 'He knows, right?'

I shrug. If Trace is unwilling to come around with me, he can squirm a bit longer, thinking his girlfriend is flirting in front of him.

"Pizza or burgers?" Amelia asks.

"I don't—"

Oh no. Where are we? I haven't been paying attention to the route we're taking and now my fingers and toes are tingling. Light flickers through the windows and in seconds the weight crashes over me. Out of the corner of my eye I notice Quinn sink lower in his seat, but it must be my imagination. The weight lifts and I'm pushed toward the roof of the car, lighter, lighter, then—

—my leg drills the coffee table in front of me. I turn to face Quinn, who's sitting next to me, the soda in his hand spilled all over his chest.

He smiles. "You too?"

# chapter 23

I can't believe it! Quinn flickers too? This means—well, this is huge. There's more than just me and Dad who have freakazoid brains, although it's more family, so maybe we're all still freaks. I look at Quinn, my mind making connections faster than I can keep up with them. "Is this how—I mean, is..." I shake my head.

He touches my arm. "I feel the same way. And yeah, I'm pretty sure that's what killed my mom, but I didn't figure it out until just now."

My mouth falls open. "You never talked to her about it?"

"I was just a kid when she died. I hadn't flickered yet. When you told me what your dad's health has been like over the past few years, it seemed familiar, but again, that's based off memories from ten years ago. But when I saw you having the same reactions in the car—"

"I thought I saw it in you, too!"

"So here we are. We should call Ripley's Believe It or Not."

"The museum?"

"I think it used to be a show. My dad always says that when something unbelievable happens, and this ranks at the top of unbelievable things."

"So, have you..." I pick at a hole just starting in the knee of my jeans. "Have you told anyone about it?"

He shakes his head.

"Does your dad know?"

Another shake. "You're the first person."

I smack his arm. "Seriously? You've never told anyone?"

His eyes widen, and it's the most serious I've seen him since he arrived. "You have?"

I launch into the story of the kidnapped girls and enlisting Cameron to help, trying—and failing—to stop Katie from killing herself, and my research with Martinez.

A broad smile lights his face. "You're like a superhero."

I snort. "Hardly."

"Did you listen to what you just told me? Total superhero." He stretches his arms in front of him, then leans his elbows on his knees. "So that's three people outside the family. And you trust them?"

I don't look at him.

He grips my arm. "Who?"

"Martinez."

"The doctor?"

I look at him, tears burning my eyes for no reason other than apparently I've become a big crybaby. "I know with everything in me that Cam and Amelia would never tell anyone, so it has to be him. Plus he's the only one with anything to gain."

He cocks his head. "I feel like you're leaving something out."

So I tell him about the email, and the look of fear that settles onto his face almost matches the panic lodged in my chest.

But then his face relaxes and he smiles. "It's a good thing you've got a sidekick."

"What are we, Batman and Robin?"

"More like Wonder Woman and Scooby Doo."

I tousle his hair. "Don't knock Scooby. He always catches the bad guy."

"You really think your doctor would sell you out?"

"I don't want to, but he's the only one who makes sense."

"So now what?"

I stretch out my hands, fingers laced, and crack my knuckles. "Simple. We foil his plan."

◆ ◆ ◆

I know I'm being a coward, but I skip this week's appointment. After the non-kiss and everything else I've decided about Martinez, I don't know if I can sit through an hour in his office. I tell Mom it's because the last batch of assignments that Amelia brought home include instructions that outline the photography portfolio we need to put together for graduation. I went through a lot of my photos when I started submitting them to newspapers, but the sheet says we need an overarching theme, something I can't say I've ever thought about.

For the millionth time I wish Dad was here. This is the type of thing he loved to help me with. Computers and technology, not so much, but we could spend hours discussing anything visual, especially photography.

At the bottom of the page is a note from Shelly offering to meet outside of class to discuss my portfolio. Before I can debate it, I grab my phone and text her.

> Me: Got your note. When can you meet to talk
> about portfolio?

My limited driving privileges don't get reinstated until Monday, but I'm sure I can convince Quinn to drive and just hang out at another table while Shelly and I meet.

I'm halfway through an English essay when my phone dings.

> Shelly: Kind of last minute, but what about
> tonight?
> Me: Perfect. 8pm at a coffee shop?
> Shelly: The one by the paper. See you there.

Now to enlist my sidekick. I finish my thought in the essay, then hit save and go downstairs to find Quinn.

He didn't take much convincing. As exciting as it probably sounded when he first decided to stay with us an extra week, the reality of being cooped up in our house has to be catching up to him. "You realize you won't actually be talking to Shelly, right?"

He pouts, thrusting out his lower lip. "You're going to make me sit by myself?"

I sigh. "Fine. But don't distract her with your charming self. I really need help with my portfolio."

He draws a cross over his chest with his finger. "I promise I will be an unobtrusive chauffeur. I will sip my latte and not utter a word."

"Latte? Really?"

"Don't tell me you drink it black?" He shudders.

I smile. "The way nature intended."

Shelly's already there when we get to the coffee shop, her dark hair perfectly mussed, her slouchy boots effortless, and her long sweater casually comfy.

I sigh.

Quinn nudges me. "You okay?"

"I strive to be that cool."

He rolls his eyes. "Please. Give your hair another couple months and you'll totally surpass her."

"You're delusional." We approach the small table where Shelly is sitting. There are only two chairs, but Quinn doesn't let that phase him. He flashes a dazzling smile at a girl sitting by herself at a nearby table and returns moments later with a third chair.

"Shelly, this is my cousin Quinn. He came from Portland for my Dad's funeral and now we can't shake him."

Quinn holds out his hand and Shelly takes it, looking a little uneasy. "Shelly." She shakes his hand but looks at me. "Biz, I'm so sorry about your father. I can't even imagine."

I shake my head, cutting off any other sympathetic remarks. "Can we just talk about my portfolio?"

She nods once, seems to think about it, and then her usual smile is back in place. "Of course." She reaches into her bag, pulls out a packet of papers, and slides them across the table to me. "This outlines the requirements for the graduation portfolio. It's pretty much the same as what Mr. Turner used for the past several years, but I tweaked a couple things so you and your classmates can incorporate the projects we've been working on since..." she waves her hand.

Quinn sits up straight. "Since what?"

I narrow my eyes at him, hoping he reads my silent message to shut up. "He's the kidnapper I told you about."

His mouth opens, then closes quickly. "Got it."

Shelly, of course, knows nothing about my involvement with the kidnapped girls beyond the fact that I was in his class and my former boyfriend slash friend slash who-knows-what's little sister killed herself because of what he did to her. "Did you hear they scheduled his trial?"

My eyes widen. "No! I knew it was coming up but I hadn't heard." I know I've had a lot going on lately but I feel like I've let down Katie by not knowing the second it was announced.

"End of April. It was in the news a couple days ago. Depending on how long it takes, it might be over before graduation."

"Wow. That would certainly cap off a bizarre senior year."

Shelly cocks her head and gives me an odd look. "Do you plan to attend the trial?"

"I don't know. I haven't decided." Even though I flickered out of Turner's van so he technically never drugged and kidnapped me, I don't know if I can sit in the same room and pretend that nothing happened. I can't even imagine how Maddy and the other girls feel. At least I got away.

"If nothing else, you should consider attending as a photographer."

Quinn smirks. "Bizarazzi."

I roll my eyes at him. "I'll think about it." With my camera as a shield, seeing Turner might almost be bearable.

We spend the next half hour looking through the requirements. In theory, it's straightforward—twenty photos that highlight my strengths—but it's the overarching theme that has me worried. "When you say theme, do you mean all the same subject?"

Shelly laces her fingers together on the table and leans forward, and I reflexively lean toward her. "No, it's more abstract than that. Like, something that ties all your photos together. For mine I did perspective. All the shots I submitted were of everyday subjects, but I shot them from an unusual angle."

"Like the fireman with the kitten."

"Yes," Shelly says at the same time Quinn says, "Two of my favorite things."

I kick Quinn under the table and he gives me a 'what?' face.

He raises an eyebrow. "What about light?"

Shelly face breaks into a smile. "That's a great idea. I've always loved the way your photos capture the relationship light plays with whatever you're shooting."

Quinn nudges her arm. "And don't forget the shadows. I t's almost like she can feel the absence of light and wraps you in its emptiness."

"Seriously? I'm glad you two have decided what I'm doing." I don't disagree with the idea, but the conversation is running away without me.

He shrugs. "I'm just saying you have a gift."

"Yes, she does."

I stare at the two of them with their matching smiles and nodding heads and finally concede. "Okay, light it is."

We spend another ten minutes outlining how I should go about selecting photos before Shelly gets a text and announces she needs to leave. I hug her goodbye. "Thank you for your help. I want this to rock and I don't think I could sort this out on my own."

Walking to the car, I punch Quinn in the arm.

"Ow! What was that for?"

"For alluding a little too closely to my 'gift'." I air quote the last word.

"It's a brilliant idea and you know it."

"I'm not saying it's a bad idea—it actually is quite brilliant—"

"Aw, shucks."

I roll my eyes. "But I'm nervous for anyone else to find out about me. About us. And I thought you were, too."

He straightens his shoulders and pauses in front of my car, the carefree image I've grown accustomed to turning more serious. "I am."

♦ ♦ ♦

Later that night, we have even more reason to be nervous: I got another email.

# chapter 24

You can't change what's already in motion. The truth will come out.

The words run through my head on a loop. Today's the first day I'm allowed to drive and I'm doing my best to concentrate on the road—to prove to Mom and everyone else that I'm a responsible adult—but I can't stop thinking about the email.

> You can't change what's already in motion. The truth will come out.

What does that even mean?

I slow to a crawl when a minivan emblazoned with a sticker stick-family with thirteen hundred kids pulls out of a driveway, and the engine sputters when I accelerate. Dad stopped driving years ago but I can still smell his cologne when the air kicks on and I'm grateful Mom let me take it.

I texted Amelia before school to see if she needed a ride, but Trace isn't giving up his duties that easily. It's still a couple weeks before her cast comes off but I get the feeling she'll be riding with him even after she's able to drive again.

My day gets a teensy bit better when I head to my locker and find Cameron lingering nearby.

"Hey." His half-smile makes my stomach do a little flip-flop.

I hesitate with my fingers on the lock. "Hey."

He moves closer and leans a shoulder on the locker next to mine, just close enough for me to get a whiff of his shower gel.

"So, if you need, like, a ride or something, you know you can ask, right?" He dips his head so his hair falls in his eyes and I swear his cheeks are turning pink.

I've never been more disappointed to tell the truth. "I got my license back today. Well, limited license. School and community service only."

His smile fades, but is back in a heartbeat. "So maybe I could get a ride?"

"What happened to Old Berta?"

He shakes his head and places a hand over his heart. "It's not looking good. She's been coughing a lot. I think she might have pneumonia."

I bark out a laugh. "So how were you going to drive me to school?"

He shrugs. "I'd figure it out if you said yes."

"Well now I kinda wish I had."

His eyes lock on mine and my breath catches as the warning bell rings. "I'm going to hold you to that." He straightens, pushing off the wall of lockers. "See you later?"

"Yeah, sure." I watch as he joins the flow of students as the second bell rings.

I'm still daydreaming about my conversation with Cameron when I join Amelia at our table in the cafeteria.

She raises an eyebrow. "You look dazed."

"I am dazed."

"Spill."

I shrug, trying to play it off as nothing, but Amelia knows me too well. "I think he asked me out."

"You don't know for sure?"

I replay our earlier conversation and Amelia takes a bite of her sandwich, thinking while she chews. Before she says anything, she nods across the room. "He's staring at you."

I whip around, expecting him to look away, but he holds my gaze. My heartbeat picks up its pace.

Amelia shakes her head. "You two...It's like you've reverted back to seventh grade. You need to jump him and get it over with."

"What?!" My voice is way louder than I intended and the cafeteria goes silent for a second.

She takes another bite. "I'm just saying."

"But what about the whole risking-my-life thing?" I can't say the thought of having sex with Cameron is the worst idea she's ever had—much better than the kiss with Martinez—but I don't know if I'm ready to forget what happened.

Amelia rests her hand on mine. "Look. I don't mean to sound like what he did was okay. It wasn't. But it's not like he asked you to help him pass a test or something. He was trying to save his sister's life."

I drop my gaze. "I know."

"Forgiveness isn't a bad thing. Talk to him. Give him a chance."

I peek over my shoulder at Cameron. He's laughing, his hair pushed out of his eyes so I can see his face, and my entire body tingles. Then just as quickly sadness pushes away the excitement. "My dad said the same thing."

Her smile softens. "We both know how smart he was."

"I'm not making any promises."

Amelia laughs. "I'm not the one you should be promising yourself to."

I push the food around my plate and look her in the eye. "I love you. You know that, right?"

She takes another bite and mumbles with her mouth full. "Yup."

I'm still debating the pros and cons of getting back together with Cameron when my second-to-last class ends. The pros slide through my mind with each step toward my locker.

He's funny.

He's smart.

He's hot.

He loves photography almost as much as I do. (Okay, that was three steps.)

He's been my best friend forever.

I miss him.

I miss him a lot.

But the one negative won't release its grip.

He was willing to let me die.

I know Amelia's right. He had a really good reason, but I can still picture the coldness in his eyes when I told him I wouldn't go back a third time. Until that moment, I'd never questioned his loyalty to me, but everything changed the day Katie died.

"You look like you need a hug."

I look up to find Cameron waiting at my locker, his back against the metal, one foot propped up so he looks like he belongs in a teen rom-com, not our boring school hallway. And if this was a movie he'd sweep me into his arms and kiss me and the credits would roll while the kids in the hallway cheered, but I'm not ready for this conversation. "Yeah, I suppose I do."

He drops his foot and pushes off the locker. His eyes search mine like he's not sure if I gave him permission or was merely agreeing with him.

I want to fold myself into his arms, but the memory of that day is still fresh in my mind. I cross my arms over my chest.

He touches my chin, lifting my head so I'm looking at him. "What's wrong?" His dark eyes are wide, concerned, and I can feel myself getting pulled closer. Instead I step around him and open my locker.

"It's been a long day." I dump books in my bag. While I'm bent over I take a deep breath, and do my best to shake off this funk. I need to talk to him. Get it all out in the open and then we can see if there's anything left of us.

His hand brushes my back and I freeze. The heat from his skin seeps through my shirt and spreads through my body. I straighten, and he's staring into my eyes again.

I smile. "You buttering me up so I'll give you a ride?"

He returns the smile. "That depends. Is it working?"

I nod my head a little too enthusiastically. "Yeah."

He loops his arm through mine and guides me toward the parking lot. "Good."

The electricity between us keeps getting stronger as we approach my car, and by the time I'm pulling onto the street I'm seriously considering Amelia's advice to skip class and take advantage of Cameron.

Okay, maybe she didn't tell me to skip class, but I'm sure she would approve.

Cameron laughs and I jerk my head at him. I wasn't saying that out loud, was I?

"What?"

"You're arguing with yourself again."

"Yeah, I suppose I am."

"What about?"

"That's a conversation for another time. Not when we're on our way to class."

He shifts in his seat. "I'm intrigued."

I need to change the subject if we're ever going to make it to the newspaper. "Have you started your portfolio?"

"Sort of. I think I have my theme, but I haven't really gone through my photos yet."

"Same here."

"Do you want to work on it together?"

I glance at him and take a quick breath. He's so unbelievably beautiful, with his perfect jawline and full lips and those eyes that I could stare into forever.

"Biz, you're killing me here. If you want to wait until later to talk, we can, but I'm not letting you get out of it."

My throat goes dry. "Okay. And yes, I'd like to work on our portfolios together. You probably know my stuff as well as I do."

He drops his head. "Most of it, anyway."

True. He hasn't seen anything I've shot since Katie died.

I pull into the newspaper parking lot and rest my hand on his. "I'm a complete ass. I haven't even asked you how you're doing. Since Katie."

He looks at our hands, then his gaze drifts to the floor in front of him. "It's hard. The whole time she was missing we always had this sliver of hope that she might come home someday. Then she did, but she was ripped out of our lives again. I don't think my parents will ever be the same."

"Cam, I'm so sorry."

He looks at me, tears shining in his eyes. "I know."

We walk side-by-side to the entrance. Whatever heat started between us at school has cooled now that we're both thinking about his sister. Several people stare longer than normal when we walk in together, including Shelly, but I ignore them as we take our seats at opposite ends of the table.

I pull out my notebook, determined to focus on class and not think about Cameron, but I swear I can still feel the electricity between us. Deep down I know I want things back the way they were. I prop my head on my hand and will myself to concentrate on Shelly, but my head turns a fraction of an inch so I can see Cameron.

I groan internally. This isn't helping.

Or maybe not so internally. Shelly pushes a hand through her hair and a flash of silver on her wrist catches my eye. "Biz, you okay?"

"Um, yeah. Sorry." Where have I seen that bracelet?

She glances at her notes and continues talking, but not before throwing me another concerned look.

Cameron turns his head my way and cocks an eyebrow.

I shake my head, heat flooding my cheeks. What is wrong with me?

Shelly continues her lecture, which involves a series of pictures of things that are broken, dying, or otherwise completely falling apart. "Can anyone tell me the overarching theme of these photos?"

Ahh, so that's what this is about. Maybe I should pay a little more attention.

Shelly scans our faces and runs her hand through her hair. The silver bracelet catches my eye again. I know I've seen that someplace before.

Kaya raises her hand and Shelly nods at her. "Death."

Several people giggle, but Shelly nods again. "You're

close. They represent a transition, the end of an era. Even the termination of usefulness."

The guy across from me exhales. "Whoa, that's deep."

More people giggle, but Shelly ignores them, instead narrowing her gaze at us. "I want you all to think bigger with your themes. Go beyond high school." She clicks through the next three images: an adult hand clasping a child's, a man dangling from a cliff face, and a doctor examining a patient. "How about these?"

I clear my throat, swallowing past the sudden dryness. "Trust."

Shelly smiles. "Correct." She steps away from the computer and paces the length of the table, spinning the bracelet on her wrist. "You're here because you're the best from your class, but I want you to be better. Sure, you can turn in a portfolio with a simplistic theme and you'll pass and graduate and put this all behind you. Or—" she stops and stares at me, and I shift in my seat. "You can create something you'll look back on years from now and be proud of."

The familiar excitement zips through me. Photography is so much more than just being in the right place at the right time and snapping the perfect picture. With careful thought and planning, you can create something that will speak to people, maybe even move them to think in a different way. I can feel the possibilities opening up, the ideas flying past me almost too fast to catch, and hope I can grab onto one that will do what Shelly's talking about.

That would make Dad proud.

I press a hand to my throat. I can't lose it in here.

Shelly casts another glance my way and seems to sense that I'm having a moment. Her eyes soften and her mouth turns into a small frown, but in a heartbeat her smile is back and she's clasping her hands together, addressing the class. "My offer to meet privately is still open. I've already met with a few of you and I strongly encourage you to give your themes the thought they deserve." She moves back to her spot at the table and closes her laptop. "See you all next week."

I push back my chair and sling my bag over my shoulder, my thoughts a jumble of portfolio themes and how I can accomplish what I want combined with Cameron and how I can accomplish what I'm thinking about him.

"Biz, can you stay a few minutes?" Shelly asks.

I glance at Cameron, who nods at the exit. "I'll wait outside."

"Thanks." I rest my bag on the chair and lean a hip against the table. "What's up?"

Shelly presses her hand to her throat, mimicking my earlier gesture and sending the bracelet sliding down her arm. "I didn't mean to put you on the spot like that. Are you okay? You seemed upset." Her dark eyes search mine and for the millionth time I'm grateful that she volunteered to teach our class.

"I'm okay. The pictures you showed actually gave me some good ideas for my portfolio."

"Are you thinking of changing your theme?"

"No, but you sparked an idea for me, of how I can take the light and dark theme and make it bigger." She tilts her head, so I continue. "You suggested me taking pictures at Turner's trial, so I started thinking that I could use shots from there and compare them to the babies I'm photographing at the hospital. I can still use actual light and shadows to highlight the subjects, but also use the deeper theme of good versus evil." I feel a little out of breath. When the idea came to me I wasn't sure if I could pull it off, but saying it out loud and watching the reaction on Shelly's face tells me that this is good. Really good.

"I love it." Her hand slides to her chest.

My gaze drifts to her bracelet. "Are you sure?"

"Yes. Biz, this is exactly what I was talking about. This is what gets you scholarships to school, not just acceptances." She moves closer and rests a hand on my arm. "I want to help you make this the best it can be."

I can't fight the goofy smile that plasters itself to my face. "Okay. Thank you."

She smiles back.

I pick up my bag and turn to leave, then turn back. "You're good at this."

"At what?"

"Teaching." I wave my hand. "Inspiring kids to want more."

She bites her lower lip and her eyes get shiny. "Thank you for saying that. It means a lot, especially coming from you."

"Why me?"

She shakes her head. "You really don't know?"

I shake my head.

"Biz, you're the most talented student in here. Sometimes I feel like I'm stuck in this town, but being able to help you, to help shape your future..." She looks down at the table. "That's exciting for me."

Pinpricks of sweat dot my hands. Telling myself to learn to take compliments and actually doing it are two totally different things. "You shouldn't stop once this class is over."

Her eyes dart to the ground. "I'm not sure if I'll still be around next year."

My mouth falls open. "Are they firing you?"

"No. I'm ready for bigger things. Now go enjoy your weekend." She laughs as she shoos me toward the door and glances behind me. "And have fun with him."

I turn to find Cameron waiting inside the door and my heart stutters. "Thanks, Shelly," I say, turning back to face her. "I'll let you know when I'm ready to meet—" The words die on my lips.

I know where I've seen that bracelet.

# chapter 25

It doesn't make sense. Why would Shelly's bracelet be in Martinez's car? Could she be his sister? They kind of resemble each other but as far as I can tell, she's not Hispanic. Plus her last name is Graham, not Martinez. This is stupid. There are probably a million of those bracelets at the mall. Just because she happens to own a bracelet that looks exactly like the one he tried to hide from me—although did he try to hide it? Or did he just move it out of the way?

"What did Shelly want?"

I look up at Cameron, the conversation from thirty seconds ago already in the back of my mind. I shake it to clear my thoughts as he opens the door and we step outside. "She wanted to make sure she hadn't upset me by singling me out during class."

"Did she?"

"No. The opposite actually. She gave me a great idea for my portfolio."

"So why do you still look upset?"

I unlock the car and we climb in. "I'm not sure." How do I explain what I don't understand? I tell him about the bracelet connection.

"You think she knows Martinez?"

"They talked when he arranged my community service at the hospital. I don't know, maybe they met in person." And she rode in his car and took off her bracelet because why? A flash of jealousy stabs my gut, but I look in Cameron's eyes and it settles. Priorities, Biz.

He rubs his thumb over his jaw. "That seems weird."

"I know. It's like worlds-colliding weird. Then she made a comment about not being here next year. She made it sound like she's moving away."

"Maybe she got a job at a bigger paper. Has she ever said anything about leaving?"

"I've gotten the impression she feels stuck here, so that would make sense." I pull onto the street, but realize I don't know where I'm going.

Cameron seems to think the same thing. "Do you...uhh...do you have plans right now?"

"I'm supposed to go straight home after class."

"I thought you weren't grounded?"

"No, that's from the judge. I can drive to school and community service, but nothing else."

He bites his lip, then a smile lights his face. "So you can go out, you just can't drive?"

I nod, not following. "Yeah."

He points at a parking lot. "Pull over."

I do, still confused about what he's thinking. When I park, he climbs out of the car and half-runs to open my door. He does a low bow, sweeping one hand out like a court jester. "Madame."

When I don't immediately move, he straightens. "I can drive your car, right?"

I laugh out loud. Why didn't I think of that? "Duh, of course!" I squeeze past him and hustle to the passenger side. By the time I'm situated, he's got the driver's seat slid back to make room for his long legs.

"Where to?"

"The boat ramp?"

He smiles, sending ripples of excitement racing through me. "I was hoping you'd say that."

I try to keep my emotions in check. I can't get swept up too quickly. It would be too easy to give in to whatever he's decided he's ready for with me, with us, and lord knows if I spend too long staring at that smile there'll be no turning back.

He takes a meandering route to the boat ramp, avoiding the Strand, and my heart clenches. His hand flexes on the gearshift with each change in speed, like he's imagining driving his manual instead of my dad's boring automatic, and my fingers twitch, wanting to feel his hand in mine. When we finally park near the water, I fling the door open and scramble out of the car. I need air to clear my head.

Gravel crunches as he joins me at the water's edge. His shoulder brushes mine as he stops next to me. "I haven't been here since the last time we were here."

I watch him out of the corner of my eye, unsure where he's going with this.

"Can we sit?"

"I don't have a blanket."

He kicks at the ground and nods at a spot that still has a little grass. "What about over there?"

I let him lead me to the grass, then sit next to him, leaving plenty of space between us. Once I'm situated, legs crossed, he slides closer until our knees are almost touching.

He clears his throat. "I wanted to tell you that I'm not mad anymore. It took a long time for me to get here, but I forgive you for not helping Katie."

It's like he kicked me in the chest. "You forgive me?" My voice is flat, my anger barely under control. My pulse pounds in my ears and I clench my jaw to keep from saying something I can't take back.

He hangs his head and exhales a long breath, and if I wasn't so mad I might melt at how adorable he is. "Yeah. At the time I didn't understand why you refused, and part of me still doesn't, but—"

I need to get away from him. I push to my feet but he stops me with a hand on my leg.

"Wait. Where are you going?"

"I can't listen to this. I thought—" I brush my hand against the sudden tears that make everything blurry. "I thought you were going to apologize, not tell me it was my fault she killed herself."

Confusion and pain darken his eyes. "Please don't go. I'm trying to fix this." He tugs at my pantleg until I sink back onto the ground.

"But you still don't get it, do you? I risked my life to help her and the only thanks I got in return was you telling me that if I loved you, I'd commit suicide to save her."

He flinches and I immediately regret my word choice, but I've never been known for saying the right thing at the right time. "I'm sorry. I didn't mean it that way, but did it ever cross your mind what you were asking me to do?"

The shock fades to sadness. "I guess in the back of my mind, but I thought you were the only one who could stop her. I didn't know what else to do." He reaches for my hand and I pull away. He stares at the space between us before meeting my eyes. "I'm sorry. I never meant to hurt you, and I never meant to drive you out of my life." His voice cracks. "It's been hell without you, Biz."

My anger falters. This is what I wanted. He said all the right words. But there's been too many wrong words for me to give in just like that. "It's been hell for me, too."

"Do you think you can forgive me?"

"I want to."

"But not yet?"

I shake my head. My eyes burn from tears that want to fall, and for once I don't fight them.

He scoots closer and slides an arm around my shoulders, pulling me against him. "I'm sorry." He presses a kiss to the top of my head, then rests his cheek against the same spot. "I'm sorry."

I let him hold me. The little voice in my head insists that I need to keep pushing him away, that I'm giving in too easily, but being in his arms feels right. Safe. I snuggle against his shoulder and breathe him in, and he kisses my forehead again.

"Since we're getting everything out in the open," he clears his throat. "You were right about Sarah."

My head snaps up and I stare at him. "You were cheating on me?" My stomach pitches and I'm thrown back into a spiral of jealousy and anger. Why would he tell me this now?

"No!" His eyes widen and he rubs his hand up and down my arm. "No, I swear."

"Then what was I right about?"

He drops his gaze and his cheeks color. "That she liked me."

"Oh. Duh." Boys are so clueless. "How did you finally figure it out?"

"After Katie—" he swallows hard, "—died, Sarah was over all the time. At first it was nice having someone other than my parents to talk to, especially since you weren't talking to me, but then it became pretty obvious that she liked me and wanted to be more than just friends."

I know I shouldn't ask, but I can't help myself. "How did it become clear?"

"She kissed me."

"Oh." I suddenly feel very small, even though I have no right to be jealous. And if we're getting technical, what I did with Martinez was worse.

"Nothing else happened. I told her I was tired so she'd leave. After that I made excuses not to hang out."

"She doesn't seem like the type to give up that easily."

He smiles, like he's remembering something. "No, she's not. But I can be stubborn, too."

My stomach twists again, but this time it's from nerves. If we're confessing things that happened while we weren't talking, I need to tell him about Martinez.

"Are you mad?"

I shake my head. "I can't say I'm thrilled at the idea of you two making out, but it's not like we were together."

He dips his head to catch my gaze. "We didn't make out, it was just a kiss."

Now I really feel like shit.

"I'm sorry, Biz, but I want to be honest with you."

"Then I need to be honest with you, too."

His lips tighten. "Do I want to hear this?"

"Probably not."

He closes his eyes. "Are you sure you want to tell me?"

I can only imagine the sordid things running through his mind. Yes, I have to tell him now. "First, some back story. You know the freaky email I told you about?" He nods. "I still don't know who sent it, and I got another one yesterday."

"What? What did it say?"

I wave away his question. "Let me get this out. So as I told you, there are only a handful of people who know about me and therefore could try to blackmail or threaten me, or whatever it is they want. I know it's not you or Amelia or my parents, which only leaves one person."

"Martinez."

"Yeah."

"Did you confront him?"

I nod. "He spun things around so the email didn't seem like a big deal, and he's yet to convince me that he's not involved. Then the night before my dad died, they had a private conversation and I freaked out that he convinced Dad to tell him secrets about flickering—stuff he'd never told me—so I flickered to stop Dad from talking to him."

"This is the weirdest confession I've ever heard."

I swat his arm, hoping he doesn't want to return the favor when I get to the kiss. "I'm getting there. I wanted to find out what Dad told him, so Amelia convinced me to..." I trail off. The heat coming off my cheeks is enough to scald Cameron, who's watching me intently.

He clenches his jaw, waiting for me to continue.

"To kiss Martinez. To try to find out what he knew." I wait for him to say something, but he just stares at the ground. I should give him a minute, but uncomfortable silences are a special kind of torture for me. "She had this crazy idea that I could use my feminine wiles to get him to confess everything." I force a laugh. "Like I could have that kind of power over anyone, especially looking like this. I flickered the next morning so he doesn't remember—"

"Stop." Cameron holds up a hand. "Please."

I freeze, mouth still open.

His face has gone pale and he finally meets my gaze. "I don't want to hear about you and Martinez."

I snap my mouth shut.

"Isn't there some kind of oath that says he can't date his patients?"

"We're not dating. It was one kiss." One unbelievably hot kiss, but still, one kiss. Or maybe several kisses, but just one time. "And because I flickered and didn't do it again, he has no idea."

He rubs his hands over his face. "This feels like weird science-fiction territory. I know you've always gone back and changed things, but I never thought about the implications of you manipulating people."

His words hit me like a slap. Is that what I did?

"Did you—" he swallows. "Did you get him to confess?"

"No." I bite back the fear that my feminine wiles are so lacking that it barely affected him, but I'm not sure that's true. If things had continued, I may have found out what I wanted, but there's a line I'm unwilling to cross, even if it means I never find out the truth.

He picks at a piece of grass between us. "Your dad was right not to trust him."

Thoughts of Martinez scatter and the grief I've held at arm's length comes crashing around me. I take several breaths, determined not to cry, but my voice comes out strained. "I did manage to tell my dad not to talk to Martinez. Or at least not to divulge any secrets on his deathbed."

"So what now? Are you still going to your appointments?"

"I skipped this week, but then..." I hadn't made the connection before. "I got the second email a couple hours after I was supposed to see him."

Cameron straightens. "Do you think it's him?"

"It has to be. Maybe he freaked out that I wasn't there and is worried that his precious research might be in jeopardy." I shift so I'm facing Cameron. "Quinn offered to be my sidekick while I figure this out, but he's going home in a couple days." I drop my eyes. While I may not be ready to trust him with my heart, I do trust him. "Do you think you could help me?"

He reaches toward me and covers my hand with his. This time I don't pull away. "If it means getting Martinez out of your life, I'd be honored."

I snort out a laugh. "Have you ever liked him?"

"I liked him plenty when he saved your life, but ever since then I haven't trusted his motives. It's like once he learned the truth about you, he was only focused on what it could mean for his career."

"Yeah, I know what you mean." There are so many things I could say, but sitting here with Cameron, sort of holding hands, is the best I've felt in weeks. Maybe months. I don't want to risk saying anything else to break the spell that's been cast over us.

Cameron rubs his thumb over the back of my hand, sending chills up my arms. "So do you and Quinn have a plan?"

I meet his gaze, a smile playing on my lips. "We didn't get past our superhero costumes."

"Well, it's a good thing I'm here." He looks at our hands and stops rubbing. His smile fades, and I hold my breath.

So many things could come out of his mouth—some good, some bad—and I don't know if I'm ready for what follows whatever he's going to say. I'm still holding my breath when he finally speaks.

"I am here, you know. For you."

My heart feels ready to burst. I believe that I can trust him again, but I can't let go of how badly he hurt me. I swallow past the lump in my throat. "I just need more time."

"I can do that." He lifts my hand and brushes his lips across my fingers.

"That's cheating."

The corner of his mouth lifts and he shrugs. "I never said I play fair." He kisses my hand again then stands, pulling me to my feet. "We should probably get you home, ya big delinquent."

I stumble and he catches me against his chest so both of his arms are wrapped around me. I look up into his eyes and my heart does a fancy quickstep. His head lowers and his lips part ever-so-slightly, but I pull away. "Not yet."

His head continues to lower, but instead of kissing me, he tucks his cheek against my neck and inhales. "Okay. But promise me one thing?"

"What's that?"

"You let me know the second you change your mind."

# chapter 26

Life has a cruel way of continuing, no matter how desperately you need a week or a month to hide in your room and deal with all the crap that's happened. The earth keeps spinning, teachers keep assigning homework, and babies keep being born. Mom and I haven't really talked since Dad died, and I'm beginning to worry that she's either going to completely snap or never, ever talk about him again.

Every day Mom goes to work and I drag my butt to school, but behind closed doors it's like time stopped since the day we went to the lake. Quinn has been a welcome distraction, but even he's noticed how distant Mom has been.

"Does she always ignore you like this?"

I double-check my camera bag for extra batteries, then zip it closed and take a bite of my bagel. I have to be at the hospital in less than an hour, and since I'm planning to be there all morning I need to fuel up now. "I wouldn't say she ignores me."

"Biz, I haven't heard her say more than two words to you all week." He picks at his bagel and pops a piece into his mouth. "It's weird."

I agree—it is weird—but I feel the urge to defend her. "She's always had to take care of Dad so I've done my own thing. Now that he's gone I'm sure she's just trying to figure out what to do with herself."

"And talking to her daughter isn't an option?"

I pick up my bagel but drop it back on the plate. "What, did you climb inside my head or something?" Hearing him voice how I've felt my entire life makes it real, like it's not all my imagination.

"I don't mean to pry, I'm just telling you what I see. It's okay to wish you had a different relationship with your mom. Believe me, there's a lot I wish I could talk to my dad about but after twenty years, I know his limits." His jaw clenches and I can't help but wonder if his dad knows the real Quinn or if they wrote each other off years ago.

Is that how I feel about Mom? That she wrote me off?

No, I don't think so. "It's like she only has the capacity to give all her love to one person, and that person was Dad."

"Your mom loves you."

"She does in her own way, but I'm not the love of her life. And that's okay." I shrug, pretending it doesn't hurt to admit my mother will never love me the way I want her to. I trust that she'll provide for me as best she can, but the closeness I see with other mothers and daughters is something I'll never know.

"Give her another chance."

A spike of anger makes me sit up straight. I wave my hand at him, tears burning my eyes. "You said it yourself, she doesn't talk to me. I'm not going to crawl on my hands and knees, begging for my mommy to acknowledge me."

Quinn catches my hand and rests it on the counter. "Are you always this dramatic?"

My mouth falls open, ready to spew obscenities, but he's not the person I'm mad at. A smile lifts the corner of my mouth. "Sometimes."

He smirks. "Maybe she's afraid to talk to you." He leans away from me. "I'm kind of afraid of you right now."

"Oh, shut it."

"Talk to her today after you get back from playing with the babies."

"I wouldn't know where to begin."

"I don't know, tell her it was hard being in the hospital." He tilts his head, watching for my reaction.

"That wouldn't be a stretch."

"Okay, so it's settled."

I push back my chair and slide my camera bag over my shoulder. "I better get going."

He follows me to the door. "Biz, I'm telling you. Don't let this be how things are. Yes, she's the parent, but no one's perfect. Show her that you need her."

I can feel the energy draining out of me. If I stand here much longer I'll crawl back into bed instead of doing my community service, and then I'll have even more trouble on my hands. "I'll think about it."

A smile brightens his face. "Great! Now go have fun with the babies." He swats my ass, making me squeal as I open the door.

I wouldn't call the neo-natal wing fun, but it is a nice change of pace from my house. I skip Dr. Ward's office and head straight to the heart of the neo-natal wing.

Jonathan isn't there, but the nurse who greets me, a petite redhead, seems nice enough. "There are two families here who agreed to let you photograph them, and another family will be here in a few hours."

"Thanks. Who should I start with?" Even though I was here last week, the sheer volume of machines and wires makes me nervous. Whenever Dad was in the hospital, the tubes were confined to one machine. The neo-natal ward is crawling with technology dedicated to keeping these tiny people alive, and I'm terrified that one wrong step from me will send it crashing to the floor.

The nurse points to a couple huddled around an incubator. "Beth and Thomas Stinton. Their twins were born two weeks ago, two months early.

"Twins?"

"Two girls. Beverly and Tamara." She checks her computer monitor, then touches my shoulder. "Follow me." She leads me to the family and a gasp escapes me before I can stop it.

"They're so tiny." I'm sure this is the exact opposite of how I'm supposed to react, but how do you get used to seeing people small enough to fit in a grown man's hand? You don't, that's how.

"Beth, Thomas. This is Biz, the photographer I told you about."

Thomas unfolds himself from his chair and extends a hand. "Thank you for doing this. We had all kinds of ideas for photos for when we brought the girls home, but they had a different plan."

I shake his hand, unsure what to say. He's treating me like a professional, like an adult, so my hesitation must not be as obvious as I think. What's the saying? Fake it 'til you make it? I can totally do this. "I'm honored to be your photographer." I hold out my hand to Beth, who seems less certain about me, but rather than making me self-conscious, her hesitation puts me at ease. She knows I'm not really a pro so her expectations are probably so low that I'd really have to screw up to disappoint her.

I rest a hand on the glass separating the girls from the rest of the room. "Are they able to come out?"

The nurse checks the printout spooling from a pair of monitors, running her finger down the paper. "Vitals look good for both of them. We're clear for at least an hour." She lifts Baby Number One and settles her into Beth's arms, then repeats the process with Baby Number Two. I'm not sure who has which baby, but based on the look of pure adoration on their parents' faces, I don't think it matters.

I step closer to study their faces and am struck by a sense of awe. They are so pure and innocent, so unaware of anything dark or evil that could change their lives in a heartbeat. Then the monitor beeps, proving me wrong. These two have seen more trauma in their painfully short lives than many people ever will. They will be perfect for my portfolio, but can I really use them? It feels almost sacrilegious to take advantage of their innocence for my own gain.

Kind of like Martinez.

I shudder, and a wave of nausea hits me. Once again I'm left wondering if I have the cajones to be a professional photographer. It feels cheap, almost profane, to use people this way.

Thomas tilts his head. "Should we get started?"

I clear my throat. "Yes, sorry. I was deciding which angles would be best since there are two of them." I nod at a small couch in the corner of the room near a window. I don't think it was there last time—perhaps Dr. Ward had it moved in there for the session. "Let's get you situated on the couch over there."

Once Beth is seated with both of her daughters in her lap, the tension in her face fades, revealing a mixture of rapture and exhaustion that must be all she knows right now. I take a few shots even though Thomas is still standing—*click-click-click*—and Beth frowns.

"I want Thomas in the pictures, too."

I move aside so he can sit. "Of course. The spontaneous moments are the hardest to recreate, and I want to make sure I capture everything." If I explain what I saw she'll get self-conscious and I'll never get a good picture out of her. "Thomas, if you're ready, wrap your arm around Beth's shoulders."

He obeys, and I get to work.

When we're winding down, the light outside shifts, casting a shadow over Beverly and her parents so only Tamara is bathed in light. The juxtaposition of dark and light—my breath catches. It's perfect. Then the light shifts again and Tamara lets out a wail, while her sister remains calm. The symbolism is tripping over itself: terror in light, goodness in dark. I take a few more shots before lowering my camera.

"I think we're good." I hand Beth my card, a square of paper I printed at home with my name and email address, and feel a surge of pride. To them I'm a professional.

"Thank you. You can't know how special this is for us."

"I'll send a proof sheet within a week. Once you let me know which photos you want I'll bring you a disk."

Thomas leans forward, cradling Tamara's head against his chest. "How much will all that cost? The director told us this is free, but we don't expect handouts."

I nestle my camera into the camera bag. "My time and the disk are free. I don't provide prints, so the only expense will be getting them printed."

Beth's face lights up, her eyes shining with tears. "How can we repay you?"

It's now or never. "Would you mind if I use some of these shots for my portfolio? It's for graduation."

They exchange a look and for a moment I worry my phenomenal idea is shot to hell, but then they both nod.

"Thank you."

The other family is ready for me so I switch memory cards and dive into round two. Mother Nature doesn't repeat the dramatic lighting, but I'm able to shift the father until his head falls into shadow, leaving only his son illuminated. By the time we're through, I'm exhausted.

I find the nurse. "Is there time for me to take a break? I could use a snack."

She checks her watch. "You've got at least an hour before they arrive. Go have fun."

Fun in the cafeteria, yeehaw. I take the stairs to stretch my legs, my thoughts bouncing from the photos I just took to what I'll have to take for the opposite perspective.

The evil.

Turner's trial is soon and as much as I want to avoid it, I know I have to go. Not for me, but for Katie and Cameron and the girls I helped save. It'll be my first real test to see if I can put aside my personal feelings and capture an event as a photographer.

"Biz?"

I stop in my tracks before walking into the lab coat in front of me. Martinez. "Hey."

He nods at the camera hanging around my neck. "Taking pictures today?"

"Actually, I was donating blood. This is my security blanket."

He purses his lips. "I missed you this week."

Why the hell didn't I think of an excuse in case I ran into him? "Yeah, well…I had a crappy day and I had to meet Shelly to go over my portfolio." I watch for any signs of recognition at her name, but his expression doesn't waver from irritated curiosity. "Sorry. Didn't your receptionist tell you I canceled?"

"She did, but you could have called or texted me yourself. It's like you were avoiding me."

Not one to beat around the bush, is he? "I wasn't ready to be in the hospital so soon after my dad…"

His irritation slides off his face and in a heartbeat he's closed the distance between us and envelops me in a hug that feels nothing like the embrace from the night we kissed. His arms and chest are still rock solid, but his hands rest politely on the middle of my back. "I'm so sorry. I know I saw you that night, but it just occurred to me that I haven't seen you since then." He grips my shoulders and pushes me back so he can look in my eyes. "How are you holding up?"

I have to look away. The intensity in his gaze is too much. I keep telling myself that nothing happened, but standing this close to him, the buzz of the first floor fades and I'm transported to his office in the middle of the night.

"I have a few minutes now. Do you want to talk in my office?"

I shake my head. "No. There's nothing to talk about. He died, and I'll never see him again." I drag the back of my hand across my eyes, begging the tears to stay away a little longer. So far I've managed to keep the butterflies at bay but if I start crying he'll hug me again and who knows what will happen.

He touches his finger to my chin, forcing me to look into his eyes. "You know my door is always open."

"I do, thanks." I pull away. "I promise I won't skip next week."

He points at me as he backs away. "I'm holding you to that."

I shuffle into the cafeteria, grab a coffee and an apple, and silently high-five myself. For the first time in as long as I can remember, Martinez didn't make me weak in the knees. I find a table near an outlet and plug in my battery charger, then rest my camera against my chest and flip through the photos. I immediately delete any that are blurry—no amount of retouching can save a poor shot—then begin critiquing. When I reach the series for my portfolio, I pull out a small notebook and write down the image numbers of the ones I think will work. The lighting is so drastic between the twins that the little voice in my head whispers that it might be enough to demonstrate my theme without needing to photograph the trial.

But that would be a cop out. I can do this.

As if to encourage me, my phone vibrates. I finish scrolling through the photos, close my notebook, open my mail app, and almost fall out of my chair.

Ms. Clement,

Thank you for submitting your photos. We apologize for the delay in getting back to you, but we'd like to feature all three in an upcoming series about teen photographers.

We pay $50 per image and would love to see more work.

Best,

Joe Johnson

The Free Press

One hundred fifty dollars? And they want to see more? I check the date when I submitted the photos he's talking about. It was months ago, back when I was gung-ho on my career and sent pictures to newspapers all over the country. Before Katie died, the accident, Dad...when everything seemed to fall apart around me.

I send a quick reply thanking him and promising to send more soon, then make a vow to myself: No more moping. No more being afraid of what I might achieve if I actually try. And if I can't do it for myself, I'll do it for Dad.

# chapter 27

"I can't believe you're leaving."

Quinn nestles a pair of shoes into his suitcase and gives me his charming smile. "What can I say? I'm needed at home." I raise an eyebrow, and he laughs. "Okay, my boss threatened to fire me if I didn't get my, quote, pretty little butt, end-quote, back to work." He sets the suitcase on the ground and sits next to me on the couch. "Just between you and me, I'm not so sure women's retail is the best use of my skills anyway."

"You never told me why you decided against college."

His face grows serious, and it makes me nervous. Quinn's smile is a permanent feature and without it he appears older, more weary. "That's because you asked before I knew that you flicker." He taps the side of his head the same way Dad used to do, and a sense of déjà vu passes through me. "Unfortunately I wasn't as cautious as you about flickering and my headaches have gotten worse in the last year. I barely made it through my first semester of college."

"Seriously?"

He nods. "I knew the migraines were side effects, but I didn't know..." He flexes his fingers against his legs. "I wish I'd known about you and your Dad a long time ago. I'm afraid it's too late to turn this ship around."

I scoot right up against him and wrap my arm around his back. "Don't talk like that. You're not even twenty-one." I poke him in the side. "You have plenty of life left in you."

He puts his hands in his face. I've never seen this side of him and I hate that he's felt like he had to put on a cheerful pretense for me and Mom. "I guess I'm regretting being so careless." He turns his head to look at me. "Haven't you ever done anything you regret?"

I snort. I can't help it. "Me? Never."

"You can't even say it with a straight face. What'd you do?"

"There's too many to list."

"So start with the first one that popped into your head."

Martinez. "I don't think so."

He leans against the couch, the happy, teasing Quinn back. "Now you have to tell me." This time he pokes me in the ribs. "You're blushing. This must be good."

Ugh. Can I really tell him? I was hoping I'd die with only Amelia and Cameron knowing the truth about my failed seduction slash manipulation of my super hot brain doctor.

He bounces on the couch, his hands gripping his knees. "Look how happy you've already made me! Come on, spill it."

"Okay, but you cannot tell anyone. And you can't judge me. Or tease me. Or, I don't know, ask me too many questions."

"I fear you're building this up so it won't seem like such a big deal."

I take a deep breath and close my eyes, but that makes it too easy to remember the kiss so I snap them back open. "Okay, fine. The night before my dad died, Martinez had a private chat with him and I was worried he got Dad to confess something about flickering. Something he'd never told me. Plus this was right after I got the threatening email so I was a bit out of sorts."

"I recall you sharing the out-of-sorts-ness."

I roll my eyes. "Amelia and I were convinced that Martinez was keeping something from me so she persuaded me to—" I stop.

"Did you break into his office?"

Why didn't we think of that? "That probably would have been a lot easier."

"Ooh! Go on."

I twist so I'm facing the couch and bury my face in the cushions. "Amelia brainwashed me into thinking I could find out what Martinez knew by trying to seduce him."

Silence.

I risk peeking at him. His eyes and mouth are wider than I've ever seen them and he's staring at me. "Don't look at me!"

"Did you?"

"Did I what?"

He pokes my arm. "Don't play coy. Did you seduce him?"

I straighten. "If you recall, I still don't have confirmation that he's the one sending the emails, so that would be a negative."

He leans close and waggles his brows. "But did you try?"

There's no stopping the blush that floods my cheeks. Even my neck is burning.

He pushes my arm. "You did!"

"Maybe."

"Don't deny it. You totally did, you little minx."

"We may have made out in his office."

"I need popcorn." He starts to get up but I yank him onto the couch.

"There will be no popcorn."

"This is so much better than I imagined. I was expecting you to say you cheated on a test."

"Well, who hasn't done that?"

He makes a tsking sound and shakes his head. "Biz, do I need to stick around to keep you out of trouble?"

I cross my arms and shiver at the memory of Martinez's arms around me. "I doubt even you could help."

"You still haven't told me what happened."

"Do I have to?"

"Yes."

I take a deep breath and spit it out. "It was the middle of the night and I was already planning to flicker the next day to warn Dad not to talk to Martinez. I didn't expect him to still be at the hospital when I texted him, but he was."

"How convenient."

"There's always been this, I don't know, flirtation between us, and being in his office in the middle of the night with him looking all hot in his EMT uniform—"

"Hold the phone. He's an EMT? I thought he was a neurosurgeon."

"He goes on runs some nights. It's a long story."

"That is hot."

"You're not helping."

"So he was all hot in his uniform..." he prompts.

"Actually, the uniform was earlier. By then he was in regular clothes but his hair was still wet from his shower—"

"My thighs are tingling."

"And, I don't know, I may have bumped into him or something and the next thing I knew we were full-on making out."

He flutters his lashes. "Was it good?"

I nod, unable to verbalize exactly what I'm feeling. At the time, the kiss was the hottest thing I'd ever experienced, but now that things with Cameron seem to be okay and my trust in Martinez is pretty much destroyed, the memory is tainted. "I left before things got too out of hand, then flickered first thing in the morning and did NOT repeat it."

"So he has no idea?"

I shake my head. "And I want it that way."

"Understandable."

"So my one and only attempt at using my feminine wiles to manipulate someone completely blew up in my face. That is what I regret."

He raises an eyebrow. "You regret that you did it, or you regret that it didn't work?"

"I think I'd still regret it even if he had confessed everything, but I'll never know. Now I just have another crazy memory that never happened."

"Another?"

"My former photography teacher and my non-kidnapping. That still ranks as the freakiest thing that's never officially happened. And now his trial is almost here and I don't know if I can face him."

He rests a hand on my arm. "Just remember that he may be evil, but he has no recollection of what he did to you. He has no power over you."

I study him, looking for a hint at what must have happened to him to make him so understanding, but he's not sharing. My phone buzzes and I check my message.

Amelia: We're here. You ready?

Me: Be right there.

"Amelia and Trace are here. Do you need to do anything else before we go?"

He looks around the room. All evidence of his stay is packed away in his suitcase. "Let's go. I'm dying to try this world famous pizza you keep talking about."

When I open the door, Amelia tackles me, sending us both flying into Quinn. We land in a heap at the bottom of the stairs. "You got your cast off!"

She giggles. "Surprise!"

Quinn squirms out from beneath us. "What the hell just happened?"

Amelia sits up. "You don't know how long I've been waiting to do that!"

Quinn looks at me. "This is normal?"

I beam at Amelia, tears shining in my eyes. "Definitely." Maybe things really are getting back to normal, or at least as normal as they ever can be.

"Then hello!" Quinn launches himself at Amelia, wrapping his arms around her as he falls so they end up closer to the door.

We're still lying on the floor laughing when a throat clears in the doorway. Amelia disentangles herself and smiles at Trace. "Hey, babe. You ready?"

He shakes his head, smiling. "This never gets old."

She pushes to her feet and plants a kiss on his lips. "And that's why I love you." She grabs Quinn's hand and pulls him to his feet before helping me up. "Let's go, I'm starving."

Amelia and Quinn carry the conversation in the car, both gesturing with their hands and talking over each other, and it strikes me how similar they are. Loud, boisterous, full of love for the world—totally the opposite of me. I don't know what it is about me that they seem to like, but I'm grateful they can see past the sarcasm and negativity to care about me.

"Hey, Biz," Amelia says. "I think my lip gloss rolled under the seat. Can you try to find it?"

I cock my head at her in confusion, but one glance out the window and I understand: we're approaching the Strand. Trace doesn't know what it could do to me, but she does. "Be right back!" I bend over so my head is wedged against the back of the seat. "Quinn, can you help me?"

"Are you serious?"

"Very." I grab his collar and yank him to me. I whisper, "You need to cover your eyes for this stretch of road." I close my eyes as added protection. After several moments something plastic bumps against my fingers. Amelia's lip gloss. She must have rolled it to me under the seat. "Found it." I hand her the tube and give her a grateful smile.

"You're the best."

I look her in the eyes. "No, you are."

Trace groans. "You two need privacy?"

Ugh, sometimes he is such a jock.

Amelia swats his arm. "Don't be jealous."

Trace pulls into the nearly empty Fricano's parking lot and we pile out of the car. Amelia stumbles and Trace is at her side in a heartbeat, tucking his arm through hers. "You okay?"

Quinn laughs. "Oh, sure. She trips and you come to her rescue, but she does a flying tackle into the house and you're nowhere to be seen."

"No offense, dude, but she's a lot cuter than you."

I nudge Quinn's side and touch the side of his face. "I don't know, have you seen these cheekbones? And I'd kill for those eyes."

Amelia stares at me. "You do realize you look just like each other? If it weren't for the fact that he's a foot taller, you could be brother and sister. Twins even."

I study Quinn. Sure, there's a resemblance, but I attributed it to him looking like Dad, not me. "Well, we do have the same haircut."

"You're practically the same person."

I smile up at Quinn. "I'll take that as a compliment."

Quinn smirks. "Not me. You're a mess. I'm only here because we're family." He's so deadpan that for a second I think he's serious, then he winks.

"I'm really gonna miss you."

Trace opens the door and the scent of greasy cheese pulls us inside. Quinn presses his hand to my lower back, escorting me inside, and lowers his head to whisper in my ear. "Me too."

Once we're seated, pizza and breadsticks and gallons of Coke dominate the afternoon and I laugh so much my stomach hurts. I could spend all day here, surrounded by my friends, not worrying about anything but right here, right now.

"Are you sure you have to leave?"

Quinn pushes his plate away from him. "They might have to roll me onto the plane, but yeah."

Amelia props her elbows on the table. "Do you live near the ocean?"

"Not far."

"Biz, we should totally take a road trip after graduation. Wouldn't it be amazing to visit the ocean? And Quinn, of course!"

He smiles. "I see how it is."

Getting out of town does sound amazing, and hanging out with Quinn in his world would be a good warm-up for going away to college. "Do we have to wait until graduation?"

Amelia twirls a strand of hair around her finger. "Screw it. Who needs a diploma? Let's go!"

I laugh. "I'm sure my parents—I mean, my mom—would be okay with that." I try to cover my slip but the light mood fizzles.

No one speaks.

I break the silence. "Quinn, would that be cool if we came? Do you have room for us?"

He looks between me and Amelia. "For you two, yes. That one," he nods at Trace, "I'm not so sure about."

Trace's brows furrow and we burst out laughing. By the time we're driving back to my house, my face hurts from smiling so much. It's almost enough to forget the grief that's been my constant shadow since Dad died.

Later, when I'm saying goodbye to Quinn at the airport with Mom by my side, he pulls me into a final hug. "Promise me you'll talk to your mom. You're all she has left and while she may not know how to say it, she needs you."

I sigh against his shoulder. "Fine. I promise." I'm not sure how much good it will do, but I do know one thing: the loneliness I've felt in the house since Dad died is not how I want to live the rest of my life.

"Good." He kisses the tip of my nose and gives me a final squeeze. "Be sure to keep me posted on your love life, and let me know if you really want to come out this summer. I'd love to have you." He releases me and turns to Mom, pulling her into a hug, then he grabs his bag and walks out of our lives.

"Love life?" Mom asks.

I take a breath, ready to deflect her question with a sarcastic comment, but instead I do the opposite: I tell her the truth.

# chapter 28

I spent the rest of the week dreading my appointment with Martinez, but I promised him I'd show up, so here I am. When his receptionist leads me to his office, I can't help but remember when Martinez was the one leading me down this hall. In the dark. In the middle of the night.

Will I ever be able to push that out of my mind?

The door is open so I step inside and mumble a greeting to his back before climbing onto the examining table.

He swivels around, and a smile brightens his face. "I have to admit, I wasn't sure if you were going to come."

I run my thumbnail along the seam of my jeans. "I didn't think that was an option."

He rolls the stool closer. "Biz, we've talked about this. You're an adult. You're here voluntarily." The hint of something dark and brooding flashes over his face as his smile fades. "Has something happened that's made you not want to be here?"

You mean like not being able to stop thinking about you being pressed up against me, kissing me better than I've ever been kissed in my life? I can't look at him when I'm thinking that. "No. I guess I'm just having a hard time with Dad."

He leans forward so his elbows are on his knees. "Do you want to talk about it? I know that's not why you're here, but I'd like you to think of me as more than just your doctor."

And now I'm thinking of him kissing me again.

"Biz, you know you can trust me."

"Can I?"

He straightens, crossing his arms over his chest. "What's that supposed to mean?"

I didn't mean to bring it up, but the words are out of my mouth before I can stop them. "I got another threatening email. And it coincidentally arrived the same night that I skipped your appointment."

"Are you accusing me of sending the emails?"

His directness sends me backpedaling. I don't have a plan for a confrontation. "Not accusing. I'm just wondering out loud."

He stands, sending the stool clattering against the wall. "Biz, we've talked about this before. What benefit could I possibly stand to gain by scaring the subject of the most interesting study I've ever done?" He paces the small room, his broad frame filling every inch of available space and making it hard for me to breathe. "I understand how frightening it must be to know that someone is threatening to reveal your secret, but I'm here to help you." He stops next to me and levels his gaze at me. "I thought you want to prevent what happened to your father from happening to you?"

I can't help but notice that he technically hasn't denied it. "I do, but not at this price." I look away. "I'll just stop flickering and then I'll only have to live with whatever damage I've already done. I won't inflict any more."

"Just like that, you'll stop flickering?"

I look him in the eye, but I'm picturing Quinn. His despair over knowing he's already done irreparable damage to himself has motivated me to stop cold turkey. "I'm not saying it will be easy, but I want more for my life than wasting away inside a dark house."

"And you think that's all your father accomplished?"

A lump catches in my throat. I was supposed to avoid talking about Dad and now he's got me criticizing him. "No! That's not what I meant."

"You wouldn't be here if it weren't for him. If you truly want to make sure you're father's life meant something, don't give up on our research."

"I'm not giving up."

"But you are. You're letting some anonymous person bully you into giving up."

If he wants to over-stubborn me into not quitting, that's the way to do it. After all the crap I put up with after getting my head shaved, giving in to bullies is the last thing I want to do. "I hadn't looked at it as bullying."

He holds up his hands. "I'm just saying how it looks to me. You don't even know what this person wants, do you?"

I shake my head. "The emails have just said that they know my secret and that the truth will come out. And that it could kill me." Ironic that I'm more worried about my secret getting out than the fact that it will kill me.

"So quitting our research won't accomplish anything other than putting your life at greater risk."

"I wouldn't say it's putting my life at risk, but I guess I can see your point." The little voice in my head interjects that if Martinez is the one behind the emails, I'm doing exactly what he wants. But the emails haven't said anything specific about what I'm supposed to do, and really, if someone knows my secret and has decided they're going to tell people, there's not much I can do to stop it. "So what do you have in mind?"

A smile lights up his face, and the sinking feeling in my stomach gets worse. "I want to record you again." He grabs his tablet from the drawer and in a few taps, shows me the display. "It's a head-mounted camera. People use them for all sorts of things, and this way you won't have to hold a camera when you flicker."

"You want me to flicker again? I just said that I don't want to do any more damage to myself."

He leans against the counter, arms crossed again. "I need— we need another video to support the hypothesis I've established. We're so close to—"

"You have a hypothesis? About why I flicker?"

"It's not fully developed, but I've drawn comparisons to another condition and I think another video would solidify my findings."

"What other conditions?"

"There's something called the bucha effect that's common with helicopter pilots. The steady rate at which the helicopter blades rotate cause a strobe effect with the light, and that can cause reactions similar to epilepsy."

"So I should avoid helicopters."

He closes his eyes for a second, ignoring my comment.

"So how do these helicopter pilots avoid the strobing lights?"

"They cover their eyes. Or close them." He presses his lips together. "The same thing you do."

My heart sinks. For a second I thought he might actually have an answer.

He clears his throat. "If we time it right, you'll flicker back into your room, which should minimize any inadvertent side effects."

"You mean like landing in a car?"

I expect him to laugh, or at least crack a smile, but he doesn't. "Yes." He moves toward me until his hip is resting against the table. "I know this scares you, but it's what your father would want."

I sit up straight. Dad wanted me to be safe, not flicker to help Martinez. "How can you know that?"

"He told me. The night before he died." He rubs his hand over his jaw and I can't help but feel that he's manipulating me right now. Lying to my face about what Dad told him just to get me to make him another recording. "He didn't want you to repeat his fate and asked that I do whatever I can to keep you safe."

Okay, I can see him saying that, but Martinez is twisting it around to suit his needs. "And you think flickering for more research will keep me safe?"

"I think it's our best shot at getting what we want."

Again with the redirect. If he is deceiving me about his intentions, he still manages to never flat out lie. "And we want the same thing?"

He throws up his hands and exhales. "Biz, how many times are we going to do this?"

I jump to my feet so we're face-to-face. "Until I believe you. This is me we're talking about, not some rat in a lab experiment. Last time you wanted a new video you said, 'Ooh, just one more,' but now it's just one more again. What if you're wrong and this one more time is the difference between me living a relatively normal life and becoming a vegetable by age twenty-five?"

The color drains from his face, but he doesn't back down. "I don't think I am."

"You don't think you're wrong or you just don't want to be wrong?"

"You're mincing words. It's the same thing."

"Not to me it isn't."

He lifts his hands and rests them on my arms. "Biz, I took an oath to do no harm. Asking you to do something for research, knowing it could cause irreversible damage, goes against everything I stand for. What else do I need to say to make you trust me?"

I pull away and his arms fall to his sides. "You say all the right things. It's your actions I'm not so sure about."

He opens his mouth to protest but I hold up a hand. "I'll do one more recording for you, but that's it. No more after that."

His eyes brighten but he's smart enough not to smile. If he did I might punch him in the teeth. "Great! I'll order it tonight and we'll coordinate in a couple days when it arrives."

"Okay." I lean against the table feeling like I've been duped, once again, into doing what he wants.

He squeezes my shoulder but doesn't let his hand linger. "This is the right decision. We're close, I can feel it."

I wish I felt the same way. Instead I feel like I've signed my soul over to the devil. "I better get going. I still have homework to catch up on."

"I was planning to review the other video with you. Don't you want to see it?"

I walk to the door, and pause with my hand on the handle. "You watch it. I think you'll enjoy it more than I will." I push into the hallway before he can say anything else.

Is he truly close to figuring out why I flicker? I should feel excited, but instead I feel so drained of energy that I can barely make it to my car. I wasn't lying—I am scared that the next flicker could be the beginning of the end for me—but I have a new motivation for going along with his plan: whatever Martinez finds out could help Quinn.

On the way home, I call Shelly with the hope that talking about photography will take my mind off Martinez.

"Biz, hey. What's going on?"

"I was hoping we could talk about my portfolio. I took some great shots of the babies and I'm wondering if two main subjects would be enough to demonstrate the play off light and dark."

"Are you thinking Turner would be your only dark subject?"

I grip the steering wheel tighter. Now's the time to see if I can push aside my emotions for the sake of my future career. "Yes."

She pauses. "I'd like to say yes, but I think it's smarter to make that decision after you take the photos. I'm not questioning your ability, but sometimes even the best photographers aren't able to make every shot work. Keep thinking of other subjects for the dark portion of your project."

Turner's the darkest thing in my life, but what she's saying makes sense. "Okay."

"How's everything else? Did I see you and Cam talking the other day?"

The heaviness in my chest lessens a tiny bit at the thought of Cameron. "Yeah, but nothing has happened there. Yet." I laugh. "Frankly, between school and the extra time with Martinez, I barely have time for a social life."

She pauses again, but this one feels awkward. Uncomfortable.

"Are you still there?"

She laughs, but it's not her usual carefree laugh. It sounds forced. "Yeah, sorry. I got—my phone beeped. I have another call."

I didn't hear a beep but I don't say anything. If she wants to get off the phone I'm not going to stop her. "Okay. I guess I'll see you tomorrow in class."

"Be safe, Biz."

Be safe? What the heck is that supposed to mean?

# chapter 29

"Maybe she meant don't crash your car while talking on the phone."

I called Quinn as soon as I got home. Between agreeing to record myself and Shelly's weird-ass comment, I need advice from someone who understands what I'm dealing with.

"Or, wear protection when you sleep with Cam."

I snort out a laugh. "I don't think that's what she meant."

"Maybe not, but it's good advice."

"Noted. But seriously, what could she have meant?"

"What did you say right before she said that?"

"Just that I'm so busy with school and the extra time with Martinez that I don't have much time for a social life."

"Hmm." He's silent for a moment. "Does she know him?"

I gasp. "The bracelet." I rush to explain. "When I was in Martinez's car I saw a bracelet that looks just like one Shelly has."

"You were in his car? Why haven't you told me this?"

"It was when he recorded me flickering. He could have left the bracelet where it was and I probably wouldn't have noticed, but he made a point of moving it, which is the only reason I remember it. Then I saw her wearing a similar one a week later."

"So they could know each other."

"I think it's a stretch. I'm sure there's probably a bazillion of those bracelets floating around town."

"But he would only try to hide it from you if he thinks you'd recognize it."

"True."

"Do you think they're banging?"

"Quinn!"

He laughs. "It's a fair question."

Images of Shelly, with her perfect hair and adorable body, mash together with what I know of Martinez's body and the sudden twinge of jealousy angers me. I don't want to be jealous of him. "They're adults. They can do whatever they want."

His voice softens. "Does it bother you?"

"Maybe a little," I admit. "But I don't want it to. Like you so eloquently pointed out, Cameron is back in my life. Nothing can ever happen between me and Martinez so—"

"Except it did."

"I knew I shouldn't have told you that."

"I'm not judging. I'm just pointing out that something did happen between you, even if he's unaware of it. It's okay to be jealous, it's what you do with those feelings that matters."

"When did you get so smart?"

"Last year. Before then I was as clueless as you are."

"Very funny." I sigh. "I wish I could talk to Dad about this. He had a way of pointing out the obvious and making things seem not so screwed up."

"I get it."

I pause, and the sound of his breathing carries over the line. "Do you miss your mom?"

"Not as much as I used to, but yeah, I do."

We're silent for a moment, both lost in our thoughts, when my phone dings. "Hang on, let me check my text." I switch screens.

Martinez: The camera arrived after you left. Any chance I can drop it off at your house?

Me: Already?

Martinez: Expedited shipping.

Does he really think I'm so stupid that I would believe

he ordered the camera after we talked and an hour later it's already arrived?

> Martinez: I'm heading to dinner. Can I drop it off
> on the way?
> Me: Now?
> Martinez: If you're home.

This feels too rushed, but I already agreed to it.

> Me: Okay.

I switch back to my call with Quinn.

"That was a lot of typing."

"It was Martinez. He's dropping off the camera right now." My head swirls with a thousand doubts, the biggest being the fact that he lied about not already having the camera. "Is it too late to back out of this?"

"No! You don't owe him anything."

"I feel like I do."

"Biz, don't do anything you're not comfortable with."

"But he saved my life."

"He's a surgeon. It's his job to save your life. This stuff—" I picture him waving his hand in the air. "This goes beyond any Hippocratic obligation."

"I know..."

"I don't think you do." He pauses. "You clearly have your doubts about this and from what you've said, you don't trust him the way you used to, so listen to your instincts. What are they telling you to do?"

"Not to answer the door when he gets here."

"Then that's what you should do. Or shouldn't do. You know what I mean."

But when Martinez texts that he's outside, I fling open the door and step into the night.

# chapter 30

Martinez is wearing a dark button-down shirt, jeans, and dress shoes, and is leaning against his car like he has all the time in the world. When I close the door behind me, he quickly approaches. We stop in front of each other on the sidewalk, and I hate myself for checking him out. This outfit is even hotter than the EMT uniform.

He holds out a white plastic bag and I peek inside at the brown box.

"This is it?"

"The instructions are in the box, but it's pretty self-explanatory."

"And there's already film or a disk or whatever?"

He smiles, and I glance away to stop my heart from any form of erratic beating. A movement in the car catches my eye, but the light over the garage hits the windshield in a way that makes it impossible to see inside the car. "I picked it up at a store near the hospital and they made sure it's charged and ready to go."

So he didn't lie about ordering it ahead of time. "I thought you said it had expedited shipping?"

He's still smiling. "Yes, I expedited the process by driving to the store rather than ordering it online."

I snort as I grab the bag.

"Plan it out so that when you flicker, you go back to your

room." The smile fades and the intensity in his gaze increases. "I was serious when I said I don't want you to get hurt."

"Yeah, yeah. I'll have the video for you at our next appointment."

"Thanks, Biz."

"Have a good night." I turn and head up the sidewalk. I'm opening the door when I hear his car door open.

"Be safe."

I whip around, but he's already in the car. That cannot be a coincidence. I stare at the car as he backs out of the driveway. Someone is definitely in the passenger seat, but it's too dark to see who.

I text Quinn.

> Me: The eagle has landed, and gave me the same warning as Shelly.
> Quinn: The plot thickens.
> Quinn: Be safe.
> Me: Shut it.

I toss the bag on my bed and refuse to look at it until the weekend. Right now I need to focus on the schoolwork I claimed is taking up all my free time.

Which is easier said than done.

I'm still behind in most of my classes, but all I want to do is work on my portfolio. After twenty minutes, I push my Trig notebook aside and turn on my monitor. The image program is already open but instead of looking at the latest shots from the hospital, I scroll to the beginning of the school year, back when Turner was still my idol and all I had to worry about was people finding out my secret.

Come to think of it, not much has changed. I mean, everything has changed, but even after all that's happened, my biggest fear is still being outed as a freak.

I come across the sports-themed pictures from last fall, including the ones of Trace scoring a goal that I used for my full-page project. I click a couple buttons and email them to Amelia with the note "Enjoy." Next is the football game that I went to with Cameron. That's when I first found out about Turner's daughter disappearing, which, from what they've said on the news, is what pushed him over the edge and made him kidnap those girls. I shake off the memory and focus on the shots of the players. Even though I took them this school year, it feels like they're from a lifetime ago. Both because I can tell my eye has improved and because everything seems so innocent.

I keep scrolling and jump at the face that fills my screen.

It's the man who kept showing up at games and staring at me. The one I thought might be the kidnapper. A sense of unease passes through me. I know he didn't do anything wrong, but for a while he had me truly scared, when really the man I should have been afraid of was walking around the school.

I click away from his face and Cameron fills my monitor. Half his face is in shadow—a perfect example of light and dark in one image—and he's staring into the distance, lost in thought. His hair's a little longer than it is now but his jawline, lips, and eyes are as delicious as ever. His face grows blurry and I blink away tears. He believes we can get past the last few months, and as much as I want to hold back, I'm tired of fighting it.

I belong with him.

I grab my phone and text him before I can change my mind.

Me: You busy?

I scroll through more photos but my fingers keep leading me back to his picture. We had just started dating when I took this, and I was terrified that I'd ruin our friendship by pushing him away like I did with the other boys I'd dated. Now I realize he was never going to let me go.

Still no answer.

I'm about to Google 'how to retract a text' when my phone finally buzzes.

Cameron: What's up?

Me: I'm a little freaked out.

My phone rings.

"What's wrong?" His deep voice is safe, reassuring. Exactly what I need right now.

"It's probably all in my head, but I told Martinez I'd record myself flickering with this fancy head-cam he gave me and now I'm freaking out that maybe it's not the best idea and I don't know if I should ever flicker again because of what happened to Dad but what if this is the only way I ever find out why this happens to me? And I miss you." I take a deep breath, hoping he didn't catch that last part. "Are you still there?"

He chuckles. "Yeah, I'm here."

"So I'm freaking out."

"I'd say so. I didn't mean to laugh, but that was a lot all at once."

My lips curve into a smile that reaches all the way to my heart. How did I go so long without talking to him?

"You miss me?"

"You weren't supposed to hear that part."

He clears his throat and I imagine him running his hand through his hair, maybe even blushing. Like I am. "So if I followed all that, you're afraid to flicker again but you're going to for Martinez?"

"Pretty much."

"He can't make you, can he?"

"No. In fact, he keeps reminding me that I'm an adult and can make my own choices, but the way he says it is like he's trying to reverse psychologize me into doing what he wants."

"So you feel pressured?"

I glance at the bag on the other side of the room and struggle to catch my breath. "Based on the constant ache in my chest, I'd say yes."

"I don't get it. Why would he risk your health? It seems like he just wants more data for his research regardless of what it does to you."

I can't help but notice the irony in Cameron worrying about Martinez's intentions with me. It's like the tables haven't so much flipped as spun in a giant circle, so now Cameron is the one worrying about my safety and pointing out that Martinez is only looking out for his own interests. "That's how I'm feeling, too, but he said he's close to figuring out what makes me flicker."

"Do you believe him?"

"I think so. But then there's the whole threatening emails thing and none of it makes sense. I asked him again if he sent them and he redirected without answering."

"But you're still going to record yourself?"

I close my eyes. "Yes."

He's quiet for a moment. "Do you want me to drive you?"

I nod, and I can feel the tears starting up again. He drove me the first time I told him about flickering, then again when we tried to save Katie. The last time he grabbed my hand at the last moment and ended up flickering with me. "Only if you promise not to hold my hand."

He pauses. "Just while we're driving, right?"

My heart flutters. "Right."

"So when's the day?"

"I told him I'd do it before our appointment next Thursday, so the beginning of next week?"

"You don't sound sure."

"Tuesday. Let's do it on Tuesday."

"It's a date."

A weird, twisted, time-traveling date that could lead to my eventual death, but yes, a date.

# chapter 31

The following Monday, I'm a good little restricted driver and go home straight after class. Cameron's coming over an hour after class tomorrow and considering I'll have a camera strapped to my head when I flicker, I want to give myself plenty of cushion to make sure I end up back in my room.

Mom's in her room when I get home, which seems weird, and I start to knock on her door, but stop. I need to spend the next hour in my room. I throw myself onto my bed and study the camera. Martinez was right, it's super easy to use. I slip it onto my head and turn it on. He ordered an extension piece that allows the camera to face me, rather than out at the world like most normal people record. Who wants to film their face? Whatever. I roll my eyes at the camera before plugging it into my computer to make sure it works.

Yep. Eye rolling. Good.

I spend the rest of the hour finishing an English essay that I've been warned will not have another deadline extension, then go find Mom. Her bedroom door is still closed so I knock lightly and press my ear to the door.

"Come in."

I turn the knob and am startled by the darkness. "You okay?"

The bedside light comes on. She's lying on her side with her back to the door, hugging a pillow to her chest. Dad's pillow. "I have a headache."

I crawl onto the bed so I'm lying behind her and slide my arm over her hip. "That I understand. Can I get you anything?"

She laces her fingers through mine and squeezes like I'm the only person left in the world. Which I suppose I kind of am.

A lump catches in my throat. I squeeze back.

Her voice is so soft I almost don't hear her. "Can you stay in here with me?"

"Of course." I scoot closer so my body is pressed against hers and tuck my face against her neck. The scent of lavender fills my nostrils, sending me back to my childhood, back when she cuddled me and held me close when I was healthy—not just when I had a migraine.

We lay like that until she falls asleep, then I gently slide away, careful not to wake her. An empty glass sits on the nightstand, so I bring it to the bathroom and fill it with water. Even this small gesture feels strange—I don't think I've ever taken care of my mom, and the realization hits me hard. I've always blamed her for the distance between us, but everyone has a point at which they can no longer give. Maybe my constant refusal of her affection eventually pushed her away.

And she does still give. Anytime I've had a headache, she's right there trying to make it better. I smooth her hair off her face and press a kiss to her temple. She makes a small noise but her eyes remain closed, so I tiptoe out of the room and close the door.

◆◆◆

Tuesday. D-Day. Why am I so nervous? I've flickered more times than I can count and this isn't even the first time I've recorded myself, but this feels...I don't know...bigger. More important. More dangerous.

I assumed Cameron would meet me at my house, but when photo class ends he grabs my hand as we're walking out and tugs me away from the parking lot.

"There's no reason you have to kill half an hour at home, right?"

His hand is warm and I lean against him as we walk. "No, I guess not. So what do you have planned?"

"No plan."

I'm not sure if I believe him—this is the same person who snuck me into the zoo on our first date—but any time with him is fine by me.

We wind our way to the sandwich shop with the killer milkshakes and he holds the door open for me.

"I should have guessed."

"You've got me hooked."

I cock my head at him, wondering if he means that in more ways than one, but he's already walking to the counter to order.

"Chocolate with peanut butter?"

My stomach grumbles in response. "Sounds great."

The girl behind the counter gets to work on the shakes, and he turns to face me. "Are you nervous?"

How can he tell? "A little."

His mouth is set in a firm line as he studies me. "So you really think flickering once more could cause permanent damage?"

"Oh, that nervous." I laugh and shake my head. "Yeah, I, uh, got some other information that has me worried that the damage could start much earlier than I originally thought."

"Did Martinez tell you that?"

I drop my gaze. Telling him about Quinn isn't my business—it's Quinn's secret to keep—but I want Cameron to understand why I'm so freaked out. "My cousin Quinn. He flickers, too, and he's started having side effects like my dad."

Cameron's face pales. "How much older is he than you?"

"Two years. He said it's gotten worse in the past year."

He pulls me toward him, wrapping his arms around me so I'm tucked safely against his chest. "Do you know if he's ever double flickered?"

"He's never had surgery, but I don't know about the double flicker. I could ask."

"If I somehow caused you permanent damage..." He shakes his head against mine. His arms tighten and everything around us fades away.

"Cam, you didn't know. You were trying to help Katie."

"But if it hurt you—" his voice breaks and he presses his cheek against the top of my head.

"Um, your shake is ready."

We break apart, yanked abruptly back to reality.

She's only holding one shake.

"Where's yours?"

The corner of his mouth lifts into the half-smile that makes my heart race. "I thought we'd share. You'll be gone in a few minutes anyway, and I'm not letting you take it with you."

I smack his arm, but my hand drops to my side when he takes a sip. It's been ages since we've kissed, so sharing a straw is the next best thing.

"Mmm." He tilts it toward me and I stand on my toes to reach the straw. His eyes never leave mine as I put the straw in my mouth and I swear to god drinking a milkshake has never been more erotic.

He nods at the door. "We should get going."

I nod dumbly as he slips his hand into mine and leads me back to the newspaper. Once we're in the car, he hands me the shake.

I take a long sip and a piercing pain shoots through my eyeball. For a second I think it's a migraine, but it subsides as quickly as it came and I laugh at myself. Ice cream headache.

"You don't have to do this. I still think that if Martinez truly cared about your well-being he wouldn't ask you to risk your health."

I set the cup in the console between us. "He cares. At least I have to assume he does. This will help with the research, to figure out why my head's so messed up."

He reaches out and runs his fingers through the baby curls at the top of my neck. "You're not messed up."

I raise an eyebrow and he laughs.

"Okay, but only this part of you. The rest is perfect."

I tap the top of the shake with my finger. "I think you're drunk."

His smile softens. "Maybe a little." He turns on the car. "Ready?"

"As ready as I'll ever be." I pull the camera out of my bag and look at him. "Do not laugh at me."

He covers his mouth with his hand. "Never."

I slip it onto my head and fiddle with the settings while we pull onto the street. Once it's situated, Cameron covers my hand with his.

"You'll be okay."

I wish I believed him.

Fate is smiling on us and I flicker on the first try. No dramatics, just tingling, then heaviness and floating, then—

—I'm back in my room. I yank off the camera and plug it into the computer to copy it to my hard drive, and hit play.

You know how when you're watching a movie or TV show and the characters start crying, sometimes you cry too? Apparently the same thing happens when you watch a video of yourself. I wipe away tears I didn't realize were there, turn off the camera, and head to Mom's room.

This time I need the hug.

# chapter 32

On Thursday, I'm still not sure I want to give Martinez the video. It's too late to take back any further damage that might have happened when I flickered, but once I hand over the video, I feel like all of this will be out of my control.

I don't feel any better by the time I'm at his office. His eyes light up when he sees the contraption in my hands, and he seems to be restraining himself from snatching it away from me.

"Did it work?" No hello. No how's it going.

I nod.

He watches me, waiting.

I take a deep breath and thrust it at him before I can change my mind. The whole point of this research is to figure out my brain. If the video can help, there's no sense in me keeping it.

His brows furrow. "You don't seem happy about giving this to me."

I don't want to get into another fight, I just want this to be over. "You know I'm not comfortable with this."

I expect him to give me another speech about how I can trust him blah blah, but he retrieves a cable from a drawer and connects the camera to his tablet. In seconds my face fills the screen. Tears and all.

He glances at me out of the corner of his eye. If he comments on why I was crying I might lose it, but he doesn't say anything.

I suddenly feel very small. Insignificant. This is supposed to be about me and he's acting like he's doing me a favor.

After what feels like hours he finally looks up, a broad smile lighting his face. "Biz, this is fantastic. We did it!" There's a passion in his voice that I've never heard before and it makes me squirm on the table. It's like the room is slipping out from beneath me and no matter how desperately I cling to the walls, I'm going to fall.

"Excuse me one second." He types onto the tablet.

I peek over his shoulder. It's an email app, not notes about the video. He's never sent an email during our appointments. Add that to the list of bizarre behavior.

He finally sets the camera on the counter and swivels to face me. The eagerness in his eyes scares me.

I've made a huge mistake.

"I—I think I have to go." I slide off the table and try to squeeze past him, but he stops me with a hand on my arm. For once my body doesn't betray me with stupid butterflies and a quickening heartbeat. No, it's telling me to run.

So I do.

♦♦♦

"You look like shit." Cameron's leaning against my locker the next day, his head dipped close to mine so the guy at the next locker can't hear.

"That's because I feel like shit." I barely slept last night. I told Cameron about the appointment as soon as I left, but I spent the rest of the night worrying that this mistake is worse than I first thought.

"Are you wishing you hadn't given it to him?"

I grab my books and slam the locker shut. We fall in step as we head to first period. "Yes and no. I'm beyond freaked out that he's the person behind the emails and I don't know what he has planned, but then I remember the whole reason we started this research was to prevent me from ending up like my dad, so then I'm okay. At least for a few minutes. Then I start to panic again." As if to emphasize my point, my lungs tighten and I struggle to take a breath.

Cameron stops me with a hand on my arm. It's nothing like when Martinez tried to stop me last night. Not scary or threatening, but safe, comforting.

I resist leaning into him and look into his eyes.

"Can you get it back?"

"He copied it the second I handed it over."

"Hmm." He chews the side of his lip. "I don't know what to tell you."

I loop my arm through his and tug him down the hall. Being late isn't going to make this any better. "That's because there's nothing to say. I hate the cliché 'what's done is done' because I've always been able to go back and change things, but I don't want to rely on that anymore. I need to learn to live with my actions, good or bad, and deal with the consequences." I smile up at him. "You know, the way the rest of you have to do it."

"You sure you're ready for that? Failing tests sucks."

I laugh. "No, I'm not ready for that. Speaking of which, I have a quiz first period." I stop at the hallway that leads to my class. "See you later."

He leans toward me and my heart nearly leaps out of my chest, but his lips only make it as far as my cheek. "You betcha."

◆ ◆ ◆

I don't see Cameron again until I'm getting out of my car at the newspaper. He's leaning against Old Berta, arms crossed, looking completely irresistible.

"Do you practice that at home?"

He tilts his head. "Practice what?"

"Looking so adorable."

He runs his hand through his hair and a hint of color appears on his cheeks. "For hours."

"I figured." I nod at his car. "When did Old Berta make a comeback?"

"A couple days ago, but I don't think it'll last." He pushes off the car and beats me to the front door, which he holds open for me.

"If I didn't know you better, I'd think you're trying to woo me."

He presses a hand to his chest. "Moi?"

We're actually on time today so the table's only half full. "Sit by me?"

"I'd love to." He slips his hand into mine as we make the short walk to our seats.

Shelly beams at us from the end of the table. "Hi, guys."

I drop my camera onto the table and sit, my eyes never leaving Shelly. She's someone I would describe as high-energy—always moving, and if she's sitting, always fidgeting—but she is literally bouncing on the balls of her feet. She hasn't stopped smiling since we arrived and her eyes are even brighter than normal.

Kaya scowls at Cameron before taking Cam's seat at the other end of the table. Apparently our carpool bond is gone.

Shelly begins class by showing us samples of portfolios, but as she clicks through the slides, her gaze bounces around the room. We haven't had a new assignment in weeks and I can't help but wonder if it's because she's looking for another job and doesn't have time to prep for class, or if she no longer cares about us. True, we're supposed to be working on our portfolio, but I have other classes with big projects for the end of the year and those teachers still make us do regular homework. But Shelly isn't exactly a real teacher, so maybe the school will just give us all As to make up for everything we've been through this year.

Cameron's hand drifts to mine and he laces our fingers together, his thumb tracing a lazy loop across my skin. After that I don't hear another word Shelly says.

When she dismisses class and the kids around us get up to leave, Cameron doesn't move. Instead he shifts in his chair so he's facing me. "Do you have plans later?"

I glance at our hands for the millionth time and smile. "That depends."

"On what?"

"If you're finally asking me out."

He smiles his half smile. "I am."

"Then no, I don't."

He shakes his head. "You kill me, you know that, right?"

I stand, tugging him to his feet. "What did you have in mind?"

He doesn't answer until we're outside. "It's a surprise."

I still have no idea what he has planned when he picks me up that evening.

He drives us on a meandering route through town. "My dad hinted that I might get their car as a graduation present, but I'm not holding my breath."

My blood runs cold. The last time I was in his dad's car was the day Katie died. Cameron thought I was agreeing to flicker for the third time when really I just didn't want to be left behind at their house. I shake off the memory. "You're not going to give me a hint about where we're going?"

"One hint. There's food."

I lean my head back and close my eyes. "That's all I need to know."

"You're no fun."

I peek at him out of the corner of my eye. He's sticking out his lower lip like a two-year old. "Okay, fine." I pull on his arm, making us swerve. "Pleeeeease tell me where we're going. I can't stand the suspense one more minute."

He straightens his shoulders and smiles. "That's more like it. I'm not telling yet, but we're almost there."

We're nearing the land of the delicious milkshakes. I don't think they're open for dinner, but I'm not about to question his plan. Minutes later, he pulls into a parking lot next to a low brick building covered in strings of white lights. I start to open my door but he stops me.

"Be patient." He runs around the car and opens my door, holding out a hand.

I take it, suddenly nervous. With everything that's happened I wasn't sure if we could start over, but judging by the bass line my heart is pounding out as we approach the entrance, this definitely feels like a first date. Italian music plays from tiny speakers above the door and red-checkered cloths cover the tables. A man in a suit greets us at the door. Cameron tells him his last name and we're whisked to the only empty table, which happens to be in the front window.

"Impressive."

He shrugs, but a slow smile shows how pleased he is. "I figured it's time we step it up from paper-wrapped cheeseburgers and orange soda in disposable cups."

"What's wrong with orange soda?"

"Nothing, it's the paper cups I don't like."

Like magic, a waiter appears with two glasses of orange carbonation. I take a sip. It is better out of a glass. "Doubly impressive."

"This bodes well for me that you're so easily impressed."

I laugh, nearly shooting soda out of my nose. My eyes widen. "What else do you have planned?"

The corner of his mouth lifts. "Nothing in particular, I just wanted to see soda come out of your nose."

I dip my finger in my glass and flick it at him, then quickly look around. But I don't really care who's watching. The dark cloud that's shadowed my life seems to lift when Cameron is near me and it's like I can finally breathe again. Even so, a food fight in an adult restaurant probably isn't what he had in mind for our romantic date. I wipe my hand on my napkin. "Sorry."

A couple drops hit his cheek, so he wipes them with a finger and licks it off, before sticking his finger into his glass and flicking it at me. "I'm not."

I burst out laughing and several people turn our way. "You win this round."

He waggles his brows. "I'm already planning for round two."

And I'm blushing.

The meal passes too quickly. I want to sit across from him for the rest of the night, watching the way his eyes light up when he tells a story, but when he grabs my hand and leans forward to kiss my knuckles I decide maybe sitting closer to him would be a much better idea.

When we're finally outside, I start plotting how to kiss him. Our first kiss was completely spontaneous and perfect and my hands start sweating just thinking about how I could top it, but now we've stopped walking and Cameron is looking down at me with the half-smile that I love.

"You okay?"

"Me?" My voice comes out a squeak. "Never better."

"I can hear you arguing with yourself."

Our old joke. I know he can't actually hear what I'm thinking, but heat creeps up my cheeks anyway. Although, the little voice insists, if I tell him we could get past this hesitation. "About that."

He raises a brow.

"I was just wondering..." Nerves tumble over my stomach and I take a quick breath. His gaze dips from my eyes to my lips and I close my eyes, steeling myself to just go for it, but he beats me to it. His hands are on my jawline, cradling my face, and his breath whispers over my skin.

"Shh."

My eyes flutter open as his lips press against mine and all the nervousness melts out of me. I slide my arms around his waist, slipping my hands inside his jacket, pulling him closer.

His kiss is cautious, unhurried, like it's perfectly natural for us to be kissing in the middle of the sidewalk. I part my lips and his tongue lightly touches mine, but then he moves his mouth over my cheek, my eyes, and finally my ear. "We should probably press pause until we're not on display." He nods over my shoulder and I twist my head so I can see without moving my arms from around him. We're standing in front of the very large window of a very busy restaurant filled with people who are all watching us.

I bury my face in his shoulder. "Omigod."

"Is that Shelly?"

I lift my head. "Where?"

"Don't turn around yet, but at a table inside. Not by the window."

I wait a beat, then pull away and pretend to adjust my jacket in the window's reflection.

"Subtle."

I scan the restaurant for Shelly's dark hair. "We both know that's not my—No way." That can't be right. I narrow my eyes and it's totally him.

"What?"

"Martinez is in there."

"Where?"

"At a table by the—oh shit."

"That's him with Shelly?"

"Yes." I forget that Cameron only met Martinez right after my surgery. At the time he was so overwhelmed with finding out Katie was alive and learning about me flickering, plus my whole brain surgery slash almost dying situation, that it's no wonder he doesn't recognize him.

"What are they doing together?"

A million reasons fly through my mind but none of them make sense. Neither does the stab of jealousy that pierces my heart. They're both adults. They're allowed to go to dinner—and do whatever else goes with dinner when you're an adult—with whomever they please. As far as Martinez knows, our kiss never happened, and even if it did, he's entitled to date anyone he wants. But why Shelly? I understand why she'd be interested in him, but something doesn't feel right about them being together. I grab Cameron's hand and tug him away from the window. "Let's go."

"You're not telling me something."

"I don't know what's going on." I'm walking faster, the excitement from our kiss just moments ago shattered by what I can only describe as a feeling of betrayal.

"You're losing me."

I stop abruptly. "I'm sorry. Everything's hitting me all at once. My concerns about trusting Martinez, plus the emails and whatever the hell they're supposed to mean. I feel like all the pieces are falling into place but I can't for the life of me figure out the answer."

"What can I do?" He rubs his hand up and down my arm and I'm grateful he didn't try to fix this with a hug. I'm so wound up I think I might explode if I'm confined right now.

"Figure out what the hell Martinez and Shelly are up to and if they're behind the emails." I hadn't linked Shelly to the emails until the words left my mouth, and it feels like the ground drops out from beneath me. But this theory makes other pieces fall into place. Especially her abnormal excitement in class today—the day after I gave the new video to Martinez.

"Do you really think she could be a part of that?"

I hang my head. My feet seem separate from my body. I see them standing on the sidewalk, toe to toe with Cameron's, but it's like I'm looking down at myself from ten feet in the air. Like this isn't really happening to me. "Can we go?"

He loops his arm through mine and we fall into step the rest of the way to his car. He opens my door and pauses with his arm on the top of the door. He bites his lip, his dark eyes concerned. "Do you want me to bring you home?"

The last thing I want is to sit in my room by myself and worry about this, but the mood from earlier is broken. "Not really, but I don't think I'll be good company."

He lifts his hand to touch my cheek, then lets it drop to his side. "You're always good company. But if you don't want to stay out, I understand."

"No, that's not what I meant." I touch the side of his jaw and the tension in his face relaxes. "I don't think I'll be able to stop thinking about all this, but," I raise my eyebrows, "if you're up for a challenge..."

He takes a step closer so we're almost touching. "Name it."

"I challenge you to make me forget, even if just for a little—"

His mouth is on mine before I can finish my sentence.

The hesitation from before is gone and it's like the months we were apart never happened. I rise to my toes so I can wrap my arms around his neck, and he tightens his grip around my waist so we're pressed against each other. He deepens the kiss and my fingers tangle into his hair, making him moan softly. He breaks the kiss but doesn't move his head. "This still isn't private enough."

My stomach does a flip at the thought of why we need more privacy, but I'm not ready to stop. "Mm-hmm." My fingers are still locked in his hair so I pull him closer to kiss him, taste him, breathe him in. If I can fill all my senses with him maybe I'll be able to forget everything else.

He turns us so my back is against the car and presses so hard against me that it nearly takes my breath away. I run my hands down his back, trying to pull him still closer, and his hands move from my face down my neck, exploring every inch of me. His shirt magically comes untucked and I slide my hands inside, the fire in my belly spreading to every nerve ending. He gasps at my touch, then grows bolder, reaching under the hem of my shirt to touch me, and now it's my turn to gasp. I wrap a leg around his, silently urging him to throw me onto the car and have his way with me. He bends his knees, lowering his body so all the important parts hit exactly where they're supposed to, and my mind spins. All I know, all I want, is Cameron.

A car near us honks as someone locks it, jolting us back to reality.

I lean my head against his shoulder, lowering my foot to the ground. "Jesus."

"You can call me Cam."

I snort.

"Do I win?"

I nod against his chest. "You could say that."

He leans against me until our breathing—and other things—returns to normal, and I slide into the passenger seat.

Parked in front of my house, our goodnight kiss is tamer than the one in the parking lot.

"I loved our date. Thank you."

He lowers his head to kiss my neck. "There's more where that came from."

"I'm holding you to that." I finally disentangle myself and head slowly to the house. The chill I expect to wash over me, the one I used to feel when leaving his car after a hot date, never comes. Instead it's like his arms are still wrapped around me, holding me close.

# chapter 33

By the next morning, all that's left of my earlier panic is the vague sensation that I should be worried about something. And not just one something, lots of things. Because not only am I confused about Martinez and Shelly and whatever the hell is going on between them, but I totally forgot that Turner's trial starts on Monday.

In two days.

I knew it was coming, but I'd only been thinking of it in terms of my portfolio. The part about having to go to the courthouse and physically see him and the spectacle that I'm sure will be happening outside—I'd somehow blocked all that out.

Mom finds me moping in the living room. She pauses before joining me on the couch, then sits in the middle next to me, careful not to sit in Dad's spot on the opposite end. She opens and closes her mouth several times, and finally sighs, folding her hands in her lap. "I'm not good at this."

"That bad?"

She smiles on reflex, but it sinks into a frown. "No. I just... We've never really shared what we're thinking. I want to, but I don't know how I'm supposed to start."

I silently thank Quinn for his insistence that I talk to her. "Just spit it out. That's usually the easiest way."

"Okay." She takes a breath and shifts so she's facing me. "Are you planning to go to Mr. Turner's trial? Because if you are and you'd like me to go with you, I will."

"You don't have to miss work for that."

She shakes her head. "I'm sure half the town will be there. And I'd like to support the Joneses."

"Of course." In the back of my mind I knew Cameron's family would be there, but I hadn't pictured them actually walking up the steps of the courthouse, past the cameras and reporters, and sitting just feet away from the man who tormented their daughter to the point that she killed herself. "Have you talked to them?"

"Just briefly. Mrs. Jones asked that we sit with them. I think they need all the moral support they can get."

I touch her hand. The gesture feels awkward, but maybe it will get easier with time. "That's very thoughtful of you."

She covers my hand with her other one. "I want to be there for you, too. I know that because of the flickering you were technically never kidnapped, but it will be hard for you to see him in person."

"Thanks, Mom. I am freaking out a little." Maybe she's not as out of touch as I think.

"I'll be by your side for as long as you want me there. And if you decide you can't stay, I'll leave with you, too." Tears shine in her eyes.

I drag my free hand across my eyes. "I want to be there for Cam and his parents, and the other kidnapped girls, too, but every time I think about seeing him, about sharing the same oxygen, I get all panicky inside." I press my fist against my chest, willing the knot to loosen, but it's not moving.

"No one's forcing you to do anything. If we get there and you realize you can't do it, just say the word." She wraps her arms around my shoulders and pulls me into a hug.

I bury my face in her shoulder like I used to when I was little and hope her strength will be enough to get me through the next few days.

◆◆◆

It turns out the first day of a trial is filled with motions and jury selection, none of which the public is allowed to watch, so Mom and I are huddled with Cameron and his parents around the corner from the courthouse. The TV news vans stationed across from the front steps didn't notice them when they arrived, and we figured the longer they go unnoticed, the better.

As lunchtime approaches, men and women in suits begin filing out of the courthouse and the reporters swarm. Mr. Jones rests a hand on Mom's shoulder. "That's our cue to sneak off for lunch. In a few minutes all the local places will be packed."

We beat the crowd to a sandwich shop around the corner, and Cameron and I lag near the entrance while our parents order. Cameron scratches the back of his neck. "Do you think it will start today?"

"I have no idea. I've heard of it taking a long time to pick a jury in cases where everyone in town already has an opinion. I can't imagine anyone who lives here not already deciding that Turner is guilty."

Mrs. Jones waves at us. "Kids, you need to order quickly."

We join them at the counter and I order a boring turkey on wheat. The menu covers the entire length of the wall and based on the number of people marching down the sidewalk I'd never decide on something else in time.

"Make that two," Cameron says. We move toward the end of the counter and stand beneath a sign that reads 'Pick Up.' Mom's already grabbed a booth along the wall. It's built for four people, but considering the restaurant will soon be standing-room only, it'll have to do. When our food's ready, I squeeze in next to Mom, and keep sliding so Cameron can fit next to me. He picks up his drink and takes a sip, but leaves his sandwich untouched.

I lean close so his parents don't hear me. "You're not eating?"

He shakes his head and touches his belly, then lets his hand fall onto my thigh. "There's too much in my head."

I poke my half-eaten sandwich, no longer hungry. I've kept my mind off why we're here by focusing on him and his parents, but now that we've stopped moving it's crashing down all around me. We didn't see Turner this morning because, as Mr. Jones explained, the defendant isn't present for jury selection, and the anticipation is growing worse with each passing hour.

Mom makes small talk with Cameron's parents about the end of the school year. "I can't imagine what it will be like when Biz goes away to college in the fall. I haven't been alone since before her father and I were married."

Their faces pale, and I realize where their minds have gone. When Cameron leaves for college, they'll still have each other, but they'll be alone in a different way. They should have had another child at home for five more years.

Mom's hand flutters to her mouth. "I'm sorry. Here I am yammering on about myself when..." she trails off, and Mrs. Jones catches Mom's hand.

"It's okay. You've suffered your own loss. Let's not start comparing." She smiles at us. "There are two wonderful children here who need our love and support."

Mr. Jones glances at the door. "Speaking of support, we might want to get out of here. It looks like the press has arrived."

I force down another bite and we slide out of the booth, pausing long enough for the reporters to study the menu. Once their backs are to us, we make a beeline for the door.

Mr. Jones turns in the opposite direction of the courthouse. "I could use a walk. Sound good?"

Mom falls in step alongside them, but Cameron grabs my hand, holding me back. "We'll meet you there."

They study us as if unsure how much support their children need at this moment.

I wave them off. "We'll be fine. Go." I look up at Cameron. "We really should get out of here before they notice you."

"I know, I just wanted a few minutes alone with you." He starts walking the same direction as our parents, but slowly enough that we'll never catch up to them. "I'm having a hard time believing the trial is here. Ever since the day we found out Katie was alive, all I wanted was to see Turner behind bars. Then after she died..." his hand tightens on mind and I press myself closer to his side. "When I think back to how he looked me in the face in class, day after day, when all that time he had her. I wished he'd never been arrested so I could kill him myself."

My mouth falls open. I understand hating Turner but I never imagined Cameron would actually take matters into his own hands. "Would you really?"

His head jerks toward me like he forgot I was here. "What? No, not really. But that doesn't mean I haven't fantasized about it."

I remember waking up in the back of Turner's van, bound and gagged like a pig. And that was only ten minutes of my life. Katie was with him for four years.

"But now that the day is finally here and we're going to see him, all I want to do is run." He stops near an alley and looks down at me, tears in his eyes. "I don't want to see him, Biz. I don't want to look at him and imagine all the things he did to Katie. I can't do it."

I reach up and touch his face. A tear wets my fingers. I pull his face toward mine and press a kiss to his lips, then another to his jaw. "You can do this. Katie needs you to be here for her."

A sob breaks free and he pulls me close. I stroke his hair, murmuring unintelligible sounds until he quiets. "I'm so glad you're here."

I'm still not one hundred percent sure that I want to be here—heck, I'm not even twenty percent sure—but if it helps Cameron, I'll do it. "Are you ready to head back?"

He wipes his eyes on his shirt sleeve and cracks a smile. "Sorry. I guess that kind of built up."

I poke his chest. "Your secret's safe with me."

The heaviness lifts on the walk back to the courthouse, but as soon as we round the corner it's back in full force. A familiar-looking reporter standing near a news van at the end of the row glances at us, then does a double take before elbowing her cameraman.

"Oh shit, Cam, we've gotta go."

"Hey! Excuse me!" She runs surprisingly fast considering the height of her heels, and the camera is already on her guy's shoulder, filming our panicked escape. Other reporters turn our way but she seems to be the only one who recognizes Cameron as one of the victim's family. Of the victim who killed herself.

We sprint around the corner, weaving through government employees having a final smoke before returning to work and random people from town waiting for the show to begin. The doors to the courthouse are in sight when a police car pulls to a stop at the curb. Cameron stops so suddenly I slam into his back, nearly knocking him over.

"It's him." Cameron's face pales as his gaze locks on the backseat of the cop car.

Adding to the surreal scene: Officers Buster and Reece—the cops who arrested me—are in the front seat. My focus bounces between them and Turner while three uniformed men hustle down the courthouse steps to the car. Two fall back and scan the crowd while the third, the one in front, opens the back door of the car and reaches inside.

Turner steps into the sunlight. He's wearing the same tweed jacket and slacks he used to wear in class, and if it weren't for the bizarre setting I'd think he's here to give a lecture. He lifts both hands to shield his eyes and I realize they're cuffed in front of him. His eyes dart around the crowd, not focusing on anyone, and I'm grateful he doesn't see us.

But Cameron sees him. Before I realize what's happening, Cameron leaves my side and charges at Turner. If he were running Buster and Reece might have seen him, but so many people press forward when Turner appears that no one notices the teenager with both hands fisted until he's lunging for Turner. One punch lands squarely on Turner's jaw before two of the uniformed men grab Cameron.

"You killed her! You killed Katie!" Fresh tears stream down Cameron's face. He tries to jerk his arms free, but the guards have a firm grip. "I hope you rot in prison. I used to hope they'd kill you but you deserve whatever they do to you in jail."

Aside from clenching and unclenching his jaw, Turner shows no reaction until Cameron stops screaming. He tries to take a step forward but he's held back by the guard. "Cameron, I loved Katie like a daughter. You have to believe me. I never wanted anything to happen—"

"You loved her? You destroyed her!" Cameron lunges at him again just as his dad pushes through the crowd.

"Cameron, stop. Don't waste your breath on this...this... monster." He faces Turner and for a moment I'm afraid there aren't enough police to hold him back. "You don't get to speak to us. Not ever."

"I never meant for her to get hurt. She was the special one—" His erratic gaze lands on me and it's like everything slows down. He tries to take a step toward me, his expression calm, but the guard is still holding him. "Biz. You came."

He never kidnapped me.

It didn't happen.

I take a step back but there are too many people. I can't escape. I lock eyes with Cameron but he's still being restrained, so I spin around and slam into a solid chest. Strong hands grab my arms, keeping me from falling. I look up and lock eyes with Buster.

The crease in his forehead deepens and my stomach knots, preparing for a lecture, but his grip on my arms loosen and the creases in his face relax. "Are you okay?"

I nod, not sure what to think of this Buster who doesn't glower and growl at me.

"You staying out of trouble?"

"Y-yes. I'm volunteering at the hospital."

He nods once, then moves past me, toward Turner.

I look around for Cameron, but the crowd has filled the space around the cop car. My chest constricts, making it hard to breathe.

I need to find someone safe.

I need to find Mom.

I push through elbows and shoulders until I finally spot her beyond the crowd, standing with Mrs. Jones near the foot of the courthouse steps. I shove past people until I'm at her side and throw myself into her arms. She strokes my hair and in that moment it's like none of it happened. But of course it did. Just because I flickered doesn't mean I didn't experience it. I'll live with the memory of being kidnapped for the rest of my life, just like I'll never fully erase the memory of kissing Martinez. Just because I undo something doesn't mean I can forget.

The low murmur in the crowd grows louder, and I look up as Turner passes, flanked by the three uniformed guards. A man grabs at Turner's arm, revealing a bullet-proof vest beneath his jacket. Several women yell at him as he passes but he doesn't flinch. It's like he doesn't hear them.

Cameron and his dad join us at the foot of the stairs. I step away from Mom and wrap an arm around his waist. "I don't think I can go inside." The two Turners I know refuse to meld into the handcuffed man climbing the steps.

"Are you sure?"

"I'll wait out here. Text me if you really need me in there." I'm afraid he'll be upset, but the panic at being in the same room with Turner outweighs anything else right now. "Maybe tomorrow will be easier." Even as I say it, I know I'll never step inside that courtroom. I don't need to hear the things he did to those girls. Katie already told me.

Mr. Jones rests a hand on Cameron's shoulder. "We need to get inside."

Cameron brushes his lips over my temple. "You sure you'll be okay out here?" He juts his chin at the herd of news vans across the street. "They might attack once you're alone."

I laugh. "I dare them to try." I squeeze him tightly. "Good luck."

He moves to his mom's side and grabs her hand, and together the three of them make their way up the steps.

Mom gives me another hug. "Do you want me to stay out here with you?"

"No, go with them. They need all the support they can get."

Her gaze bounces between me and their quickly retreating backs.

"Go, before all the seats are taken."

"Okay, I...I love you."

The statement surprises me. It's not something she says often and when she does, it comes out forced. But not today. Today I can feel her concern for me in her touch and her words.

"I love you, too."

I don't watch her go inside. Instead I sit on the bottom step, daring the reporters to attack.

# chapter 34

It doesn't take long. A tall thin man with short dark hair approaches a few minutes after the doors to the courthouse close. I straighten my shoulders, preparing myself for the worst, but he doesn't rush at me with a microphone. Instead he saunters over and nods at the spot next to me on the step.

"May I?"

"Sure?"

"Why didn't you go inside?"

I nod at his cohorts across the street. "What, you have a bet going or something?"

"No, but they are curious. I told them we'd never find out if we ran at you like a pack of banshees, so I volunteered."

I smirk. "Brave man."

He mirrors my expression. "Oh yeah."

I try to come up with a witty response, but I don't have the energy for it. He's being respectful so I decide to throw him a bone. "Turner was my teacher. My friend's—my boyfriend's—sister is the one who killed herself."

He stiffens, but quickly masks any surprise he feels. "Katie."

Her name doesn't sound grotesque coming from him, not like it did from the reporter who hounded Katie before her death. "Yeah."

He studies his fingernails. "So why are you out here?"

"I planned to go in but when I saw him getting out of the car..." I shake my head. Small bits of information are one thing. A full confession is not happening.

"Did you like him as a teacher?"

I nod. "His was my favorite class. Still is." He cocks his head. Apparently he hasn't stored away that piece of information. "Photography. Well, photojournalism, but I'm better at the taking-pictures part."

"No kidding. So you want to be one of us?" He lifts his finger to point at the reporters, but does it in a way that doesn't look like he's pointing. To anyone watching us it's just a casual gesture, part of the conversation.

I look at him full on for the first time since he sat down. "I don't know if I have it in me. I've had some pictures published but this," my pointing is far less subtle, "isn't what I want to do."

"We're not all ambulance chasers. Some of us, present company included, are actually quite civilized." He pretends to straighten a nonexistent tie and I laugh. I actually laugh.

"How long have you been schmoozing people?"

"Schmoozing? Is that what you think I'm doing?"

I raise an eyebrow at him.

"Okay, maybe a little, but I'm genuinely interested in people and I like to get to know them. I graduated from State a few years ago but I've been pestering strangers since my sophomore year of college."

"Practice does make perfect."

He gasps, but the shocked expression doesn't last long. He nudges me with his elbow. "You'll do fine in this business. It's the creampuffs who don't make it past the first month."

"Thanks, I think."

"One last question?"

"Could I stop you?"

He smiles. "No." He nods at the empty space next to me. "If you're a photographer, as you claim, why don't you have your camera at the biggest trial of the year?"

"It's in the car."

"Not good enough." He pushes himself to his feet and holds out a hand. I take it, and he pulls me up. "If you're going to spend the afternoon out here with us, you may as well look the part." He winks. "I might even give you a head start when Turner leaves the courthouse."

My head spins at the mention of his name and I can feel the blood drain from my face.

"Are you okay?"

I shake off the nausea that threatens to pitch me back onto the steps. "I'm fine. Are you really going to give me a head start?"

He laughs. "I will, but I can't make promises about the rest of them. I wasn't kidding when I called them a pack of banshees."

I follow him down to the sidewalk, careful to place each foot precisely on a step. "Thanks for the pep talk. I really appreciate it."

He holds out both hands, one of which has a business card.

I cross hands to shake one and take the card with the other. "What's this for?"

"We're always looking for interns, that sort of thing. Shoot me an email when you're ready."

I scan the card. He's from one of the big-city papers that ran the fox photo last fall. "You guys ran my first popular photo."

He raises an eyebrow.

"The fox and the baby duck."

He takes a step back. "You're the fox girl?" Surprise and what looks like a hint of admiration brighten his face, and I admit it feels good to be known as something other than a freak.

"The one and only."

"Then I imagine we'll be in touch. Now go get your camera and don't make this afternoon a waste of time."

I give him a mock salute. "Yes, sir!"

My enthusiasm fades after three hours on the hard steps, but as soon as the courthouse doors open, I'm on my feet, camera ready. When Turner steps into the fading sunlight, I take a deep breath and press the button. *Click-click-click.* I take another breath and step closer, determined to get the shot. A man in a suit guides Turner by the elbow as they ease their way down the steps. Toward me.

The clouds shift, opening a shaft of light that blinds him. It's the perfect shot. Light and shadow, right there on his face. Except he's not looking at me. He takes another step down and the light shifts. If he comes any closer the shot will be gone.

All it will take is something to make him look up.

A noise.

A car horn.

Anything.

"Turner!" I shout.

With that one word I feel like I've transformed from a kid who likes to take pictures to an actual photographer. He looks right at me and I hold down the button until the camera whines in protest.

Then I turn and run.

Mom finds me at the car. Cameron and his parents are right behind her, and I hurry to Cameron's side. "How was it?"

He shakes his head, eyes heavy. "Awful. It was just a bunch of preliminary stuff, but even that was horrible. They did the opening statements and if you didn't know the truth, his lawyer would have you thinking this was all just a big misunderstanding."

"I should have been there for you."

He touches his heart. "You were."

A sarcastic comment leaps to my tongue, but I hold it back. The weariness on all their faces tells me I had the far easier afternoon and joking right now would be a huge mistake.

He touches my camera bag resting on the hood of the car. "Did you get the shot you needed?"

I nod, trying to contain my excitement. "It's exactly what I need for my portfolio."

He pulls me into a hug. "I'm glad. Now let's get the hell out of here."

◆ ◆ ◆

That night I send the three best shots to the *Chronicle*, but part of me doesn't care if they get published. My talk with the reporter at the courthouse has given me a burst of determination and I feel like nothing can hold me back from what I want.

But that's not the only thing motivating me.

Something inside me changed when I saw Turner through my camera lens. It's like whatever connection we had has been severed and he's no longer intrinsically linked to photography in my mind. Now when I'm framing a shot, instead of his voice in my head, I hear my own.

# chapter 35

Mom usually wakes me up by knocking on the door, then waiting a minute for me to groan before slowly opening the door. Not today. This morning she knocks much harder than normal, startling me from sleep, and bursts into the room and stands over me, waving her tablet. "You need to see this."

"Good morning?"

She paces the length of the bed.

I push up on an elbow. "Mom, what's going on?"

"This is...this...I don't even know what to say." She stops and stares at the screen, then hands it to me.

It's the *Chronicle* website. I scan the headlines for whatever it is that's completely freaked out Mom and notice my picture of Turner with a story about the trial. "The picture?" She shakes her head and I sigh. It's too early for a game of I-Spy. I scroll down and that's when I see it. The lead headline for the science section:

> Neurologist Claims Link Between Epilepsy and Time Travel

"What?!"

"Keep reading."

> A local neurologist claims he's discovered a connection between what's traditionally understood as epilepsy and a relatively unknown scientific solution first discovered by Kurt Gödel, which, when combined with a specific strobe

effect of sunlight, causes time travel.

Dr. Ricardo Martinez has not revealed his subject, but writes at length about his research methods, initial findings, and the risks involved with the alleged time travel. Martinez describes Patient X's condition as "founded in solid science" but admits that his findings will be hard for the scientific community to accept.

"I think I'm going to be sick." I fling the tablet to the end of the bed, as if putting space between it and me will somehow make the article less real.

Mom sits on the edge of the bed. "I feel like I should have asked this months ago, but did he sign a confidentiality agreement?"

"I remember talking about it, but I don't think we ever did. He smooth-talked me into trusting him like he always does." How could I be so stupid? That final video somehow had the evidence he needed to finish this paper that he— "Did this say he's published a paper in a journal or something like that?"

"No. Just the interview." She looks dazed, like this might be the final straw that's pushed her over the edge. She's held it together better than I expected since Dad died, and she was rock solid at the courthouse yesterday, but now she seems numb.

"How could he do this to me?" This betrayal is far deeper than anything I've ever experienced. Maybe even more than with Turner, because I've never believed that Turner intended to hurt me—I just got in the way. But Martinez...He set out from the beginning to use me to help his career. "All the crap he fed me about wanting what's best for me and wanting to save my life was just a lie to get me to do his stupid experiments."

Mom's eyes widen. "Did he make you do something you weren't comfortable with?"

Ha, if she only knew. "Not really. He asked me to record myself again last week and when I gave him the recording, he was more excited than I've ever seen him. I didn't want to do it and I guess I should have listened to my instincts." I shake my head. "What's that saying about hindsight?"

"It's twenty twenty."

"Yeah. Of all the times I've flickered to undo stupid crap that I've done, this is the one where I really should have gone back."

Mom rests her hand on mine. "I'm glad you didn't."

"How can you say that? You want people to find out about me?"

"No, but you've had an advantage most people don't, and that advantage has made it more difficult for you to learn to face the consequences of your actions head on." She squeezes my hand. "Everyone else has to live with their stupid decisions."

"I've been thinking about that a lot lately. As awesome as it's been to go back and change things, I don't want to end up like Dad."

She studies me, her eyes watering. "He'd be very happy to hear you say that. His biggest regret was not being there more for you."

"What are you talking about? He's the one who was always there." As soon as I say it I realize I'm basically telling her she's never been there for me. "I mean, you are, too, obviously. But he shouldn't have felt that way."

She averts her gaze. "Is that how you feel? That I haven't been there for you?"

What's the saying? Speak now or forever hold your peace? This moment might never happen again and if I'm not honest now, we may never be able to move past it. "Maybe sometimes, but I understand it. You had to take care of Dad. He needed you."

"Yes, but you're my daughter. You need me, too."

"Yeah." Now that I've admitted it, I don't know where to go from here.

"Biz, I don't ever want you to feel like you can't be honest with me, whether it's about school or boys or us. You're all I've got and I want to help you if I can." She picks up the tablet and scans the article again. "You shouldn't have to deal with this alone."

"He must have broken some kind of law by talking to the press about me without my consent."

"You aren't mentioned by name so he's probably protected. Aside from confronting him, I don't know if there's anything you can do."

"Except hope no one figures out that it's me."

She rests the tablet on her leg and looks at me. "How many people know he's your doctor?"

"Besides my close friends, I don't think very many. Kids at school know I had brain surgery but it's not like they care about who did the operation."

"Then I think your best option is to distance yourself from him. Stop the research immediately."

I push myself into a sitting position. "I don't think I can be in the same room as him without punching him in the face."

Mom laughs. "I think telling him off will be enough. Although it would be nice to see that perfect face a little messed up."

I swat her arm. "Mom!"

"What? I'm not blind."

A giggle escapes me, but the euphoria is short-lived. That perfect face blabbed to the world about me and now it's just a matter of time before my secret is out.

"Are you planning to go to the courthouse again today?"

I shake my head. "I wanted to, but seeing Turner was harder than I expected and since I got the photos I need for my project," I hold up the tablet, "and got one published, I think I'll just go to school." I asked Cameron if he wanted me to go, but he doesn't want to be there either. As he said, there's no point in both of us being miserable.

"Okay. I'll let you get ready." She tousles the hair on the top of my head—there's almost enough hair to tousle!—and leaves me with the tablet. I scan the article again and nearly throw up. I don't know how I missed it the first time.

It's written by Shelly Graham.

# chapter 36

Why?

Why? Why? Why?

I can understand Martinez, but what motivation did Shelly have to abuse my trust? Is that why she was always asking personal questions? To gain my trust? I can't believe she really thought I'd tell her my secret.

Oh, shit. She knows my secret.

Double shit. The entire world knows my secret.

Or if they don't now, they will.

The only good thing that could come from this is if Martinez actually figured out why I flicker. I skim the article, but all it talks about is the things that happen to my body before I flicker, and the side effects afterward. And, obviously, the flickering. I can't figure out what role Shelly played in all this, but her name's next to his so as of this moment, I hate her, too.

My phone buzzes but I ignore it.

I read the article more closely but the explanation I've been so desperate to find, the reason I risked my health making stupid videos, isn't there. Martinez hasn't solved my brain. And if I have any say in the matter, he never will.

My phone buzzes again, so I grab it from my nightstand.

Amelia: OMG. Have you seen the paper?

Me: Yes.

Amelia: Name the time and place.
Me: We are not killing him.
Amelia: How about a friendly game of meet my bat?
Me: I wish.
Amelia: What are you gonna do?
Me: Throw up.
Amelia: On him?

I laugh.

Me: If only. The Biz Show is officially cancelled.
Amelia: But no bodily harm?
Me: Not right now.
Amelia: Does Cam know? Cuz he might sacrifice Old Berta to take out the doc.
Me: No!
Amelia: I'm just saying.
Me: I have to get ready. See you soon.
Amelia: I'll bring my bat.

I toss my phone onto the bed and throw on clothes before sending a text to Quinn.

Me: When you get up, Google Martinez, then call me.

Then Cameron.

Me: I saw the paper. Don't worry about me right now. Good luck today. Maybe you'll get to punch Turner again. xoxo.

My phone rings midway through Trig class. I have it on silent so Bishop doesn't hear it, but when it doesn't stop vibrating after five solid minutes, I raise my hand and ask to use the bathroom.

It's Quinn.

I breathe out a sigh of relief. As much as Mom and Amelia want to help, Quinn is the only one who can understand the terror of the world finding out our secret. "Hey."

"What the ever-loving—"

"First, no one knows about you so you're safe."

"I don't care about that right now. How could he betray you like that? I thought he took an oath. Does that mean nothing to him?" He's yelling so loud it hurts my ear.

"I'm gonna go with no."

"How can you be so calm?"

"I'm not calm. I'm freaking out. But I'm in the hall at school and we're not supposed to use our phones during class so I have to keep my voice down."

His voice lowers several decibels. "Sorry. What are you going to do?"

I pace a small circle in front of a row of lockers. "I don't think there's anything I can do. If I file a complaint, I'll reveal my identity. At least right now no one knows the paper is about me."

"Right now."

"Yeah."

"This sucks."

"Amelia wants to beat him up with a baseball bat."

"I knew I liked her."

"Even my mom suggested punching him."

He barks out a laugh. "Go, Mom!"

"She also mentioned that Martinez was cute, which was beyond weird."

He pauses. "How are you doing? Since your dad, I mean."

I shrug, even though he can't see me.

"That good?"

"I don't know how to explain it. Nothing about my day-to-day life has changed, but everything has changed. I still can't believe I'm never going to talk to him again. I could really use his logical mind to figure out this nightmare."

"I'm sorry."

"Will I ever get used to him being gone?"

"Used to? No. Eventually you'll stop thinking about him like he's still around, but then you'll feel bad that you're not thinking about him as much as you used to. It's an endless cycle."

"You'll be happy to know Mom and I are talking more."

"That does make me happy. But what about this paper? You're really not going to do anything?"

"Besides rip Martinez a new one? No."

"Can you do me a favor?"

"What?"

"Wear that head camera thing when you do it."

I laugh far too loud for an unauthorized conversation in the hallway. "I've gotta go."

"Keep me posted. And Biz?"

"Yeah?"

"Please consider the camera."

I hang up and head back to class. No one pays me any attention when I return to my seat, and I have to wonder how much longer that will last. Medical papers, no matter how earth-shattering, aren't standard reading for kids my age, but all it takes is one overly-ambitious honors student to start talking and my entire world will fall apart.

By the end of the day, I'm a complete wreck. Anxiety has burrowed so far into me that I'm not sure I'll ever be able to exhale. I've scoured the internet for any mention of Martinez and the article, but while it's gotten a lot of attention, most of the comments seems to question Martinez's research rather than wonder about his anonymous subject. Without an actual patient backing up his claims, the general public has come to the conclusion that perhaps the good doctor is crazy.

Which suits me just fine.

After school, Amelia comes over armed with enough snacks and soda to choke a horse. If horses ate chips, chocolate, and Twizzlers.

I eye the bags as she dumps them on the counter. "Isn't that a bit much?"

She rips into the Twizzlers and tosses one to me. "It's been a while since we've had an emergency of this level."

"I don't think we've ever had an emergency of this level."

She slaps the counter. "You're right. I should get more."

I laugh. "I think we're good."

"If you insist. So," she leans her elbows on the counter. "No one has connected you to Martinez, at least not that I found. He has a lot of patients and I think it would take a fricking rocket scientist to figure out that it's you. That, plus the fact that no one believes him."

"How long do you think that will last?"

She shrugs. "I thought you were crazy when you first told me, but eventually I believed you. This could die down and nothing will come of it or his ego might get so bruised that he decides to release your videos."

My stomach drops. I knew it was a risk to make those videos, but it never occurred to me that he might make them public. "Do you really think he'd do that?"

"Did you think he'd talk to the press without your permission?"

I let out a long exhale. "I'm screwed."

"Quite possibly."

"I thought you were here to make me feel better?" I expect a sarcastic comment but her smile fades.

"I don't know what to tell you. This is some serious shit and honestly, I don't think it's going to just go away."

I lean forward until my forehead is pressed to the counter. "Sorry."

"No, you're right. This is completely out of my hands."

"Are you gonna see him again?"

"What if someone's staking out his office?"

"What, like a reporter?"

"Or an investigator. Or another scientist who wants to kidnap me and do crazy time travel experiments."

She taps another Twizzler against her chin, thinking. "That is a risk." She takes a bite, then points it at me. "Do you want me to go as your bodyguard?"

"You do have a mean tackle."

"It's a gift."

"If anything, Martinez will need a bodyguard."

"I've got a bat in the car."

I burst out laughing. "I appreciate the thought, but don't you think people might put two and two together if one of his patients attacks him days after he's published?"

"Perhaps."

I pause. "I'm gonna miss this."

She tilts her head. "Miss what?"

"This." I point back and forth between us. "When we go away to school."

She slumps into a chair. "Oh god, is it starting?"

"What?"

"The weepy goodbyes that will last until the end of the school year." Her voice goes an octave higher. "I'll miss you so much! Omigod, you're like the best person ever! Stay sweet! I can't believe we haven't hung out more because you're so awesome!" She sticks her finger in her mouth and pretends to gag.

I throw a chip at her head. She tries to catch it with her mouth but misses and it falls to the floor. "Do people actually write that crap in your yearbook?"

"They don't in yours?"

"You're a bit sweeter than me. But I do expect you to pinky swear we'll always be best friends."

She holds up a pinky and I link mine with hers. She sniffs.

"We have all summer to get weepy."

She sniffs again. "But then we actually have to say goodbye because you decided to go to school in a completely different state."

"Technically you will also be in a different state."

She squeezes my pinky with hers. "We need to do something big this summer."

"Bigger than graduation?"

"A road trip." She releases my hand as a smile spreads across her face. "We'll go visit Quinn! And we'll visit all the states on our way there!"

A road trip does sound amazing, but I can't stop the negativity that creeps in. "I don't know if Mom will let me. And I can't drive anywhere but school until July. What kind of co-roadtripper can't even drive?"

"Then we'll go in July. And..." she twirls her hair. "We could invite the boys."

The excitement builds slowly, first in my belly, then it tiptoes into my chest and up my throat until I can't stop the smile that's taken over my face. "You're a genius."

"It's the perfect celebration to your re-found freedom. We'll just point out to our parents that once we're at college they'll have zero control over what we do, so what's the difference if we start a month earlier?"

"I might leave the parental convincing to you."

"Deal." She bounces in her seat. "I can't remember the last time I was this excited. And I'm assuming that since you immediately agreed to invite Cam, you guys are back together?"

I blush, remembering our date last week.

"You better not be this secretive when we're at different schools. If I can't see your face I'll never know what you're really thinking."

"I'll try to be better. And we can video chat." I press my hands to my face to try to cool my cheeks. "It's not that I'm trying to hide it, I just…I don't know. We've been through so much that I'm afraid it's going to vanish again." And there's one other thing that's been chewing at my insides. "And what about when we go to school? I have no doubt that you and I will always be friends, but a long-distance romance is a lot harder to maintain."

She straightens. "He hasn't told you?"

"Told me what?"

"Oh, no. I'm not telling." She draws an X over her mouth with her finger.

"Seriously?"

"Nope. You have to ask him yourself."

I grab my phone and fire off a text.

> Me: Amelia says you have a secret and she won't tell me.

I set my phone on the counter and stare at it.

"You're not going to talk until he writes back?"

"Nope."

Fortunately his reply comes back in under a minute.

> Cameron: I do.

Me: OMG tell me.

Cameron: But then it won't be a surprise.

I glare at Amelia. "Are you two working together?"

She holds up her hands. "No! I swear."

Me: Pleasepleasepleasepleaseplease.

Cameron: Are you sitting down?

I sit.

Me: Yes.

Cameron: I got into RID.

"What?"

Me: What?

Cameron: I applied last fall and was gonna surprise you then, but then...

Me: Yeah.

Cameron: SURPRISE!

Me: OMG.

Amelia kicks me. "It's good, right?"

I don't know what I did to deserve a friend like Amelia, but I recognize that finding an almost-sister is a once-in-a-lifetime thing. Between texts, calls, and visits home, it'll be like we aren't even in separate states.

"This is better than good. This is..." I don't have words. I haven't wanted to admit it, but part of the reason I was so afraid to start back up with Cameron is I didn't know if I could go through another breakup. "He's really going to my school?" I cock my head. "How long have you known this?"

She presses her hand to her heart, the same way Cameron did the other day. "Me? Maybe for a while. But I didn't say anything because you hated him, or were mad at him, and I wanted you to forgive him first."

I shake my head slowly.

"Are you a little more excited for our road trip?"

"Totally."

# chapter 37

By the time my appointment with Martinez finally arrives, I've imagined every possible scenario:

He confesses everything and begs for my forgiveness.

He denies everything and doesn't understand why I'm upset.

He dodges my questions until I'm thanking him for working with me.

He declares his love for me and confesses this was the only way he thought he could ever win me away from Cameron.

Okay, maybe that one's a stretch and I swear I don't want anything to happen with him, but when I let my imagination go wild it comes up with some whacked out situations.

I'm on alert for reporters outside the hospital, but either they're hiding in the bushes or they don't care about the story. Martinez's interview has made it to the national news, but more people seem to doubt his sanity than actually believe he's discovered time travel, especially since he claims it can't be replicated.

I rest my hand on the aluminum bat that Amelia put in my car after she left the other night, letting the metal cool my skin. As tempted as I am to bring it with me, I leave it on the front seat.

When I step off the elevator, I do a quick scan of the hallway, but nothing seems out of place. Even if a reporter or someone was here, it's not like they would know the story is about me just from looking at me. This is my regular appointment and has been for months. As far as an outsider can tell I'm just another patient with a brain issue.

The receptionist gives me her usual bored look but instead of telling me that he'd be with me in a minute, she sends me right back. "He's waiting for you."

I try to mask my surprise as I walk by. Does she know I'm his mysterious Patient X? The door to his office is open a crack so I peek inside before entering. He's sitting on the stool with his back to the door and for a second I'm pissed that I didn't bring Amelia's bat. I knock once on the door before pushing it open, but instead of sitting on the table I stand in the doorway, arms crossed, until he turns around.

Part of me hoped the mask he wears concealing his evil nature would be gone and I would see his true self, but he looks exactly the same as he always does. Which makes me feel like I wasn't deceived—I'm just an idiot.

"Can you shut the door?"

I roll my eyes and sigh but do as he asks. "Whatever."

"So this is how you're going to act? Okay." He makes a note on the pad on his desk, then crosses his arms, mirroring my posture.

"What's that supposed to mean?"

"I anticipated a number of ways you would react. Now I know."

He planned out our conversation, too. I start to smile on reflex, but cover it with a cough. I hate that I have anything in common with this disgusting excuse for a man.

He gestures with his hand for me to talk. "Let's hear it."

Option three it is: dodge my questions until I thank him for working with me. "Why should I be the one to start? You're the one who talked to the freaking press about me without so much as a word of warning or...I don't know...my consent!"

He takes a slow, deep breath, then exhales even more slowly. "I didn't tell you for several reasons." He holds up a finger. "First, you aren't mentioned by name and there's no way for you to be identified."

"No way? What about the video?"

"Those are safe with me."

I snort.

He closes his eyes for a beat and I feel a tiny burst of happiness that I'm irritating him. "Second, I was concerned that the story might be received negatively, as it is."

"Meaning what exactly?"

"That it would hurt your feelings to have people pick apart your ability. To say it isn't true."

"I may be insecure, but that's because I flicker and I'm afraid people will find out, not because I'm worried they won't believe me."

"I was just trying to protect your feelings."

"By telling the world about me? I think your priorities are a bit out of whack."

"My priorities have always been the same."

"To take advantage of me?"

"To keep you healthy."

"Right."

He stands to pace the small office, brushing my shoulder as he turns back toward the desk.

"So what are the other reasons?"

He stops moving and looks at me. "What do you mean?"

"You said you had several reasons for lying to me, but you've only told me two."

"Biz, I didn't lie to you."

"You lied by omission. It's the same thing. Amelia's always getting in trouble with her parents for not telling them things and they say she's lying. That doesn't change just because you become an adult."

"Okay, there is one more reason."

I lean against the door and wait.

"I've accepted a position at a hospital in New York City."

That's not what I expected him to say. "Oh."

"As we've discussed before, I knew our sessions, and therefore my research, would end when you went away to school. I've been talking to the heads of neurology in a few big cities in preparation for a move and a position opened in New York." He shrugs. "The timing worked out."

Martinez has been very matter-of-fact since the day I met him, but right now his calm demeanor makes me want to pull out what little hair I have. "How can you stand there and explain away the biggest deception I've ever known without acknowledging how badly you hurt me?"

His head jerks back like I slapped him. "I didn't mean to hurt you."

"But you did! Can't you see that?" I take a step toward him. "I trusted you with the one secret that could destroy me and what did you do? You gave an interview to the fricking newspaper so the entire world can find out." My chest tightens and I struggle to catch my breath. I press a fist to my breastbone, willing the knot to slide back to my gut where it belongs.

"Are you okay?" He reaches for my arm but I twist away.

"Don't touch me."

He leans against the counter, the first sign of defeat. But I know now that he'll never back down. I'm just the first step on his way to the top.

"Can I ask you something?"

He holds out his hands. "Isn't that what we're doing?"

"Does Shelly know it's me?"

His jaw clenches. Since the first time I confronted him about the emails, he's talked me in circles until I forget the question, but I'm not leaving without answers.

"Did you tell her?"

His head nods once, a barely perceptible movement, and my knees buckle. His voice lowers so it's almost a whisper. "I know what you're thinking, but you can't turn me in without revealing yourself as Patient X."

The energy drains out of me. There's nothing I can do to stop him. "Yeah, I already figured that out. Very clever." But that still leaves one question unanswered. "Why the emails? What did you possibly hope to gain by threatening me?"

He sighs. "That was Shelly's idea. She's so desperate to get out of this town and make a name for herself that once she learned about my research she went on a bit of a power trip."

"So you're dating her?"

He tilts his head. "What difference does that make?"

"Humor me, oh destroyer of my faith in humanity."

He rolls his eyes and I almost laugh at how much younger the gesture makes him look. "Yes, we're dating. In fact, she's moving to New York with me. "

Un-freaking-believable. "You two deserve each other." I can't believe I ever thought something could happen between the two of us. My stomach turns just looking at him.

"Thanks."

"It wasn't a compliment." His office has always been tiny but now the walls feel like they're closing in on me. I need to get out of here. "I want you to destroy my videos, but I know you won't." He lifts a shoulder as if in agreement, and I point at him. "But I swear to god, if they ever go public, I will find you and I will destroy you."

It's an empty threat and he knows it, but for once he lets me have the last word.

I open the door, pausing with my hand on the doorknob, and finish scenario number three. "Thanks for saving my life." Then I slam the door and hurry to the elevator before I burst into tears.

# chapter 38

*FOUR MONTHS LATER*

"Can you turn his head a little to the right?" My hands remain on my camera as I instruct the mother how to position her newborn. This baby is bigger than some of the others I've photographed—almost the size of a regular newborn—but he has a problem with his heart that landed him in the neo-natal ward.

She shifts her arm so the light falls onto his face and I press the button. *Click-click-click.*

"Perfect." I rest my camera on my knee. "I think we're good."

Jonathan emerges from behind the vacant incubator and lifts the baby from his mother's arms. "Let's get him hooked back up for a bit."

I sometimes forget how critical some of these babies are. When I'm in here with the families, they're like any other baby, not a tiny human fighting for their life. I hand the parents my card. "These will be online within the next couple days. Email me the numbers you'd like and I'll drop off a disk." I shake their hands, then wait for Jonathan at the nurses station.

"We're going to miss you around here."

"I'll still stop by."

Jonathan smiles, and I remember his kindness the first time I met him in the stairwell. "No you won't. You'll be galavanting across the country for three weeks and you leave for school right after you get back."

I smile. "You're right. But I'll come here to say goodbye."

He pulls me into a hug. "I'm holding you to that. Now be sure to give Quinn a hug from me."

"I will." I pull away and glance at Dr. Ward's office door. "Is he in there?"

"Yep. Said to send you in as soon as you finished." He nudges me in the back. "Go on, get out of here."

I knock on Dr. Ward's door and jump when it opens almost immediately.

"Biz! Wonderful. Come in." He pulls out the chair in front of his desk before taking the seat behind it. "So you've finished your time with us."

"Yes. And I'd like to thank you again for allowing me to work my hours here. When the judge gave me community service I never imagined I'd be able to do something that I actually enjoy. I've learned so much, both about photography and babies, and everyone here has been so kind, especially given the reason I was arrested."

He pulls a handkerchief out of his shirt pocket and dabs the corner of his eye. "I wasn't expecting a speech."

My gaze falls to my lap. "Sorry. I'm just so grateful for the opportunity."

He folds the handkerchief, then sets it on the desk so it's perfectly aligned with the edge. "We've all done things we regret. Things we wish we could take back. You've never been anything but professional and respectful to the staff and our families, and frankly, who am I to judge?"

Well, for one, he's a director at the hospital, but who am I to argue?

"The court sent this form for me to sign and said you're to bring it with you to your appointment." He uncaps a pen that looks like it weighs more than the babies in the other room and signs his name with a flourish. "Anything else?"

"Besides my eternal gratitude? No, thank you."

He stands and holds out his hand. "Good luck, Biz. Stop by and say hello when you're home on break."

"I will." I leave him at his desk and shut his door behind me. The nurse's station is empty. I spot Jonathan helping a mother feed her baby with a bottle and wave the paper at him. He holds up a thumb and waves. The other nurses I've gotten to know over the past few months are all busy with patients so I slip out of the ward without another word.

My appointment with the judge is tomorrow, and armed with this document stating I've completed my court-ordered community service, there shouldn't be any reason for him not to reinstate my full driving privileges. I practically skip out of the hospital to my car. Martinez has been gone for a couple months so I don't have to worry about running into him. The hospital tried to set me up with his replacement, but I'm done with doctors. At least for a while.

When I turn onto my street, Amelia's car is parked in front of my house. She jumps out of the driver's side as soon as I pull into the driveway and runs to the front door. "It's about time! We still have so much to do!"

"We're not leaving for three days." She wanted to leave tomorrow as soon as my meeting with the judge was over, but Mom convinced us to wait a couple days in case there are any problems with the paperwork. I still can't believe she agreed to let me go—for that matter, I can't believe any of our parents agreed to let us go. Cameron's parents gave him a new-to-him car for graduation—not his dad's—so we'll have a relatively reliable vehicle, and we're staying with Quinn once we get to Portland, but Amelia and I will be alone with our boyfriends for three whole weeks.

Amelia pokes my cheek. "You've got a faraway look on your face. Where'd you go?"

"Oh, you know. Just a hotel room with my boyfriend. No big deal."

"Omigod, I know. We'll have to figure out how to deactivate the body cams as soon as we get on the road." Amelia's convinced that the only reason her parents consented is because they've wired her belongings with recording devices.

"I'd think the audio would be just as incriminating."

She taps my forehead. "Good point. Now hurry up and open the door. I have to pee."

We spend the next couple hours ripping apart my closet until Amelia is satisfied that she's found every road-trip appropriate outfit that I own. "Why didn't I get to do this at your place?"

She laughs. "You really want to help me pack?"

"Not really."

"I thought so. I enjoy it enough for the both of us." She throws herself onto my bed and wraps a thin blue scarf around her head. "What are you wearing to see the judge?"

"Thigh highs and a mini skirt."

"I'd pay to see that." She rolls onto her side and lets the scarf slide to the floor. "Are you nervous he won't give you your license?"

I sit on the floor next to the bed. "A little, but then I realized that if he doesn't let me drive, you and Cam and Trace will be stuck doing all the driving for the next three weeks." I look at her out of the corner of my eye. "That's why I decided on the short skirt."

She smacks me on the back of the head.

"Hey! There's delicate hair back there. Take it easy."

She touches the headband tucked behind my ears. It's just for show, but it's nice to have something other than a semi-shaved head. "It's almost long enough to do stuff. By the time you go to school you'll be able to wear barrettes."

"You know, that's what I'm most looking forward to. Not living on campus or becoming a better photographer. Nope. For me, it's all about the barrettes." Amelia kicks my arm and I grab her leg, ready to pull her onto the floor, but I freeze when my hand hits her rough skin. I let go as if I scalded her. "Sorry."

She tucks her legs beneath her, but not before I see the scar that runs the length of her leg. The scar that I caused. "Biz, I told you, it doesn't hurt anymore, it just looks like hell." She didn't wear shorts until earlier this month, and that's only because the temperature hit the upper nineties. If it'd stayed cooler I think she might have stayed in jeans and long skirts for the entire summer.

"I know, but I'm still sorry."

"Let's not do this again."

I rest my chin on her knee and bat my eyes at her. "I told you, I will continue to apologize until my next birthday, then I promise to try to stop." I assured her that a year would be enough time for me to forgive myself, even though she forgave me for the accident within hours of it happening, but I'm not so sure I'll ever forgive myself. When Martinez's paper was first published I wished over and over again that I'd flickered to stop myself from making that final video, but now I know that the one event I wish I could undo was the car accident. The video only hurt myself, and that I can live with. Even if someday it gets released to the public, I'll have to deal with it, but my life won't be over. The accident hurt Amelia in ways I may never fully understand. I'm just grateful our friendship survived it.

◆◆◆

We've been on the road for less than an hour and I'm finally starting to relax. Cameron's hand is resting on my bare leg, which is flung over his lap, and his eyes are closed. All the windows are down and for once I'm glad to have short hair because I'm the only one in the car whose hair isn't flying all over the place. Even Cameron's is dancing across his forehead.

Amelia and Cameron plotted our route so we pass as few trees as possible, but I still have my big floppy hat and dark sunglasses at my feet, just in case. Trace couldn't understand why they refused to take the roads he wanted—the ones with thick forests full of trees—so I finally caved and told him the truth. I'm not sure if he believes me, but if we're going to be together for three straight weeks I'd rather he find out all my weird shit now. Maybe I'm getting better at learning who I can trust, but telling him wasn't as hard as I thought it'd be. Either that, or deep down I know my secret might be revealed to the entire world so telling one more person isn't going to hurt anything. Trace seems happy to finally be included in our secret, and I'm glad he's finally forgiven me for hurting Amelia.

Cameron shifts beneath my leg and I catch him watching me. "Come here."

I twist in the seat so I'm leaning against his side. Our noses are inches away. "What's up?"

He rubs his hand up and down my arm, sending chills through my body. "I still can't believe we're here." His hand continues over my shoulder until his thumb rests on my lower lip. The butterflies in my stomach kick into action. You'd think I'd be used to being with him, but the slightest touch still makes me all googly-eyed.

"I've gotta tell you, I'm more excited for tonight."

His eyelids droop as he studies my mouth. "I admit, I haven't stopped thinking about that either."

Even though we've been together for months now, we still haven't slept together. Amelia thinks we're crazy for waiting, but between Turner's trial and his sentencing, and all the crap with Martinez, it never seemed to be the right time. Then once we decided on the road trip, we agreed to wait until the first night. We don't have enough money to get separate motel rooms, but Amelia promised to take a very long walk with Trace and not return until I text her that it's all clear. It's not perfect, but it's better than sneaking around in our parents' houses.

Cameron moves his hand to the side of my face and dips his head to kiss me. His lips move against mine as the wind wraps around us, cocooning us from Amelia and Trace in the front seat. I swing my leg over his lap so I'm straddling him, then wrap my arms around his neck as his slide around my back. I press closer and the kiss grows more urgent—

A hand smacks my leg. "Hey! Save it for tonight!"

"Ow, that hurt!"

Cameron bursts out laughing as the car swerves, and his face knocks into mine. "Learn to drive, Trace!"

I look over my shoulder. Trace is laughing so hard that his shoulders are hunched over. "Eyes on the road, mister."

Amelia laughs. "We've been in the car for an hour. Control yourselves."

I slide off Cameron but stay pressed against him, my fingers trailing up and down his chest. An excited energy courses through me. I feel like I'm standing on the edge of one life, about to step into the next. And not just with Cameron. Graduating from high school, putting all the drama from the past year behind me, going away to college—everything I know is changing. Even Mom is trying something new. She joined a monthly book club with a woman she met at the grocery store. It's a small step, but it's a good one, and it'll make me worry a little less about her when I'm away at school.

So many things are changing and I'm afraid that if I blink, I'll miss them. It's like when the sunlight filters through the trees, the kind that makes me flicker. Each beat of sunlight is something new, exciting. No longer something to be afraid of.

I reach up and run my fingers through Cameron's hair, pulling him toward me for another kiss. Whatever the world has in store for me, I'm ready.

# Read the first two chapters of *Chasing the Sun* by Melanie Hooyenga

## 1
### SAGE

It takes a brave man to ask his ex-girlfriend for a detailed list of everything he did wrong in their two-year relationship, but that's exactly what Paxton Juarez, former love of my life, has done.

I slam the cupboard door shut and toss a bag of pretzels on the counter, then grab a couple sparkling waters from the fridge.

Elbows propped on the counter, my best friend Naomi McGinnis peers at me over her phone. "He seriously sent a list? Like specific questions?"

I open the email app on my phone, pull up his message, and lower my voice to impersonate Pax. "Am I selfish?"

Naomi nods, her red curls bouncing.

"Did I not care for you enough?"

"Duh."

"Am I possessive? What is wrong with me, mentally? Did I care for your mental state of mind? What kind of a boyfriend am I?"

She lets out a low whistle. "Holy spaceballs. Isn't it a little late for him to suddenly care how he treated you?"

I toss my phone on the counter. "It's been a month since we broke up right after he graduated and I finally feel like I'm moving on. Why can't he just crawl in a hole and stay there?"

"He's still trying to control you," she says, her gaze jumping between me and her phone. We've been down this road before, but it always leads to the same place: me feeling horrible and stupid and weak. Naomi's house is filled with self-help books and she's spent the first half of summer break trying to convince me that what Pax and I had was not love—it was abuse.

I didn't want to hear that word at first, but she's helped me accept it and try to move on. I used to be stronger. Could think for myself and knew what I wanted, or didn't want, but now I'm left floundering.

My head drops to my arms on the counter.

"You're not answering him, right?" Her tone holds a hint of caution, like she doesn't want to tell me what to do but also doesn't want me to write back. "Sage Winters, please tell me you're not considering replying."

I shrug, face down. "It might be cathartic. You know, finally show him that he doesn't hold any power over me anymore." I peek at her over my arm.

She's smiling at my self-help speak.

"I feel so stupid."

"You're not."

"You'd never let a guy turn you inside out."

Her lips purse. "I'd like to think not. But that doesn't mean I don't let guys get to me."

My head pops up. "Who?"

She brushes me off with a head shake and the corner of her mouth lifts. "It's too soon to acknowledge." The pretzel bag crinkles as she grabs a handful. "Will you promise to wait before replying?"

I appreciate that she doesn't flat out tell me not to. Because as much as I want to be rid of Pax, I'd also really love to have the final word.

Before I can answer, both our phones buzz with a text.

Naomi reads it before I can grab my phone.

"Ooh, Kit's having a bonfire."

"Tonight?" It doesn't really matter when. I won't go. I never go. And Naomi understands this.

At least I think she does.

"Later this week. For his new neighbor. Neb. Connelly I think."

"Why do you know his last name?"

She shrugs. "I know things. So, do you want to go?"

I spin my phone in circles in time with my pounding heart. The unread text lights up the display, taunting me with a night of fun that should make me happy. It's not like I'm doing something wrong considering it. My gut twists and the pressure in my chest makes it hard to breathe. A fun side effect of Pax controlling my every move is now I panic when forced to make a decision. Combined with my nervousness around crowds—like at a party— and my body shuts down.

My silence is my answer.

"Really?" she asks. "It'll just be a few of us. Kit Cordero doesn't have enough friends to have a legit party."

I glance at the text.

> Kit: welcome to the Neb-orhood bonfire
> Saturday!

I groan. "No, but Theo does, and he'll invite half the school." Naomi's twin brother makes friends everywhere he goes and for some inexplicable reason he's besties with Kit, who still has the sense of humor of a middle schooler.

She bites a pretzel in half and chews, thinking. "It could be fun. And you need to get out of the house." She takes another bite. "Summer's halfway over and you've barely been outside."

I straighten. "I've been outside."

"Your backyard doesn't count."

"But it's a nice backyard." My voice is as weak as my argument.

"Come on, it's been months since you've gone OUT out. Just consider it. For me?" Her bright green eyes lock on mine and my resolve wavers.

"I'll think about it." I don't bother crossing my fingers with the lie, and shift the conversation to something safer. "Where are you at with the vlog?"

Naomi flattens her hands on the counter and bites her lip. "Change of plans."

"But I love the idea! You'll be the perfect—" I wave my hand as I grapple for the right words. "Teen advice person."

Her curls practically vibrate as she nods. "Oh I'm still doing it, but I've decided a podcast would be better. I want people to focus on what I'm saying, not what I look like." With her pale skin, light dusting of freckles, and poof of red hair, there is definitely a lot to focus on. But all of it's good.

"Do I need to pep talk you, Ms. Queen of Self-Esteem?"

She smiles and it brightens her entire face. "Nope. I've done a lot of research, and while video is undeniably the leader with online viewership, podcasts have a broader appeal."

I shove a pretzel into my mouth, considering this while I chew. "But the rest will be the same?"

"Still called Three Good Things. Still a mix of self-help and dating advice." She flicks invisible crumbs from her shirt. "Even if my dating life is sadly uninspired. But I need help with episode titles, Ms. Star English Student."

I blush at the compliment. Regardless of what's happened with my personal life, school has always been something I could control. I still haven't figured out what an interest in reading and writing means for a college major or a career, but I have all of senior year to worry about that.

"Hold that thought," Naomi says before hustling down the hall to the bathroom.

As soon as she's gone, my confidence wanes. My finger trails over the dark screen of my phone. No one will miss me. Like Naomi said, I haven't been around all summer. Or really for the past couple years. One party isn't going to change that.

I tap the screen and reply to the text thread.

> Me: sorry, can't make it. school shopping with mom.

Naomi bursts out of the bathroom holding her phone out like it scalded her. Her scowl turns to frustration, then concern, all in a matter of seconds.

"I'm sorry," I say. "I just can't."

She sighs as she flops into the chair next to me. "So what are we doing instead?"

Before I can thank her for putting up with me, my phone dings with a text.

> Unknown: I'm starting to get a complex that you don't want to meet me

## 2
### NEB

My hand hovers over my phone, like if I concentrate hard enough I can take it back. Because that wasn't to the whole group—it was only to Sage—and I hit send without thinking.

Before I moved here, I was confident, outgoing. Before, I didn't think twice about going to a party or hanging out with friends, even if they aren't really my friends and it's a pity party because I don't know anyone. But now everything's different.

And Sage hasn't replied.

It's cool of Kit to help me meet people before school starts. When we were kids and I'd visit Mom on holidays and over summer break, we'd play in our adjoining backyards, but once we hit high school, our casual acquaintanceship dissolved into shouted hellos from the driveway and promises to catch up.

Which we never did.

Until now.

This is probably Mom's doing. Her way of "showing she cares." She's been appropriately attentive since I moved in last month, but she stopped being a full-time parent seven years ago and her skills are a bit rusty.

Sage: who is this?

My eyes close and I let out a groan. I'm such a dumbass. She never saved my number from the group text.

Me: sorry! this is Neb

Me: Kit's friend

If my bed would swallow me now, that would be great.

Sage: oh. hi. saving now haha

Sage: sorry I can't make it, but new clothes are very important

Despite her playful tone, the excitement I felt when I first texted fades.

Me: so I hear

I look down at my flannel that's so worn you can practically see through it. At my cargo shorts with a tear in the leg from a camping trip last spring.

Me: I should probably do that too

Sage: gotta make a good impression, right?

Did I misread her? She seemed down to earth, like she wasn't into the superficial crap like some of the girls I know, but maybe I was wrong.

Sage: my advice — don't try to turn yourself into someone you're not

Okay, this is what I expected from her. It's hard to get to know anyone from a group text, but she never seemed fazed by Kit and his friend Theo.

Me: so don't dye my hair blue and pierce my nose?

Sage: unless that's what you're into

Is that what she's into?

Me: blue hair does not suit me

Sage: and piercings?

Me: not for me

Sage: so what is?

I drum my fingers against my phone. What if she has blue hair and a nose ring and I inadvertently offend her? I don't want to dig myself into a hole, but I also don't want to play games.

Me: I'm into camping, outdoors, that sort of thing. I'm all natural

And now I sound like an ad for fricking granola.

Sage: and astronomy

A prickle of something—pride, and a little surprise—crawls

through my chest.

Me: you picked up on that?
Sage: only after the first 50 times you mentioned
it
Me: it was not 50
Me: maybe 20
Sage: it's cool
Me: what are you into?

I feel bad I haven't picked up on her interests from the group texts, but she tends to play off what others are saying instead of starting the conversation.

Sage: I like observing people. and reading
Sage: boring stuff
Me: I bet you learn a lot about people that way

There's a pause that stretches into a moment that twists into an almost awkward silence. I count to ten, one number with each breath, then try again.

Me: are you a senior too?
Sage: is Neb short for something?

Our texts come through at the same time and I smile. Then I take a breath. It's easy to get lulled into a false security when texting a stranger, but Sage doesn't seem like she's ready to go below the surface.

Sage: yes
Me: yes
Sage: lol, are you gonna tell me?

I smile again, and the tightness that's gripped my heart for the past month starts to loosen.

Me: it's short for Nebula.
Sage: like the woman from the Marvel movies?

My eyes roll skyward and I silently curse Dad and his obsession with astronomy. Just as quickly, my jaw falls open. That's the first time I've had a normal reaction to him since—

Me: thankfully no. call it a parental obsession
with outer space
Sage: don't make me google
Me: a nebula is basically a giant cloud of gas

and dust. in space
Sage: wow, that had to be rough growing up
Me: I went to the same school my whole life so
most kids were used to it

At the start of middle and high school some people tried to make fun of my name—older kids flexing and all that—but Dad taught me to be proud of who I am and my name is part of that. When I didn't react, the jerks gave up. Plus nebulas are pretty badass.
Sage: I think it's cool. but I'm surprised no one
calls you Starlord

I snort a laugh.
Me: my best friend Yoshi does

Yoshi calls me that but until now he's the only one who's ever made the connection.
Sage: so is that off-limits?

I adjust against my pillow. Over the years, I've learned people are gonna call you what they want, so her courtesy of asking is surprising.
Me: he wouldn't mind if you borrowed it
Sage: noted
Me: is Sage short for anything?

I'm guessing not, but maybe she's willing to share surface stuff.
Sage: actual lol
Sage: and no. just the boring plant. not much of
a story except my parents thought it sounded
pretty
Sage: not that I'm saying I'm pretty
Sage: I'll stop now

Laughter bursts out of me, bringing tears to my eyes.
Me: it is pretty

Mom's head pokes in the door of my room. Her long hair is pulled into a knot-thing near her neck and dirt streaks her clothes. A hesitant smile plays on her lips, like she doesn't want to interrupt but can't help herself. "I thought I'd never hear that sound again."

"What sound?"

Her smile slips to a frown. "You laughing."

And just like that, the heaviness crashes around me. The feeling like I'm slipping back into the darkness that's overwhelmed me all summer. The reality that Dad's gone filling every molecule in my body, making it hard to breathe.

She must see it in my face because she steps into my room. "I'm sorry. I didn't mean to—"

I wave her off. "I know you didn't."

She nods at my phone. "Who are you talking to?"

The words 'just this girl' trip on the end of my tongue. Mom knew about Jennie because we dated for over a year. She inferred that we broke up because when I moved in, I never mentioned her. But I'm not ready to have her nosing around Sage and jumping to conclusions before I know what's going on. Or before we meet.

As if on cue, my phone buzzes with another text, but it's not Sage. It's Yoshi, saving me without even realizing it.

"Yoshi.'"

My phone buzzes again, texts from Sage and Yoshi filling the screen.

"Well, I'll let you get back to your friends." Mom sighs, and for a second I feel bad about lying to her. She's making an effort, and I haven't made it easy on her.

"Kit's having a bonfire later this week."

"That sounds fun." She picks at a fleck of paint on the door jamb like she wants to say more. We haven't talked about curfew or any other rules like that because I don't have any friends except Kit and he lives next door.

I glance at my phone as it buzzes again. Hopefully that's starting to change.

She waits a beat longer, then steps into the hall.

Ignoring the twinge of regret that hits me when she leaves, I scroll through the texts on my lock screen.

> Yoshi: my princess, tell me ur not sitting home tonight
> Sage: ::blush::
> Yoshi: me and Rick are at the pit

> Yoshi: everyone misses u
> Sage: it must suck starting a new school senior
> year

My thumb hovers over their messages as I decide who to reply to first. I go with Sage.

> Me: it's not great
> Sage: and Kit's the only person you know
> Me: he's been cool

The little dots bounce while she types, then disappear, then start up again like she's changing her reply.

> Sage: I guess he can be nice when he tries

From what I know of Kit, he's the kind of guy who tries too hard to make people think he doesn't care. I doubt we'd be friends in a different circumstance, but right now he's all I've got.

And Sage is clearly not a fan.

> Me: Is that why you're not going?
> Sage: maybe a little
> Me: I'm hurt
> Sage: I don't even know you. what if you're as
> bad as he is?
> Me: ouch
> Me: I promise we're nothing alike
> Sage: well Theo's cool. he balances Kit's Kitness

I'd picked up on that in the group text but it's nice to have my suspicions confirmed.

> Me: good to know

I take a deep breath and switch to Yoshi. He's the only friend from home who's made a point to text every day. Me leaving probably affected him more than anyone else and it feels good to know someone misses me. But I can't blame the others. I've heard from a few people, but I left the day after the funeral and since it was already summer break, I slipped out of town and out of their lives without a goodbye.

> Me: for your information Luigi, this princess is
> going to a party this week

In addition to Starlord, Yoshi also calls me Princess Peach. He hates that he has the same name as one of the Super Mario characters, and when we were kids, he claimed Luigi. Since no one else was allowed to be Yoshi and Rick claimed Mario, I somehow ended up with Princess Peach. Now I can't escape it.

Yoshi: good for you man
Yoshi: any girls there
Me: none that I know

More like none that I care about. This girl Tara who's been borderline stalking me since I moved here will probably be there. She lives in the neighborhood and our moms are friends, and if they had their way we'd be a couple before school started.

Yoshi: dude it's been forever since j
Me: who's at the pit?
Yoshi: the usual. rick says hi

He ignores my deflection and tells me what I want to hear. About my friends from another life and the stupid but hilarious physical challenges they make up to pass the time. The pit is an old gravel quarry that's nothing to look at, but it has wide open spaces and plenty of ways for us to almost hurt ourselves.

Had.

Past life.

Now I've got a bonfire with a bunch of strangers and the one person I want to see won't be there.

Books by Melanie Hooyenga

*The Flicker Effect Trilogy*
FLICKER
FRACTURE
FADED

*The Rules Series*
THE SLOPE RULES
THE TRAIL RULES
THE EDGE RULES

*The Campfire Series*
CHASING THE SUN
CHASING THE STARS
CHASING THE MOON

*Anthologies*
LOVE ON MAIN
THE ART OF TAKING CHANCES

# to you, the reader

Hearing from readers—whether on social media or through reviews or email—makes this whole writing thing worthwhile, so drop me a line.

melaniehooyenga@gmail.com
Facebook.com/MelanieHooyenga
Twitter: @melaniehoo
Instagram: @melaniehoo
TikTik: @melaniehooyenga

If Biz's story spoke to you as much as it has to me, please consider writing a review on Amazon, B&N, or Goodreads. Word of mouth is the best advertising and I'd love to hear what you think.

And if you'd like to stay informed on where I'll be and what I'm writing next, sign up for my newsletter at melaniehoo.com.

# acknowledgments

Writing is a solitary endeavor, yet creating a novel is never done alone. So many people helped me while writing the end to this series, and FADED wouldn't be the same without them.

Nadine, thank you for being my sounding board, my idea bouncer, and future Napa-invading cohort. I'm so proud of what you've accomplished and am glad I've been along for the ride.

Stacey, thank you for always pushing me to be the best writer I can be. The fact that you come with built-in teen readers is just the cherry on top! (psst, I slipped in a line from our Backstreet Boys song just for you.*)

Nancy, once again you've turned my draft into a novel ready for the world. I hope naming the smartest person in this book after you is a big enough thank you. If not, there's always more cheese.

To June, Beth, Angie, Wynter, and Lily: your input made this book better and I thank you for your time and honesty.

To my family and friends who tirelessly tell THEIR family and friends about the Flicker Effect, I can't thank you enough.

As always, thank you to my mother, Judy, to whom this book is dedicated. You've taught me to keep going no matter what life throws at you, and I wouldn't be the person I am without your support and guidance.

And to Jeremy, thank you for your unending encouragement (even if it's just so I become a millionaire and you can stop working). You may heart my books, but I heart you. You really are a big deal.

*Readers: email me if you find it. melaniehooyenga@gmail.com

# about the author

Multi-award winning young adult author Melanie Hooyenga writes books about strong girls who learn to navigate life despite its challenges. She first started writing as a teenager and finds she still relates best to that age group.

Her award-winning YA sports romance series, *The Rules Series*, is about girls from Colorado falling in love and learning to stand up on their own. Her YA time travel trilogy, *The Flicker Effect*, is about a teen who uses sunlight to travel back to yesterday.

When not writing books, you can find her wrangling her Miniature Schnauzer Gus and playing every sport imaginable with her husband Jeremy.

www.ingramcontent.com/pod-product-compliance
Lightning Source LLC
Chambersburg PA
CBHW020359110726
47899CB00006B/1777